I0587126

Syncing Back

Act 1

W. Lawrence

Syncing Back: Act 1

First printing 2024 October 5

Published by W. Lawrence

Book cover design by Tom Edwards (tomedwardsdesign.com)

Print Book

ISBN-13: 978-0-9904861-8-3

Printed in the United States of America

(bywlawrence.com)

W. Lawrence

Dedicated to my ma.

You always encouraged my writing, but I couldn't finish in time. I'm sorry you didn't get a chance to read this one.

I still miss you.

By my soul, my mother was right, saying that in all the world there was nothing so fear-some as devils! And to teach me how to be-have, she told me to cross myself when I see them.

But that's too much to ask: instead of crossing My-self I'll stick the biggest And strongest with one of these wooden Spears, and none of the others will come anywhere near me...

~Perceval

Chapter 1

Intertwined fingers caressing, gazes locked upon each other, smiles extending up to their eyes, faces flushed—and not from the ninety percent humidity outside. The pair doesn't notice me, doesn't care about anyone in the restaurant. Despite my listlessness, my aversion to touch, I want to be half of this view. Or perhaps I only think I want it; conditioned by nine billion souls, or programmed by two meters of DNA, or some confluence of the two. A waiter delivers the couple their lunches, breaks their connection, and sends them to opposite sides of their booth.

My gaze drifts elsewhere. He stares at me from across the café. Handsome, curly dark hair, boyish eyes hiding behind tiny-lensed glasses, and—if it weren't for the pistol pointed at me—I'd say a flirtatious smile. He wears a polo buttoned too high and business jeans worn to perfection, making him invisible in an indifferent Washington DC crowd. I doubt anyone in here would notice the gun obscured in the shadows next to his leg.

A small gesture of his head invites me to his table, a proposition I feel I should accept given my aversion to being on the wrong side of a pistol. I rise slowly, then hesitate, considering how fast I could make it to the door. He makes a second bob of his head in the direction behind me. My eyes follow the line of his gaze to see a man with a cloth napkin draped on his lap, a second dull gray barrel aimed in my direction.

There are more than a dozen adults and kids eating, drinking, watching their phones, talking, taking pictures. The couple is still smiling and laughing with bites tucked into their cheeks. Odds are a bullet is going to find flesh, even if not mine. I grab my plate and drink, walk over to his table, and sit down across from his half-eaten penne arrabiata. I leave both my hands in plain view of my new lunch date.

"How's your meal?"

He shrugs. "Too much fennel. Not enough pepper. Yours?"

"I don't like lead in my dish, otherwise it's fine."

He frowns. "It's precautionary, I can assure you. Like a napkin, or insurance, or birth control. I'm here to speak and to leave unfettered, same as you."

"'Unfettered'?" I scoff, taking a bite of my lasagna. "Jesus. Word of the day from the guy who looks like Studious Stanley."

"Would you mind powering down your phone?" His left hand sets a small cube on the table with a tiny light illuminated on top. His right hand is still below the table. I waver but soon power it down. The red light flips to green, and my armed companion's shoulders loosen a bit, but it doesn't last long.

I put my hands down to adjust in my seat and watch him stiffen. He speaks calmly, but his body says something else. Older than me, jittery, and with soft hands, he's untrained. An office worker or maybe an academic, and that trigger finger could easily squeeze a round off into my va-jay-jay if I make another sudden move.

"Relax there, Studious Stanley. I'm just shifting in my chair. I'm not even armed." Something about naming this stranger after a cartoon sets off a bit of mania. I'm panicking, but not anywhere close to paralyzed. Eyes down, I shovel enough lasagna into my mouth to make my cheeks puff out like a hamster. My guts are shaking, but I discover that I can't puke and eat at the same time. I hope he sees me as unthreatening.

"You always eat like this?"

I make a good show of it I'm sure, talking with my mouth full of food, "I skipped breakfast. So whatcha got for me, Stanley? I am guessing you didn't arrange this as some sort of speed dating thing... or wait, is it? Is this a speed dating event?"

"Uh, no, I wanted to, wait, what are you—"

I don't let him finish. "Okay, so I collect seashells, I like true crime, I studied computer science in school, and I'm a recovering Catholic. I'm allergic to peanuts so I have to carry an epi-pen everywhere, and I once almost died at a college party—not from peanuts—but because I drank so much that I fell out a window. And... It's your turn. Go!"

"I have a cure for your father."

I feel like the food in my mouth has turned to cement. He seems pleased to have deftly dispelled my antics and taken back the high ground of our conversation.

"This is real," he says. "You should respond."

I pick up my napkin and turn it into a nest for a masticated ball of lasagna. The waiter notices and arrives dressed in concern. "Is there something—"

I cut him short with a wave of my hand and he goes bouncing away. My eyes are locked on Studious Stanley. "My dad is in a coma. Who are you?"

Stanley puts his fork down with measured precision. "We know a lot about who you are and what you do, Ms. James, and why you do what you do. We also know your father isn't in a coma. We know he is alive and responsive, although not in the traditional sense."

"You don't know shit," I balk. "This is some fucked up attempt to mess with my head and I'm leaving."

"Timber cinder," he says quickly.

I sit back down.

*   *

I was nine when the government gave me a top-secret clearance. The status came with an air of mystery, of intrigue and stories of international spies and military UAP projects. Any normal kid would have gone berserk with excitement. *Top-Secret.*

It's not that I wasn't impressed by such things, but the circumstance of its receipt poisoned my enthusiasm such that it would take many years for me to appreciate what I had been granted—and how to use it to my benefit.

I'd like to say I was the youngest person to ever receive such a clearance, but my little sister Bella was seven when they ushered my mom, sister, and me into an antiseptic room with painfully white LED lights and a noisy coffee machine that spat into its pot. A rotund little man who looked like the principal at my school fidgeted in his chair as he gestured to the chairs opposite him. I remember he wore a teeny tiny tie that made his belly look enormous, buttons dangerously stretching against the fabric, and a nervous smile that conveyed anything other than happiness.

Behind him stood a handful of grownups, men and women with pinched expressions whose only conversations were shared in whispers amongst each other. I don't remember this man's name, but I do remember he introduced himself to me and Bella, complete with a handshake across the table. It was a handshake wholly rejected by both of us, albeit for different reasons.

Bella hid in my mother's side, terrified. I, however, was not. Grownups didn't scare me. I found them annoying, distrustful, and patronizing. This government representative with his meaty hand hovering near my face while the table cut into his portly belly was no different.

I crossed my arms and scowled at him. "No, thank you," I said.

"Amara, don't be rude!" my mother snapped. She followed with an apology, excusing my behavior on the stress our family had been under.

"It's okay," the man soothed. "These are not easy circumstances."

I recall there were two cameras, old by digital standards, and each was painted with a set of yellow numbers that reminded me of our school equipment shelf. They were aimed at the three of us, beady red eyes glaring beneath the lenses to document our meeting.

"So, which one of you is Bella?" he asked us, his tone like we were attending a puppet show. Bella gave a nervous wave with her hand barely breaking gravity from her lap. "That makes you..."

When he looked back at me, his enthusiasm stalled. "Well, then, you're Amara. Obviously. Uh, well... Girls, you know what it means to keep a secret, right?"

Out of the corner of my eye, I could see Bella nodding. A stubborn nerve swelled inside me. All this man received was a fixed stare.

"Okay. Well girls, some secrets are small, and some secrets are big. And some secrets are really, really big. The secret about your dad is one of those. We call them 'top secret.' When we tell you to never talk about your dad or write about your dad and all the stuff that happened to him, it's because the people who did that to him are still looking for him. If they find him, they might do something worse, or hurt you or your sister or your mom. Do you understand?

"While we are looking for a way to help your dad, we need you girls to keep this secret. You cannot tell your grandparents, your friends, your cousins, your teachers, your pastor, your—"

"What's a pastor?" Bella asked, raising her hand as high as her chest this time.

The man stopped to purse his lips. "You know what a priest is?"

Bella nodded.

"Same thing. Teachers, priests, nuns, principals, not even police officers. Tell nobody about this. The only ones that know this top secret are your mom, and the doctors taking care of your dad, and the people in this room. Anyone who knows this secret will always use two special words spoken in order: *timber cinder.* Can you say those words back for me?"

"Timber cinder," Bella said.

The man stared at me, waiting for me to speak. "Amara, you need to say the words back."

I sneered at this man. "Timber cinder. There. I said it."

Bella repeated. "Timber cinder. What does that mean?"

He took relief in speaking with my sister, exhaling as he spoke. "It doesn't mean anything, Bella. These are words that you would never hear together, so we pick those to be sure that we never give away the secret by accident."

"Timber cinder," Bella repeated. "Timber cinder, timber cinder, timber cinder…"

He put up his hand to silence her. "It's really important to know the words, but don't ever say them, and don't ever write them down. Only when someone says them to you first should you ever speak to them about your dad. You only have to know them. Okay?"

I hated him. I hated them all. I hated how they spoke to me, to my sister, even to my mom. I hated how they made us move and how I had to leave my friends and my school. I hated how they checked on us all the time.

It was my eleventh birthday when I realized they were reading my text messages. Not long after I realized they were reading and listening to everything. A bitterness grew within for the people who swore to protect my father, but who really protected the secret of my father.

And, yes, even then I understood the difference.

*   *

"Timber cinder," he repeats.

"Okay, okay, I get it. You know who my dad is. You know who I am. Now who are you? And who are you two working for? State? DHS? FBI? NIH? And why do you still have a gun pointed at me?"

He puts up his one free hand as if to stop the barrage of questions. "My name can be Studious Stanley for now. You wouldn't be the first girl to compare me to that cartoon."

"You wouldn't be the first guy to point a gun at my crotch," I shrug and frown. "Unfortunately."

"Well, that's... disturbing." He pauses. "But to answer your questions, we don't work for any government agency, and the reason why there are two guns still pointed at you is because we are from Millennial."

I hadn't planned to meet with members of an international terrorist group for lunch—much less the one I actively worked to track down. "You have my complete attention."

"Good," Stanley says, handing me a slip of paper. It's the first time I'm noticing the latex fingertips. "I'm here to strike a bargain with you. The data packet your division is dissecting right now at DHS... You call it zero-zero-four-four-two. I need you to stop and kill the analysis. Also, there is a piece of physical evidence stored and tagged under that number. That needs to be brought to me. When you do, I will inject your father to bring him out of his condition."

"And how do I know this isn't some bullshit just to screw up our investigation?"

"If we wanted to screw the investigation up, I would just shoot you here and the man behind you would set you on fire before the EMTs arrived."

That happened to an FBI agent six months ago with nobody claiming credit. Maybe Stanley knew about it from the news and merely implied involvement to scare me. Maybe. He's uncomfortable with the threat, but it doesn't matter. Stanley is delivering a message, and it has its intended effect.

I nod.

"Once we've confirmed you've destroyed the files and you've handed over the evidence, you'll take us to the location where your father is being stored, and I'll administer it. You've got until 5 pm."

"How would I even get the message to you?"

"We'll find you. Go for a walk after work. Head to the wharf. Phone number?"

"I guess asking for yours is out of the question?"

"It's a safe bet."

I recite my eleven digits, after which he gestures for me to leave.

Standing, I turn and start walking out but double back, slowly. "How are you going to know if I actually destroy that original data packet?"

"We'll know."

I keep my steps slow and deliberate and angle to the same waiter I'd dismissed earlier. "He's covering my bill," I tell him, gesturing back to the table while heading for the door.

As I walk out, I note the position of the cameras in the restaurant, the cameras on the street. I power my phone back on and my pace quickens to a jog. Normally I cut through the National Mall to steal three minutes of air conditioning, but I can't afford to fight past tourist families and summer camp mobs.

Stepping out of L'Enfant Plaza, I cut right and move alongside the traffic on D Street toward the GSA Building, recently cleared out to accommodate the ever-growing Department of Homeland Security. Joggers are out in force today, a veritable army clad in spandex uniforms, armed with their latest tunes or audiobooks. I weave between them, sweat breaking through my shirt in unfortunate places, catching their glances as they realize my jog has purpose beyond exercise.

The 9th Street Expressway roars beneath me as I cross the overpass. While keeping an uneven pace back to the office, I begin parsing what I know so far. The most sought-after terrorist organization in the world sought *me* out. They don't know where my dad is. And while they think we're "storing" him, they know he's awake. They are comfortable being in public, and being ID'd by facial recognition—why? And I was made aware of two Millennial members in that restaurant—who knows how many more could there have been? How close to death was I in there? I look over my shoulder: there are thirty people all walking in the same direction as me, and any one of them could be a Millennial member.

And they are why I joined DHS. After my dad's assault at the hands of Millennial terrorists, everyone understood there had to be an antidote to the drug they injected him with. Even as a child, I figured this out. When DHS recruited me during college to their Counter-Terrorism task force, finding the antidote was pitched as the number one goal, yet still a secret from the rest of the department. The government's reasons for obtaining such a thing were certainly not altruistic, but as long as I could save my father, I didn't care what their goals were. I still don't care.

I cut across the street and run along the length of the GSA building. The sun's angle pours heat and light against the windows and reflects it down on the sidewalk, white-washing me with the world's brightness dial set to 10. DC is a miserable city the British should have burned down repeatedly until nothing but swamp remained.

Studious Stanley said he would know when I destroyed the file, but if they've hacked DHS to track my actions, why wouldn't they destroy the file themselves? Do they have somebody on the inside? Or am I to be the one on the inside? And how did they know 'timber cinder'?

Turning the corner, I slow my pace to a walk. Could this be a set up? A test of loyalty to the department? A sting operation from another agency? My time in service is a blip compared to most of the agents and analysts around here. Does our government set up employees with elaborate situations to ensure they can be trusted? That would be a truly fucked up thing to do, which means our intelligence community probably does it.

Then again, even if they do loyalty tests, it doesn't mean this is one of them.

Chapter 2

I stand in the security queue, watching a snake of employees feed their lunches through the metal detector, each one hurrying to get to their desk before their break was over. It seems the cafeteria was serving chicken pot pie again, sending shockwaves of people out to buy something edible.

Do I help a terrorist organization or use what I know to help capture a Millennial terrorist? The first could land me in prison. The second could drop me in a grave. Either option could spell salvation or damnation for my father. My phone trembles in my sweaty grip as I thumb down through my contact list. Everett's name stares back up at me. My roomie from the academy, my best friend through training, and the only person I could think of to talk to.

Somebody behind me clears their throat and I look up to see a ten-foot gap between me and the person in front of me. I apologize and scurry to close the gap in the queue, glance up and see one of the uniformed officers looking at me. He's part of the Federal Protection Service, a separate branch of Homeland Security designated to safeguard all government buildings. Back in the day, they were private security. Nowadays, everything is law enforcement.

His purposeful glances up my tension level. Is my face flushed? If it wasn't, it is now. Half the blood in my body pumps into my face. I must look like a tomato. I must look like I'm hiding something.

"Need ur help", I text to Everett. "Import" I add.

"Where r u?" he responds.

"Lobby."

The queue snake continues to move, and I glance back up at the officer overseeing the screeners. He's looking at me again! Still? Maybe he's been watching me since I walked in. My mind reels back to the thought of this being a loyalty test and I wonder now if this person is assigned to observe me. Or maybe he works with Millennial. And he's staring at me still. *Shit! Shit! Shit!*

My turn for the metal detector. Phone, keys, a redneck wallet fashioned from a large paper clamp stolen from the office supply closet. I drop it all from my pockets into the tote and squeeze out a smile for the security screener with a half-untucked shirt.

"Hot enough for ya?" he makes small talk. He has seen me hundreds of times but has no idea who I am beyond my badge and my face.

"Scorching," I reply.

As he slides the tote toward the scanner, I see Everett's name appear on my phone screen and beneath it 'New Message'.

"Can I—well, just... Uhm, okay, never mind," my bumbling words are an assault of confusion on the untucked guard. I cap it off with a whispered "Shit" and walk through the magnetometer.

The officer is now looking over the shoulder of the guard reviewing my tote. I know it's mine because they move it back on the conveyor and point at me. They aren't even hiding it now. The unforeseen lunch meeting, the Millennial terrorists—it has to be a loyalty test, and I'm failing. Why else would his laser focus land on me?

Because you're sweating? Because you're acting nervous and rushed? Why else indeed.

"Excuse me, Agent..." the officer leans in slightly to view my ID badge, "Amara James? Can you step out of line and into the square please?"

He points to a painted square in the screening area where naughty visitors are sent to review the contents of their purses or backpacks. Pocketknives or mace cannisters buried deep in the bowels of a forgotten pocket.

I'm not carrying a purse or pack or even a lunch bag. The officer's hand is resting on his service weapon. A supervisor in plain clothes has joined him and there are two other armed officers being called to attend.

"What's the problem?" I ask, voice cracking. "I need to report mission critical info to my supervisor right away. It's important."

My choice has been made for me. Anything I say from now on will have to include the meeting with Studious Stanley. Would I have acquiesced to Millennial's proposition if left to my own devices? I don't know.

I look at his name tag and force a smile. "Officer Wadsworth, I'm an agent here, you understand that right?"

"I can see your badge, I know how to read," he drones.

"So can you tell me what—"

"I need you to stay in the square, Agent James," he instructs, left hand out as if to restrain me.

"I'm not trying to leave the box. I'm only telling you I have a priority message for Supervisory Agent Franciscus and it can't wait."

"Well, it's going to have to wait until we're done screening you. Do not leave the square." He grows more agitated, and I watch his fingers tighten on his pistol grip.

When I turn there are two more officers standing next to me, both on edge. "What's the problem?" the taller one asks.

I begin to answer when Wadsworth responds, "She keeps trying to leave the square. I'm going to need some help with this one."

I look down and gesture wildly to my feet. "Are you kidding me? I haven't moved a fucking inch since you stuck me in time out!" I flap my arms like a duck, as if I am trying to fly away. This does not have the intended effect of making them feel stupid.

"Don't move!"

"Put your hands at your side!"

"Hands over your head!"

All three are shouting now. I instinctively pivot to the closest when Wadsworth grabs me from behind and pushes me to the ground. Arms twisted, knee in my back, hands cuffed, all in a matter of seconds. Somewhere along the way, my hair gets caught on somebody's belt and yanks out several strands.

"I'm not resisting! I'm not resisting! Fucker! Get off my head!"

"Yeah, *now* you're not resisting," one of the officers snarks.

A crowd of govies, secretaries, and agents keep a safe-yet-curious distance from me as I kneel in the square. Could I have been part of some undercover operation? Did somebody witness me talking to Millennial and point me out while in line?

"I'm going to search your pockets now. Do you have anything that's going to poke me or cut me?"

"What? You just saw me empty my pockets. What—fuck!"

"Don't fight!" one of the officers says.

"I just went through the—ouch! Ouch! Ouch! Dick! You're pulling up on my arms again!"

"It's because you're resisting," Wadsworth remarks.

I feel fingers snaking into my pockets, pulling them inside out. Fingers in my sweat-soaked shoes. Fingers running through my hair. Fingers running along the inside of my pants.

"You find anything?" one of them asks the other.

"No, nothing," he responds. He sounds concerned, disappointed. I can't see much, but what I do see is the supervisor reviewing the biopattern station, an AI device that measures heat signatures, body movement, breathing patterns, CO_2 levels, and a half dozen other variables to create a fingerprint for those that might wish others harm. And as much as I hate them for turning a shit day even shittier, I completely understand why I'm face down on the ground now.

*   *

A week after I joined DHS, the world was introduced to Stephanie Bartles. Twenty-two years old, college sophomore, pretty and blonde, just the way the media likes them.

She was the daughter of Georgi Bartles, our U.S. Ambassador assigned to Türkiye.

Stephanie had gone missing during her spring break cruise, a mystery that turned into an international firestorm as U.S. Coast Guard raided a Canadian passenger liner in Mexican waters, only to turn up nothing. Stephanie's face appeared every day, ten times per day, on every flat screen from Iceland to Argentina. No video of her abduction. No indication of an accident. No ransom message. No evidence. No suspects.

Twenty-two days after Stephanie went missing off the coast of Cancun, she appeared in the lobby of the DC Trade Center. Nobody recognized her, even after she called out her mother's name and title. No longer a beautiful blonde college student smiling for her favorite social media platform, Stephanie's face was filthy, with beads of sweat carrying away bits of grime and sliding them down her neck. Eyes glazed, face contorted into a deranged smile, she looked around the lobby like a child walking into a colorful museum.

"Mom? Mom?" she called out. Heads turned. "I'm looking for my mom Georgi Bartles. Mom?"

FPS Officer Dominic White walked over to the confused girl, hands up in a gesture of peace. "Are you okay, Miss?" people heard him ask.

"I'm looking for my mom," she asked. "Can you help me?"

Nobody knows what Dominic White saw or heard to trigger his movements. Witnesses saw exactly what the CCTV captured: White screamed and tackle-rushed Stephanie Bartles, driving into her torso and lifting the lithe young woman off the ground. He kept running, using her

17

body to smash through the full-length lobby window and sending shattered glass in all directions.

A split second later, Dominic White and Stephanie Bartles vanished into light, and the subsequent pressure wave fractured the skulls of thirty bystanders. What the thermobaric wave didn't kill, the kinetic energy of their bodies hurled against concrete walls polished off.

Twelve of forty-four survived. Eight of those still had their brains intact enough to describe what happened that day, but their burns were so extensive it would be weeks before they could be questioned.

*   *

"What do you think you are doing to my agent?" I hear Darren Franciscus and turn my head to see him hulking toward us. One of the officers stands up and puts his hand on Franciscus's chest.

"This is an FPS matter," the man says. "Your agent violated policy and refused to be searched."

I yelled out from the tile floor, "He's so full of shit his eyes are turning brown!"

"Amara, no," my lieutenant grumbles, shaking his head. He turns his attention back to the man in front of him. "Officer, what are you searching my agent for?"

The supervisor intervenes and the two men lock horns. "She came into the lobby looking suspicious, sweating, looking around at all the security personnel. Biopat readers gave her a similar match to the Bukum Yilani bombing. We were searching her for a trigger or possible explosives."

"Wait, you handcuffed a DHS agent, *my* DHS agent for a matching biopat scan? Based on what? Sweating? For looking at you? It's a *thousand* degrees outside. She *works* here!" The supervisor tries to interrupt, but Franciscus steps forward and postures himself so aggressively I think he might put the officer's eye out with his chin. "You have about fifteen seconds to uncuff my agent and give her back her effects. Then you better crawl into your office and file a report with your direct because I'm going to lodge a complaint with your department head about thirty seconds after I get upstairs."

The cuffs are already off and I dust the humiliation off my pants. I make a large gesture of stepping out of the square, grabbing my phone and keys from the tote and dangling them in front of Officer Wadsworth who set all this in motion.

"You've got something to say, Agent James?" he postures.

"No, she doesn't," Franciscus interrupts before I can get a word in, then points his finger at the FPS officer, "And neither do you."

He stands next to me, gestures to the elevators, and the two of us walk past the gawking crowd. Eyes everywhere. Will I be able to come to work again without somebody recognizing me? Without remembering what happened? Or should I say, *misremembering* what happened?

Franciscus asks if the people waiting for their ride would mind waiting just a little bit longer, which when asked so politely, is granted with immediate courtesy. Either that or they don't want to be anywhere near me. Only when the elevator doors close does Franciscus speak quietly. "Please tell me you didn't start all that bullshit. Tell me I did not stick out my neck for you just to have my head lobbed off."

"I didn't, I swear!" I feel my voice crack. "I didn't do anything!"

The elevator opens and we head straight for his office. He closes the door and suddenly I am 14 years old again, sitting straight in the principal's office at school. "Those bi-opat scanners picked up on something, and the AI is pretty clever. Want to make a guess as to why you would trigger it?"

I tell him—everything. From when I stepped into the restaurant to the moment I got to the lobby. I tell him every temptation I had to free my father to my desire to capture the terrorists behind the offer. I even admit that the decision to come clean was rather forced on me by the officer in the lobby.

Darren remains still during my accounting. He makes one call to have a team surveil the restaurant. A second call goes out to a new agent, Yvonne, asking her to run prints and DNA on 00442. Then his attention returns to me. He takes no notes, makes no criticism, asks no questions beyond a clarifying point. When my silence fills the space, he lets his own quietude join it, mingle with it. We sit there, staring at each other.

"There's only one way to play this...you know that, right?" He finally speaks. "The attacks by Bukum Yilani have forced Homeland to set strict protocols for influenced agents and their families."

My words fall out in a whisper. "I know."

"We don't capitulate. We dig deep into the data, and we mobilize everything. You're not the only one who made a promise to your dad. *How* we keep that promise is kinda forced here, though. You get that, right?"

I make the smallest of nods.

"And this bullshit downstairs. Do not throw shade at any FPS officer. Nothing. No grunts. No eye rolls. No snark. *Nada. Entiendes?*"

I start to make an exasperated sigh.

Franciscus puts up a finger. "Not even that. You will be a stone wall that all their attitude shatters against."

I let the sigh out quietly and nod again.

"Now... For Millennial, you need to be one hundred percent behind my calls when we step out of this office. Put on your best face, because image is going to be everything when the details get to the higher ups. OIG is absolutely going to second guess everything we touch, and other agents *will be interviewed* about your loyalty. Got it?"

The sincerity of Studious Stanley's offer clings to my sweaty shirt. The opportunity to free my father after years of hell is a devil whispering assurances in my ear, and I've brushed him off my shoulder in favor of some misguided loyalty to this man, to this department. Chest aching, I steel my gaze at Lieutenant Franciscus. "Let's go get the fuckers."

He claps his hands together and points at me. "Perfect! That's what everyone needs to see."

Chapter 3

Data packet 00442 was recovered from an unidentified thumb drive at the Department of Agriculture. Most govies wouldn't have looked at it twice, but Phineas McCallister was a salty bastard who was on the lookout for ne'er-do-wells slowing down his department. Check-listing through his bureaucratic day, he went from station to station to verify the productivity of his workgroup. At the very end of a line of cubicles, an unattended station sat open with the screen on.

McCallister knew the employee to be home on parental leave, so finding it on was a red flag already. With nobody in the area, he checked the computer to discover a flattened section of plastic with color offset from the tower's case. Had it matched, he probably would have missed it. He pulled on the edge of the rectangle, felt it easily give way to reveal a USBX drive end. The piece was fashioned with the intent for subterfuge. And even though the station being left on was suspicious, McCallister was convinced he would have found it anyway because he had "a sneaky suspicion something was up." God forbid somebody were to steal aggregate corn production data, the country would collapse.

That camouflaged thumb drive now sits on an air-gapped system in the corner of DHS. Pulled from evidence and fast-tracked ahead of twenty active investigations, Franciscus and I sit side-by-side in the cramped room, the notification sign on the door changed to 'Top Secret'. McCallister joins us remotely from his office, his only view of our screen comes from a camera pointed over our shoulders.

Low-tech, jankety even, we have no idea if a virus or malware on this drive will infect our system and worm its way through the computers at DHS. Nothing was found on the Agriculture computers, and whoever placed this USBX drive certainly missed their opportunity had they wished, but protocol is protocol. What if the computer at DOA had connectivity issues and stopped the spread of a virus? Or the virus needed to be activated by a particular operating system? Or the plan was to infiltrate the DHS systems all along? That's why air-gapped systems exist: for all the what ifs.

I scroll through hundreds of files loaded on the drive. Occasionally, McCallister will shout in a too-loud voice to go back and review one of them.

"No, sorry, it looks fine. Keep going," he tells us.

Two hours of combing over files results in dead ends. No viruses, no unusual executable files. All files show copied one day before the DOA employee left for parental leave, a worthy distinction only in a vacuum of data. Were it not for Millennial's interest in the thumb drive (and its camouflaged design), we would mark it as a non-event and move on.

I turn to McCallister's face on the screen. "This new employee—the one who left for maternity—what's her name?"

McAllister tells us her first name, fumbles through some keystrokes offscreen, then clears his throat. "Yes, Danny Bahri. She moved up to us from the Ohio field office maybe six months ago? Five or six? Somewhere around that time."

"No issues? Problems? Anything that might have indicated her political affiliation?"

"No, she's kept to herself mostly. Used to work for RBCS... Uhh, that's Rural Business Cooperative Services... She was the top candidate, not that there were many."

"Top how?"

"Education. She holds a doctorate in genetic engineering. I hate to say it, but she was overqualified for the position."

I ask him, "Why do you say—"

A knock on the door and the newest member of the Counter-Terrorism Task Force walks in. He joined a few weeks ago, but our contact has been restricted by circumstance. Now he is standing behind my chair, his hulking form making me look like a child sitting near her father.

"Hey boss, I got the results you requested," he announces.

"Mister McCallister," Franciscus says, "We'll be in touch." With that he disconnects the vidchat before there can be any questions or objections.

Our new agent looks at the screen, verifies we are alone in the room, and begins, "Prints come back to Danielle Bahri living in College Park. DNA comes back to Danielle *and* Ismaya Bahri, husband of Danielle. And here is where it gets weird...

"Ismaya was reported missing *two years ago*. Now I guess it's possible the DNA is from two years ago, but I did a little digging and found the drive is new. So new that they didn't hit the market until about six months ago. That means either Ismaya performed the manufacturing on this drive and the company sat on it for eighteen months..."

"Or the husband isn't missing," I interrupt, standing up. "Weird enough to make Mr. and Mrs. Bahri suspects. I'm Amara."

He shakes my hand, "I know. Iván. Good to meet you finally." He pronounces it in traditional Latino with a long 'e'.

We move to leave when Franciscus clears his throat. "Where are you two going?"

I thumb in the direction of the door. "To follow up on the Bahri's."

"You know you're not going into the field, right? We have more experienced people to do that. You two stay here in the office. Dig, but do it from the desk. This isn't a cop show. We research, we communicate, we plan, we execute, we stay alive."

"We're running out of time," I respond.

"Only because you're still standing here. Go dig and report when you have something."

Iván and I walk briskly down the hall, and I can tell either of us would run if the other weren't there. He's tall but not as tall as I first thought, maybe four inches over me, but he's broad shouldered and looks like he played football.

"When they told me you were coming on board, I thought you were a woman. Everyone was pronouncing it like 'Yvonne.'"

"I get that a lot."

"You can just pronounce it Ivan, like the Russian name. Avoid confusion."

"Russians also pronounce it 'Yvonne.'"

"No shit?"

"No shit."

"Well *Yvonne*, I'm just glad to have another woman in the department." I tack a smirk on to let him know I'm teasing, but glance up to confirm he's being a good sport.

There is some truth to my joke, however: the department is short on estrogen. Plenty of women join DHS, but a minority go into Counter-Terrorism, and fewer become field agents. Some believe this a male-constructed barrier, a wall defending one of the last few niche professions that they feel only men can excel at, and so they guard it fiercely. I haven't seen that.

To give credit, the male sex has improved in many metrics over the years. I have never been groped or insulted because I'm a woman. I haven't even been asked out on a date by anyone I worked with—a problem for some women; not a problem for me. Sexual harassment complaints are rare. And with the exception of the fuck wad in the lobby, my run-ins with men here have been amenable.

However, these are not boys, nor are they college students. There is no harvest of political correctness you find cultivated on a campus or in a classroom. Nobody here cares if I feel uncomfortable. No amount of gender studies or sensitivity training has managed to break these testosterone-fueled brains—they remain impervious to whatever improvement society has deemed necessary. Theirs is a binary existence, and it isn't *him* or *her*. Instead, it is either *in* or *out*.

When you are *out*, you are treated with cold courtesy, assignments are quiet, and your presence on meaningful investigations is relegated to compartmentalized hell. I quickly learned here is that men communicate in a ferocious exchange of barbs, insults, and sarcasm. There is no line to be drawn. Fold in an ample supply of movie quotes, game knowledge, and sports commentary and you're allowed *in*. It is a status I am determined to retain.

Iván and I make our way down a long line of cubicles adorned with family photos, crayon art, football paraphernalia, tri-screen monitors, and piles of folders. The analysts are already plowing through DC footage of the restaurant and every street within ten blocks of it. Finding Millennial is a top priority, and we're hitting it from the bottom up and top down. Our walk is interrupted by three different analysts asking for verification if they've caught 'our guy.' The answer each time is no. When Iván and I finally stop, it's at an empty cubicle with a laptop and a folder labeled *Welcome to DHS*.

"Estoy al cruzar," I point to the cubicle on the other side of the partition. Iván looks at me with a blank stare, so I repeat myself. "I'm cattycorner to your cube. Grab your chair and follow me, unless you have all your logins."

"I don't even know what I'm missing, so you lead the way."

Between interruptions, we dig into Danielle and Ismaya Bahri. Social media is set to private for both of them, so every platform gets a DHS emergency request. I know which companies will respond like lightning struck and which ones will drag their heels. We'll get the data no matter what now that Millennial is involved though. Every picture deleted, every comment edited, every heart emoji, every profile they looked at but never acknowledged with a click because they were afraid their spouse would get jealous about looking up an old school sweetheart. Those logs exist for every human being, and the data intersects in ways that feed hungry algorithms so that the platform knows its user better than they know themselves. Thanks to the Stored Communications Act, the courts will invariably give us whatever we need, and then we'll know our suspects too. These emergency requests get us off the starting block just a tiny bit faster. And the way the clock is ticking, we'll need every minute.

Mitch accesses camera footage from an intersection near the National Mall, and while we don't see our subject, we do see an image of someone pixelated beyond recognition. Pedestrians on the right and left, front and back, all walk by in perfect clarity, all while this 8-bit version of a human being steps worry-free down a road bristling with cameras. Every second of footage is pixelated with privacy emitters, and any CCTV or even video captured by cell phones will be rendered useless. These devices are not cheap and require a sophisticated operator to ensure that they are employed properly.

"It's an egg scrambler. Anti-tech zealots using advanced technology to avoid apprehension," Mitch quips. "Bathing in irony here."

"We got 'em too. Coming out of the restaurant right after you, Amara." Singh calls out and I trot over to see. Five heads crowd in behind mine as we inspect the video footage. It's Studious Stanley alright (I recognize the edge of the polo shirt, the jeans), followed by Gun-Toting-Gary. They each receive ridiculous names for now until we claim their idents. Their faces are not only pixelated, but hands and ears and even the back of their heads. Flashes of light that are invisible to human eyes pierce the confused image and white out the camera shots at certain angles.

Mitch stands up and smacks a clipboard across the aluminum cubicle walls, and in response a dozen heads pop up to see. "Listen up! They're using scramblers to hide their faces from cameras, but we can follow their dumbass cube heads, so get Singh's camera coordinates and let's figure out where they go. Move it, everyone!"

By 3:15pm, Franciscus is back with news of an emergency warrant granted. Every platform we can think of has been subpoenaed and the information feeds us with a firehose. Every cubicle is occupied now, an army of analysts and agents combing through emails, private messages, posts, photos, memes, video, location data, edits, drafts, deletions. The data stampede into the Counter-Terrorism task force, and we devour them like starving wolves.

By 3:30pm, DNA swabs and fingerprints from the restaurant are submitted for DataMatch, one of our many tools that cuts across multiple agencies and jurisdictions. International databases are added and rescinded as the U.S. falls in and out of favor with various countries, but despite the speed at which it all operates, it isn't fast enough for my tastes.

By 4pm my fingers tap at my desk so loudly that Desmond next door lets out an exasperated 'please!' My mind keeps dragging my concentration to the restaurant, to the offer made by Studious Stanley. Millennial must know by now that I am working against them. Or do they? Stanley said they would know, but perhaps he was bluffing? He certainly wasn't bluffing about the things he knew.

Shen is the first analyst to notice the geospatial metadata focuses on Washington Union Station, far from the office at the Department of Agriculture, farther still from

Danielle Bahri's home in Maryland. And the dates line up with when the drive was discovered.

I piggyback off Shen's data and try to locate Danielle Bahri. She posted pictures of being at home with the baby thirty minutes ago, and a stream of hundreds of 'hearts' and 'likes' bombarded the album. The dates on the photos' exif data show they were taken two days prior. This isn't criminal, but when you have a suspect posting two-day old pics and passing them off as just taken, it's smoke from a fire.

By 4:15pm, fingerprints and DNA confirm me and 114 other individuals from the restaurant. I'm pulled from my work on Bahri to scan through each ID file: none look remotely like Studious Stanley or Gun-Toting-Gary. I have to confirm with Darren at least three times. Yes, I am positive. No, I'm not under too much stress. Yes, I can attest to this on a report.

By 4:24pm, Daniels across the room has confirmed that at least 15 people on our DataMatch file aren't even within 100 miles of Washington, D.C., and eight of them have never been to our lovely Capitol. And while they have nothing to do with our investigation, the discombobulated data means we can't trust anything fed to us from these efforts. Groans go up in a chorus from across the cubicle farm until Darren tells them all to shut it.

The break we catch comes in on the back-end of our investigation at 4:37pm. Shen manages to geolocate Bahri in Washington, D.C., blocks from her employment office. He's on a roll, and everyone feeds off his leads. I open up the files just sent to me from Franciscus. They're marked 'footage' with today's date. It's video from the Department of Agriculture.

"Mitch," I call out, "The same egg scrambler is being used by Bahri. Her face is blurred out, but her phone is giving her away. She's has got to be working with them."

He wheels over, chair squeaking and straining. "Unless it's somebody with her phone. Can you even tell if it's a woman? Color of her skin?"

"No, but—"

"Seems awfully convenient she's smart enough to wear a scrambler but dumb enough to let us track her phone."

"Fuck."

Franciscus rounds the corner wearing his vest and pistol. "Amara! Mitchell! Grazelli! Zingg! And... Fagundes! To the Insecurity Room now!"

As we worm through the cube farm, Iván asks me in a low tone, "Insecurity Room?"

"You never know if you're going to leave it with your head held high or your ass in your hands," I say.

Iván laughs nervously but stifles his amusement as we funnel into Insecurity. As we move past Franciscus, he calls for two more teams, only these he dispatches to the armory. The analysts are the only ones left in the cube farm, noses buried in their computers, as the glass door closes behind us.

As the others settle in, he leans in and asks in a low tone, "So why does he call you by your first name and everyone else by their last name?"

"Because there are three analysts and two agents named James in here and every time he calls me by my last name, five other heads pop up like prairie dogs."

Darren claps the room into silence and focus. "We are at double-redundancy plus one. You five are Bait Team. Millennial has indicated that they will catch up with Agent Amara when she leaves today. We're going to give them that opportunity. Capitol PD is vacating all patrols along your route so they don't spook our would-be's. All of you are going out for drinks on foot. Take H Street heading for the bar on 200 North Street Southwest. This is on the way to the wharf where she's expected to go."

"You mean *Kelly's*?" Mitch interrupts. "That's like five miles away..."

"It's not even two miles, you fat fuck," Franciscus barks.

"...and it's a hundred fucking degrees outside!" Mitch ignores the insult and continues to talk over him.

"Yeah, a hundred degrees. Lose some of that water weight and maybe you'll pass your fucking physical."

There's an intimacy to this exchange, one that nobody else in the office could pull off. But Mitchell is seasoned and knows Darren Franciscus well enough to deliver his own barbs—and when the time to talk shit has expired.

"Keep weapons concealed and only draw if absolutely necessary. Civies are everywhere and we don't want a gun-fight in our glorious Capitol—"

"Or worse," Grazelli adds.

Franciscus nods, "Exactly, or worse. We know Millennial employs improvised weapons and high yield explosives. We will have eyes on you all, with two more teams in the field. Team 2 behind and Team 1 in front."

"No drones?" Grazelli asks.

"No drones. Avionics has them all out for repairs. And before you ask, *yes,* I mean 'all', and *yes* I will be putting somebody's head on a stick."

Somebody lets out a long *'fuck'* but I don't catch who.

"Grazelli, you're senior in this team. You're taking a walk, that's it. Drinks with the guys..." I put up my hands in mock offense and Darren Franciscus waves them down.

"Don't even start, Amara. We all know you piss standing up."

That gets a laugh out of everybody, a tension breaker that loosens our neck muscles. Franciscus sends a flurry of text messages out and then refocuses on us once the chatter abates.

"Okay, get serious now. Hey! Eyes on me. Millennial is expecting our lady here to have done some nefarious shit on their behalf. She has risked her life to bring this intel to us, and we want to capitalize on it." Franciscus throws me the quickest of glances, and I understand that he is painting a picture of me as unwavering, uncompromising, unimpeachable.

He goes on, "We can be the first ones in the world to actually capture one of these fuckers. The HUMINT we get from a single Millennial terrorist can save countless lives. Act casual on the walk. All we know is they want to make contact with Amara. Earbuds in, pay attention, and we might get lucky. Act casual but stay alert. Nobody burns today. Got it?"

"Got it," we all answer.

"Get out of here, then. We've got a job to do." As our group starts to head out, Franciscus puts his hands in front of both Iván and me. His tone changes, his face changes. "Amara, you and I both know what's at stake and how hard this is going to be if these guys make contact. Keep your head, okay?"

I nod.

"And Iván, let me make this abundantly clear. There is no acceptable outcome that involves her dying and you living. None. You picking up what I'm putting down, noob?"

"Yes, Sir." Iván looks at me wide-eyed as we turn to leave. He whispers, "What's a noob?"

"I have no idea, but I know it's you."

Chapter 4

Compared to the assaulting heat from lunchtime, this walk is almost pleasant. Grazelli and Iván walk about fifty paces in front of me, shirts untucked to conceal their pieces. Iván wears a backpack while Grazelli carries his worn leather 'lucky' satchel.

I walk by myself, put in my ear buds and groove to some imaginary tunes as I go, surf my phone, hoping anyone watching can see what I'm doing. Just little ol' me, out for a stroll waiting for terrorists to make contact on the busy streets of Washington, D.C. *La dee da...*

Mitchell and Zingg are roughly twenty paces behind, chatting it up and doing their best to look like they're ready for the weekend. Mitch would probably drink a beer on the walk if he could, whereas Everett Zingg looks nervous. He's as green as I am. We graduated from the academy together and he's a good friend to me. I hate the idea that he's in back, that he could be snuck up on if Team 2 doesn't do their job right.

The sun angles low and warms our backs, but at least we don't have to squint to watch for suspects. And there are suspects everywhere. The man staring at me over his sunglasses as we pass each other. The two men in suits standing at the corner where no bus stop exists. An older woman wearing a coat on a day where most people in shorts are about to have heat stroke. A black van with black tinted windows slowing as it creeps alongside the sidewalk, a predator stalking from behind, only to speed up and drive away out of sight. A man who looks like the gunman from the restaurant steps from one of the offices, about ready to innocently collide with me and pass a note or burner phone as he does. Instead, he puts up his hands and steps back in surprise, pattering off at a brisk pace across the street and never looks back in my direction. Not the same man.

I am mentally exhausted after only a mile. Callouts from the other teams mention nothing of consequence, providing numerous opportunities for me to fabricate scenarios. The approaching woman carrying a water bottle is actually a terrorist armed with gasoline who will douse me with it, toss her cigarette at me, and watch me writhe in the conflagration. As she draws closer, I see she is actually vaping, and the water bottle remains in her hand.

I'm feeling like we might reach Kelly's after all, which would be both a relief and a disappointment. Millennial has decided not to make contact—or never intended to in the first place—or has been spooked off by the phalanx of agents who seem to be drawing closer the further we move down the street.

"We've got location pings on Danielle Bahri's social media accounts, everyone," Franciscus announces over the radio. "Union Station 22 minutes ago, somewhere on First

Street 10 minutes ago. Hang right on First on your way to Kelly's. Cell account intel incoming: stand by for a change of plans."

Our team turns down First Street as the sun plays peek-a-boo between the rooftops. Maintaining our casual stroll has faltered. We're all looking around far too often.

"Multiple cell phone pings for Danielle and Ismaya," Franciscus chirps. "Look alive, people. We are switching gears. Apprehending the Bahri's is now our top priority. Pics are uploaded to your phones. Team One, take 550 First Street. Team Two, take 425 Second Street. Bait Team, take 500 First Street. Everyone be careful."

Team Two unloads from their SUV in front of us and fans out across the multiple buildings. We jog past them to the next building and head for the lobby, but Grazelli grabs both Iván and me and pulls us aside.

"The boss wants you both out here on recon."

"What?"

"He called me just now, direct. You're to stay out here, keep an eye on things. If Millennial makes contact, click into your buds three times and we'll come running."

"But—"

Grazelli is already walking away, "No buts. These are orders." And with that, he's gone.

I look at Iván. He shrugs. "Hey, I'm the new guy. Maybe they're worried about me screwing things up."

"Yeah, that's what it is," I say.

The street and sidewalk are packed, but I look around for any sign of the Bahri's—or anything that may be suspicious. All I see are suits and civvies rushing to get home.

And then I see him.

He stares at me from across the street, hands at his sides, Mets baseball cap, and green polo shirt tucked into a pair of chinos. It isn't Ismaya Bahri, but the second man from the restaurant. I stare for a long time, not sure if I truly see what I see. I could have sworn I saw him before when we first started walking, but the nose and hair were wrong. But maybe it was him and my memory is shot. Or maybe I'm now seeing what I want to see.

I blaze across the street, deftly avoiding the cars only to have a bicyclist clip my arm and spin me around. The bike torques 180° yet the rider manages to stay on. He yells something but for the life of me I can't understand what.

My target has already ducked into an office building so new you can still smell the paint on it. Scaffolding wraps around the entire west side with caution tape roping off the sidewalk from cone to orange cone.

Iván is calling after me, and then I hear him over my earbuds calling for backup to 490 First Street. The office building steps are long and shallow, and bounding up makes for uneven strides. The last one catches my toes and the world turns ninety degrees. My palms hit the new concrete and barely save me from losing my teeth.

I leap to my feet and burst through the heavy plastic tarp serving as a doorway. There are only painters and electricians in the lobby, completing their finishing touches.

"Where'd he go?" Blank stares. I fumble at my belt, unclip my badge, and hold it up high. "Where did he go? A dónde fue él?"

Two men point to a hallway with an arched ceiling.

"Amara!" I hear Iván call from behind me.

I call over my shoulder, "This way! Mets cap! Green shirt!" And then I am running in dim light, or maybe my eyes have not adjusted from the brightness of a D.C. afternoon. The hallway terminates in a rectangular room with open elevator shafts guarded by scissor gates on one side. On the other side, a hiss spills out of the pneumatic door closer, and I turn to see the metal door latching with a *click*.

"Amara!" Iván calls from the hallway. "We gotta wait for backup!"

I push open the metal door, race down a stairwell, through a second door, bumbling into a basement area where the elevator shafts terminate. Pallets of construction material checker the open space along with stacks of pipes and conduit. There are pipes running across the walls, the ceilings, large ones, small ones. Pipes ping from the next room. Pipes ping above me.

I hear a secondary noise—like a hum. For the first time beyond the shooting range, I draw my service pistol and hold it in a retracted position like we learned in the academy. Heavy footfalls come from the stairwell and when the door opens Iván appears.

I hush him before he can call out to me. I point into the room where the humming originates, and he draws his pistol as well. Side by side, we move carefully, watching each corner, looking for any movement. My earbuds (and presumably Iván's) are chattering away with requests for our location and position and instructions to hold.

"Stand by, stand by, stand-fucking-by!" I whisper shout. The line goes quiet.

Iván suddenly lurches forward. When I instinctively move to grab him, I find myself tripping on the same piece of rebar he just did. How we didn't fall or shoot each other is incredible, but we regain our balance and end up back-to-back.

"Graceful," he whispers.

"No shit. Scared the piss out of me."

He breathes and a tiny chuckle escapes his throat. As we look around, he taps my shoulder. "What's that?"

We step around a stack of cinderblocks and follow a wall that runs floor to ceiling with pipes and conduit. The run of plumbing and electricity stops suddenly as they approach the middle of the basement area. It's as if they've been severed by a laser. The wall opens up at an angle to reveal a blue light, and after five feet of hinged concrete, the pipes continue their journey as if never disturbed.

I move closer and see the heavy hinges inside the secret door. Inside this tiny space is a clear plastic shell that appears vaguely man-shaped and multiple blocks of material fastened to the inside walls with wires running from one to another.

"Op, this is Agent Amara," I radio for the first time. "We're in 490 First Street lower level. There is a small room that I believe may be a Millennial crypt."

"A what?" Iván asks.

I put up my hand to wave off the question. We barely know anything about the Millennial crypts, and this may be the first time anyone has actually seen one.

"Amara, hold your position and await backup. I repeat hold your position." It isn't Franciscus's voice, but I don't question the order. "Do you have a suspect?"

"No. We chased him down here, but he's disappeared. All I have is this room thing that's right out of a scifi movie. It's making a humming noise. There's a lot of wires connecting to—no no no!"

A timer. 0:20. Now 0:19. Now 0:18.

Iván sees it and both of us turn and sprint. We scrape past the cinder blocks, manage to trip on the same rebar that tried to kill us on the way in. For the second time in a matter of a minute, we both stay on our feet and pass the threshold for this death room we've found ourselves in.

"Amara, report! We've got agents coming—"

"No! Get the fuck away! There's a bomb in here!"

Iván passes me with surprising speed, smashing into the door and flinging it wide for me to get by. We've made it halfway up the stairwell when the explosion claims the wall and the steps we just climbed. If not for the steel pillar in the center of the stairwell, the debris would have certainly riddled us with shards of concrete and metal. The concussion alone is enough to smash my body upon the steps, with Iván's weight collapsing on top of me.

Darkness, dust, a smell like motor oil and metal. The air is thick with the taste of cement and my head feels like I've been used like a punching bag. I can't see. I can't think. I can't hear. I can barely breathe. All I feel is hot air all around, cold cement stairs beneath me, and a warm drip from above. The liquid slides down my cheek, across my nose, onto my lips, and into my mouth. Blood. Mine? Iván's? Maybe both.

Chapter 5

Beep. Beep. Beep. Each tone shrinks in volume, spaced by a random interval, but holds steady in pitch. With each iteration, I click the thumb trigger until I can hear nothing. The tone volume resets but drops an octave, and the pattern starts all over again.

"Beep. Beep. Beep," I mock.

"Please remain quiet," the synthetic voice admonishes me. *"Restarting sequence."*

Bella gives me her wide embarrassed eyes I know oh so well, and gestures to the controller in my hand. She sits across from me in a room so small our knees almost touch. She couldn't visit me at the hospital so insisted on coming to my hearing exam.

"Sorry, continue," I say to the computer.

"Please remain quiet. Restarting sequence."

Bella whispers, "You don't need to—"

"Please remain quiet. Restarting sequence."

I shake my head and hiss, "Fuck this stupid—"

"Please remain quiet. Restarting sequence."

"Oh my God, Amara, just shut up!"

"Please remain quiet. Restarting sequence."

"You shut up!"

"Please remain quiet. Restarting sequence."

She makes a zipping gesture across her lips. I sneer and do my best to concentrate on the world's worst audio book.

The artificial eardrum is a nice invention. After only three days, my brain had adjusted to the implant, and after five days I noticed how poor my hearing was in my uninjured ear. I began inadvertently cocking my head to the right, relying on my new eardrum.

Another octave drop and then another. I start missing some of the tones and so the AI feeds me backward to my last perfect score until the computer was able to determine the exact range of my hearing.

"Your exam is complete," the computer plays a little song with its notification.

Bella grabs her purse and sweater, then shoots me dead with her gaze. "Thanks for making that take a half hour longer than it had to."

"I had to pee! I had two ice teas during lunch."

"Did you have to have a conversation with the computer?"

"No, that was a bonus just for you. What's your hurry? You have someplace important to be?"

"Kinda." Bella holds the door open while averting my eyes.

"What's going on?"

"I'm meeting a friend," she says.

When we reach the counter, the technician looks at my sister and asks if she's me. Bella points in my direction and

I wave, "I'm Amara James. My sister came for moral support."

"Aw, that's sweet," the technician says. "You know how scary these hearing tests can be."

I wait for this woman to walk away and then whisper to Bella, "Did she get snarky with us?"

"I think it was just with you. But yeah."

The technician returns and gives us a wave, "You're all set. Have a good day!" She doesn't want me to have a good day. She wants me to step in front of a bus.

"What was her problem?" I ask Bella rhetorically when we're on the other side of the hearing test office door.

"Maybe that you interrupted her when she was on the phone? Or maybe when you insisted on having a second chair in a room the size of a closet? Or maybe she didn't like you flirting with her hearing test?"

"Not my fault the AI likes me better."

"Truth. When it was chiming, *'Please shut up,'* it was really saying, *'I want you Amara!'*"

We leave and pass a dozen specialty offices ranging from physical therapy to canine cancer detection specialists. I see a cute little pug who looks like he's eighty years old being carried in by a sad-faced man who seems to already know what the vet is going to tell him.

"You can pet him," he offers me. "Go on, he doesn't have a mean bone left in him."

My fingers run through his coarse hair, come away a little filmy and smelling of age. I go back for seconds and cup his googly-eyed head in my hands and nuzzle his face while inhaling his terrible breath. It's a connection that loosens my heart and fills me with an urge to cry and play and laugh and comfort simultaneously. I cut it short, disconnect from the animal and his owner and avert my eyes from Bella's judging looks. She doesn't break though.

"You sure the doctor cleared you on the concussion?"

"We should get a dog," I say matter-of-factly.

"'We?' You mean 'me'. You're never at the house." Bella swings the door open and we both step into a blast of Virginia humidity.

"I'm at the house plenty."

"You got your own apartment! That's how 'never' you are at the house."

"I'm coming tomorrow, and I'll be there all week. And I would walk the dog every day I was there if we had a dog."

Our cars are parked back-to-back. It's sweltering outside and although I know the inside of the car will be downright miserable, it's not why I'm lingering.

"You didn't have to drive all this way just to go to my hearing test," I say.

"Yes, I did. You exploded your ear, got a concussion, four broken ribs, second degree burns, and somehow also broke one toe...How?"

"I have no idea."

"I'm just worried. I love you," Bella frowns. "Isn't there some other job you can do there that isn't so... Blowy-uppy?"

I can't help but smile, "Well, I promise if a better position opens up, I will transfer out of the Blowy-Uppy Department."

"Now you're just making fun of me."

"Yes, I am." She hugs me and I push her lightly away.

"Sorry! I know you hate hugs."

"It's just hot. Now go. You've got a long drive. Two and a half hours?"

"Three. I've got to go to New Jers—"

I feel the corner of my mouth twist up.

"Damn it. Fine, I'm going to go see Mom."

I pointed at her, "Ha! I knew it!"

Bella rolls her eyes and opens her car door. "I'm going. Bye!"

"Why didn't you just say you were going to go see her?"

My sister is already trying to escape, starting the car and blasting the air conditioner. I step just barely in the way so she can't close the car door. "Because I knew you would get like this. Because I wanted to have one day where we don't fight about Mom!"

"I'm not fighting! Who's fighting?" I step back and then make the sign of the blessing. "Go in peace, drive safe, enjoy dinner with your mother."

"*Our* mother."

"Semantics."

Bella tests the steering wheel to see if it is cool enough to touch, then let's out a big sigh. "Okay, I'm going. Love you. I'll tell Mom you said 'hi.'"

"Don't bother." I step back again and wave her off. "See you at *our* house tomorrow."

"Semantics," she calls out the window without looking back.

Chapter 6

Walter Reed Medical bustles with a host of nurses, therapists, clinicians, technicians, and—above all—bureaucrats. I leave the main area, cross the threshold of a restricted area, and make my way to a set of special elevators. I have been coming here since I was 10 years old, many staff members recognize me.

The Marine on duty is not one such person, and he waits diligently for the guard to complete my scan. At least the process is quicker than at DHS. It's quiet, and the only indication I pass is a tiny LED 5x5 readout with a single light in the center illuminated. He looks at my credentials a second time and politely asks what floor I am headed to.

"L3." Something about his voice sets off my tinnitus and my left ear—my natural ear—fights to cut out the ringing. I find myself cocking my head to the right again.

It has been two weeks, and the doctor told me the new phonograft procedure would take longer for my ear to heal than the traditional tympanoplasty, but eventually my hearing would be better than before the D.C. explosion.

It's a small consolation. My jaw is sore. My ribs are sore. The burn patch on my back and neck are still tender to the touch. A double dose of pain medication made it easier to keep up appearances with Bella, but now it's wearing off and moving in any direction hurts.

I get a smiling nod, and he allows me into the elevator. The last thing I see him do is hold up three fingers to the guard behind the glass who controls the elevator. There are no floor buttons inside. A call button, a keyhole, and an emergency stop are the only controls.

When the doors open, I am greeted by yet another Marine who grants me an identical smiling nod and steps aside, revealing a lime green hallway and heavy closed doors. Unlike his counterpart fifty feet above us, this man has seen me before and knows where I am headed.

When I open the lab door, I see a couple familiar faces look up briefly from their work and give me small waves. Dr. Nikonov stares at me from behind his desk and acknowledges me with the briefest of blinks.

"Amara!" Dr. Maggie Gonzales approaches me with open arms and a wide smile. "What are you doing here?"

I furrow my brow. "You told me I should come..."

"It's an expression!" She gives me the lightest of hugs, like she was embracing a Jenga tower, then hooks my arm and walks us over to a glass case. Within it is a rat covered in so many tiny needles that he looks like a porcupine. "How are you feeling? Any long-term damage?"

Dr. Gonzales worked as a scientist for the U.S. Government since before I was born. Chinese-born, in her sixties now, she married an American and managed to carve out advanced research deep underground. When my father was attacked, she was part of the team that revived him...

temporarily anyway. When it came to us visiting and interacting with him, Maggie bent over backward to make accommodations. Even more than that, she was a friend to us all. She arranged my internships and even sponsored me for my bioengineering application to MIT. It killed her when I turned down the job offer to work here, but she never wavered in her support.

I sigh. "Well, I'm walking. So is my new partner. He definitely took the brunt of it. Got badly burned. Both of us needed new eardrums, we—"

"Let's see what they did here." She grabs my chin and turns my head gently to look at my ear. "Let me guess, new phonograft implant?"

"Yup."

"Oh, you'll be so happy you got it. They should have done both ears and given you a twofer."

"I forgot my coupon. Anyway, just a lot of soreness. Burns. Nothing a bottle of pills and a box of wine can't fix."

"Don't tease, Amara. People will think you're serious."

I gesture to the container. "So... What's up with the rat-shaped pincushion?"

"This is Geraldo, and those are antennae, not pins. They collect signals from emitters underneath the cage and transmit them to nanoprobes that have taken up residence in Geraldo's blood, organs, and brain. We can tell cells to activate or shut off, speed up, slow down. We want to employ a similar dispersal of nanobots in your dad to bring him back."

"And how many needles would you need to stick in my father?"

"They're *antennae*. And the answer is none. I don't think anyway..." Her voice trails off. "No. No antennae. This is precautionary because of the size of our volunteer here. Your dad is significantly bigger than Geraldo, so directing the nanotreatment should be loads easier."

"Should? Have you discussed this with Bella yet?"

Maggie nods, "Doctor Nikonov and I conferenced her earlier today while she was on the way to your mom's. She's excited about the prospect. When your dad wakes up, we can ask him for his permission to proceed. However, given the amount of time that's passed since he was awake and everything that has happened with... You know... He may need some guidance from you and Bella."

I look around the lab. Dr. Nikonov was doing his best to look uninterested in our conversation.

"Where is Innovo on all this?"

"They're reviewing the data." She gestures to her tablet.

"Dr. Gonzales," Dr. Nikonov calls out. "Can you come over here please?"

Maggie sets her tablet down on the counter and walks across the room. As she does, I read down the data that they've been collecting. Blood and tissue samples combined with nanotreatments. Notation on the bottom indicates four of eight samples are successful in speeding up cellular activity up to ninety percent of normal.

Based on the date, these samples must be the ones taken from my father three weeks ago, since taking blood samples from my father must be undertaken with the meticulous care of a hemophiliac. Moreso, even. Any medical actions with him are only done in my presence or Bella's. It used to be my mother, but not anymore.

I note a second page and click. Eight more blood samples collected on a separate date, all with a separate collection number, and all of them tested four days after my father's tests, all with similar results of speeding up cellular activity.

I turn around and see Maggie standing in front of Dr. Nikonov, her body blocking his view of me. Their voices were up a few decibels and Maggie was becoming more agitated. Turning my attention back to the tablet, I saw the trial number was 17. I hit the back button, then back again, then found the other trials run.

Once again, there were sixteen blood samples. Half from my father, and half from *somebody*. Understanding the results from these tests was impossible without context, and who the blood was collected from was not mentioned. With each click, the trials went back —months. Years. To the same year Millennial attacked my father. And Maggie never said a word.

Chapter 7

Sensitive Compartmentalized Information Facilities—SCIFs for short—are special rooms where one could review data or video or other items not on the mainframe. Running similar to air-gapped computers, SCIFs operated with an entirely different purpose. My induction to Department of Homeland Security came with access to our own SCIF and all evidence related to Millennial, or so I was told.

Darren sat with me the first time I watched the video captured from Innovo Pharmaceutical's database. My heart pounding, my breathing shallow, my unblinking eyes fixed on the screen as I watched my father interviewing Doctor Dieterich Bruchmuller thirteen years ago. David Tsai, my father's partner at the time, could be seen turning on the camera to an already seated suspect.

I couldn't see my dad from the angle, but I heard his voice registering louder, closer, his familiar twang that only half my family found charming. "For the record, please state your name."

"Doctor Dieterich Lenhart Bruchmuller," he answered in crisp pronunciation, despite his thick German accent.

"Your position here at Innovo Pharmaceutical?"

"I'm the North American director of the pharmacokinetic laboratory."

"How long have you been working in that position?"

"Eight years in PK. And sixteen years for the company."

"And where did you work prior to Innovo Pharmaceutical, Mister Bruchmuller?"

His eyes flashed. "It's *Doctor* Bruchmuller, and surely you didn't call me all the way up here to confirm my résumé?" I always wanted to believe this was my father testing him, agitating him to see how important the doctor felt about his title. Probably not though. My father was 'raised proper' in the South and called everyone Mister.

The questions ran through typical baseline interviewing, asking questions about old dates and addresses, anything unrelated to the investigation. When he asked about Rajesh Jotwani, the doctor stiffened noticeably, his explanation that the two men attended symposia together.

"What type of events have the two of you attended?" my father asked.

"I can't imagine how this is relevant to any investigation you would be conducting, Mr. James."

David Tsai interjected, "These symposia, Doctor... Would you say that they are highly political?"

"The presentations and discussions revolve primarily around ethics. Politics is merely an extension of a people's ethical views, wouldn't you agree?"

Their questioning went on for several minutes before David asked for them to take a break. Once again, my father passed too closely to the camera to capture his face and—in a zip—he went out the door. From the decade-old reports,

I knew my dad and David left to deal with one of their suspects leaving prematurely. They weren't police, they had no holding facility, no arrest powers. They were corporate investigators, looking into missing equipment and resources from their company, and wholly unequipped to deal with what they'd inadvertently uncovered.

Dr. Bruchmuller removed his phone out of his pocket, sent multiple rapid text messages to his co-conspirators, and then stuffed his phone back in his pocket as my father returned... Alone.

Once more, my father sat down across from this man who, for all intents, appeared unthreatening in his white lab coat and wrinkled skin. No jerky motions, no threatening gestures, no violent threats or even hints of response. Martin James was considered to be Innovo's top investigator and an interviewer of extraordinary capability. If there were any hidden indicators my father picked up on, he never seemed to react to them.

If he knew the messages Bruchmuller sent just before his return, I doubt my dad would have gone back into that room, let alone come back alone. Instead, he plopped back into his chair, still sitting off-camera, and continued his questioning. All the while Bruchmuller's phone messages read out the man's guilt that would come to be.

Messages scoured from NSA files read as follows:
Bruchmuller: I'm being questioned.
Unknown person #1: We know. We're meeting at our escape point. Be here in 3 minutes.
Albert Vies: What do they know?
Bruchmuller: I can't leave without raising suspicion.
Unknown person #1: They're already suspicious. Get out!

Rajesh Jotwani: They were asking me about Bruchmuller specifically. If they call the authorities we're trapped here.
Unknown person #1: You're going to have to kill him.
Rajesh Jotwani: No! Just leave.
Albert Vies: Dr.?
Albert Vies: Dr.?
Albert Vies: Dr.? Answer or we're setting the timers.
Unknown person #1: Set them.

*   *

Beacon, Pennsylvania barely qualifies as a village, let alone a town. Northwest of Lancaster, as Amish country gives way to simply country, you'll find Exit 38 ¼. If you follow that up over the shallow Bucht Mountain, you'll be halfway to Beacon. Here you can barely see one house from another, and the only traffic you'll encounter is semi-autonomous farm equipment with names and purposes I never bothered to learn.

While driving home, I am greeted by the only four views allowed: corn, soybean, red wheat, or fallow fields. The terrain breaks from farmland momentarily as I move up a steep hill, and when the tree line disappears for just a moment, I can see our house, a refurbished Dutch colonial that dons flat white paint and few accents. The land around it used to be agricultural, but not for the last nine years. Signs posted around the property state 'For Sale by Owner' with a local number monitored by Innovo Pharmaceutical, and they never sell. If there was ever a call from an interested buyer, I was never told.

A dip and a sharp turn and another sharp turn and I am finally on our property (Innovo's property? I can't be sure.). After that, the house comes full into view along with Bella's car and a pickup truck with more rust than paint.

This of course must be Keith's, the farm boy wooing my 19-year-old sister. He should never be at our house. Given he is six years her senior, I didn't think he should be near Bella at all. The only thing he has going for him is that I can't find a single thing wrong with him. It doesn't keep me from trying though.

I step out of the car to be greeted by a sentry drone hovering behind my head. I look up, wave, and keep going. It probably identified me after I got within a mile of the house and reported that to Innovo's security department. Normally I check in with the office so we can test the system, but today I feel sore and distracted and can barely deal with myself.

As I walk up, I run my hand over Keith's hood—it feels warm, but only from sunlight. He's been here for a while.

Bella opens the front door and shuffles over to me with her flip flops and her high-pitched squeal that would greet dolphins. Hair tied up in a ponytail, tank top and cutoffs means it is another great day for my sister.

"You're home! You're home! You're home!" she cries, hugging me.

I pull away at her embrace, "Still in pain, still have burns, still recovering!"

'Sorry, sorry, sorry!'

"Why are we saying everything in threes?"

She stops and looks up. "That is weird. Okay, let's stop."

"Keith here?"

Bella sways and looks around, one of her many tells that a lie is coming. "Yeah, but he's just helping with a leaky pipe in the kitchen. He didn't go anywhere else in the house."

Keith steps out the front door, half his flannel shirt untucked and dirty jeans matching his untied, muddy boots.

Red hair, freckles, and a broad build that justified manual labor, he is a country boy through and through.

"Hi Amara, good to see you again," he says, waving to me. "I just finished replacing a couple outlets in the kitchen that went out."

I grin at Bella then turn back to Keith. "I thought you were fixing a leaky pipe?"

Keith and Bella lock eyes as he shrugs. "I thought we agreed I was doing electrical?"

She shakes her head and waves him to his truck. "Just go."

He gives us both the most awkward handshakes, then bumbles into his pickup.

"Wow! He fixes pipes *and* does electrical work without any tools? Impressive."

"He brought one tool with him." Bella turns and goes back inside.

While our mother would have been wide-eyed and churning at that comment. Then again, if she wanted to raise her children, she wouldn't have abandoned them. I just call her shameless and follow.

I'm pleased to see that the kitchen is at least clean and doesn't smell. Last time there was a sink full of dishes and two trash bags she'd left inside because of bears. I had warned her she was making things worse for herself by leaving garbage inside since a bear would go through the door like it was tissue.

"Coffee?"

"Of course."

Bella sets to the task of caffeinating us while I nose through the refrigerator. There's an obscenely large amount of disorganized prepackaged food. Cold cuts on top of tofu next to one-meal salads holding up a gallon of milk.

Bella notices. "Hungry?"

"Not really. I don't know why I'm even looking."

"So, I got a call yesterday from Walter Reed..."

"I know."

"That Doctor Niko guy was saying this nanotreatment would cure Dad for good..."

I grab a package of Buddy lunch meat and rip it open, stuffing the entire contents in my mouth. Overly salty, barely meat, it reminds me of sandwiches my father made for hiking trips.

Bella's nose is twisted up as I nosh away like some futuristic dinosaur. "I know you like those, so I bought about twenty of them. When you're done eating an entire turkey, think we can talk about the call?"

"I don't trust it." My response comes a little too quickly, partly because I don't feel like discussing what I saw, partly because I don't trust Bella to keep her mouth shut, partly because I spit a little ball of turkey out onto my chin.

Her revulsion is set aside for more familial concerns. "Why? What did Maggie say to you?"

"She said she thinks it will work, but I think she was lying."

"Why would she lie? She loves us. She loves dad."

I shrug, finishing off the food in my mouth.

"Well, there has to be a reason you think that."

"I don't know—maybe not lying. But I don't think *she thinks* the treatment will work."

"But why?"

"Oh my God! Stop being annoying. I just have a feeling, okay?"

"I'm not being annoying. You're being annoying because you are making decisions about dad without all the facts."

"I'm not making decisions! I'm just concerned. I'm allowed to be worried that Walter Reed is getting involved here where they haven't before."

Bella shakes her head and pours the boiling water into the carafe. She gives me one of her frown-smiles. "You should go see him. Go ahead. Coffee won't be done for four minutes."

I sigh. "He won't even know I'm there."

"Sometimes he knows. If I spend a lot of time holding his hand. Or sometimes I put his hand on my head and I can feel him move his fingers."

"He's sleeping this time. He won't be awake until after they synchronize him."

Bella walks over to me and hugs me. I try not to stiffen as I feel her embrace. "Go see Dad."

Sitting rooms. Once upon a time, before phones, TVs, or stereos, homes were built around the only true entertainment to be had: each other. Sitting rooms were where guests would gather and palaver, swap stories and discuss business, often with the men on one side and the women on the other.

This sitting room is truly for sitting, with nothing to distract from the guest of honor who has sat here for years. The attendant electronic devices are not designed to entertain—neither typical houseguests nor the home's residents. Monitoring systems feed to both Innovo Pharmaceutical and Walter Reed Medical Center. Cameras, pulse-ox, EEG headset, specialized keyboard, and two monitors set up for reading. And in the middle of this wired monstrosity, my father.

Martin H. James was a corporate investigator for Innovo Pharmaceutical, one of the world's largest corporations. Innovo was (and still is) a powerhouse in cancer research, robotic limbs, microsurgeries, artificial organs, and—of course—pharmaceutical drugs. Anytime you had assets, you had theft, and if you wanted to keep your costs under control, you hired someone like my father.

A couple weeks before my tenth birthday was when Millennial attacked Innovo. At the time all I understood was that my dad was working on something big. Late for dinner, leaving before I went to school, arguing with my mother when they were both home. Lots of talk about money.

I was at lunch when they closed the schools and called our parents to pick us up. We were told there were explosions at Innovo Pharmaceutical in Paramus and that all schools in the area had closed. I didn't make the connection until I saw my mother's tear-filled face show up at the bus stop.

Hours passed before we got word he was alive and at the hospital. When we finally got to see him, the entire side of his face was bruised and swollen. If he told my mother what happened then, I didn't hear it. All I remember was crying and hugging him and then talking about school because I got in trouble for calling my teacher stupid and I remember thinking *'Why are we talking about school when you're in the hospital?'*

He told us the doctors wanted to make sure he was okay because he got hit on the head really hard. I didn't know—couldn't know—who Millennial was, what they had done to him, or what that would mean to all of us.

Thirteen years later, he sits in a reclining chair, still sporting the same black eye. His body is covered in sensors, eyes shielded by special gear that sprays saline at regular intervals since it can take him up to six minutes to blink. His arms are propped by lightweight foam, as are his legs. Around each limb is an ultra-low-pressure band to ensure his blood circulates.

"Communication," such as it exists, is challenging. We tried electromyography technology to track his eyes or fingers, but his movements were too slow to register no matter how we re-tuned the sensor thresholds. We tried semantic decoders, but they don't work, since even his synaptic functions are crawling at a rate one-four-thousandth of normal. Instead, his fingers hover over a keyboard specially constructed for his condition. When awake, this is his only way to talk, and it often takes him weeks to compose a message.

Martin H. James: subject of top-secret research, anti-terrorism, and legal arguments that continue to wind through the court system.

Martin H. James: conservatee of Innovo Pharmaceutical, a decision to which my mother acquiesced to prevent him from remaining in a lab forever.

Martin H. James: my father, my ward.

I sit on a large ottoman Bella placed at his side and look at his sleeping face, his bruises looking just like they did years ago in the hospital when he smiled and hugged me and told me he'd be fine.

I realize I'm crying. I don't want Bella to walk in and see me like this, but she sees me anyway. The coffee is set aside and she embraces me, and everything I've pushed down comes rushing back to the surface.

Chapter 8

Darren Franciscus sits across from Assistant Secretary Tyesha Keownes as she scrolls through her notes. He keeps quiet, knowing any interruption will result in an elementary school scolding that he can't endure again. The Secretary prefers to meet in her office, and every portion of wall and shelf is filled with awards and commendations, photo ops with senators and business heads.

"Agent Franciscus, you would think the problem I have with Agent James has something to do with her reckless behavior in ignoring our double redundancy policy, or the millions of dollars in damages caused to the building, or even the fact that she risked another agent's life. You would think that, wouldn't you?"

"I would think those would factor in, yes," Darren answers.

"But really my problem with this whole incident is your defense of this young woman." Secretary Keownes glues her eyes to Darren's.

"Can you elaborate please?" Darren keeps his voice low and measured.

"In your S.I.R. you state that 'James called for support while pursuing a suspect she recognized from earlier in the day as a Millennial terrorist suspect.' And yet S.I.R.s submitted by Fagundes, Mitchell, and Zingg all indicate that Agent James was well within the building before she called for assistance. And that Fagundes repeatedly asked her to stop and wait."

The Assistant Secretary's micro-maneuverings grated on Darren's nerves, mainly because speaking his mind the way he wanted would mean shoving his career down the toilet.

"My report accurately portrays the mindset of Agent James. Until that day, she never drew her pistol in the field. These were unusual—"

"Unusual, I agree. But you don't think the training we provide is adequate?"

"Of course I do—"

"Then you think that she needs additional training?"

"I didn't say that. I'm—"

"Then perhaps she is incapable of being trained properly to keep loss of life and property to a minimum?"

"Amara is a great agent, and a great asset."

"Amara?"

Darren realizes the misstep. It doesn't matter that he calls all of his agents by their first and last names interchangeably. Keownes is looking for a scapegoat.

"Why are you so close to this agent Amara James?"

Although a soft accusation, the Secretary doesn't do much to hide it. But Darren actually holds the upper hand. "Amara—Agent James—was placed in my department with the personal blessing of Chief-of-Staff Joe Dorner."

"At your request, if I understand correctly."

"I can't speak to that."

The Secretary's demeanor shifts, "Can't or won't? This is my department. And I'd like to know who is working for me and why."

"I suppose you can request the information from Joe Dorner's office. If you think it is important enough."

The Secretary scrolls through reports on her screen. Darren can almost hear the wheels in her brain grinding as she tries to find something to drill down into. "You know, somebody has to be held accountable for the destruction of 490 First Street."

"I can't speak to that either," Darren says flatly. "Is there anything else, Secretary Keownes?"

She looks up at him again. "Less than a mile from here, the repeal of the Posse Comitatus Act is winding through the Senate as we speak. I've been told it will pass both houses, and—after the explosion here in DC—the President already stated publicly he'll sign it. That means change is coming, and coming soon. It's important for us both to be on the same team if our careers are going to survive."

Darren squeezes his fist so tight his fingernails pierce his palm. "Thank you for looking out for me and my career. Is there anything else?"

"No. Thank you."

Darren walks out of the office, closes the door, and then closes his eyes. He breathes deeply, counts to ten. The frustration falls away, just like his therapist says, and his head clears enough to review his schedule. Two interviews with agents from the Office of Inspector General were scheduled with his staff in an hour, and his own interview shortly after. While he understood OIG had a role to play, it felt like the destruction of 490 First Street was falling more on

Amara than on Millennial. Nobody would say that, of course. Not yet.

Amara's dad went through this years ago with the destruction of Innovo Pharmaceutical in New Jersey. Millennial planted the bombs in twelve buildings, detonated them without prejudice, killed thirteen people, and at the time Darren was the first one to blame Martin for 'instigating the event.' Had Martin James not done his investigation, not interviewed Dr. Dieterich Bruchmuller, none of that day's events would have occurred. That's how everyone felt. Initially.

The only thing that saved Amara's dad from being charged was the fact that Millennial injected him with a drug that slowed his metabolism to a crawl. Since then, Martin James has been *officially* in a coma, never expected to recover from injuries sustained at Innovo. *Unofficially*, he has become one of the nation's most closely guarded secrets. Saved from public scrutiny and criminal prosecution—at the cost of having his life turned upside down like none other.

The day Martin James slipped into a chemopreservative state, Darren watched the devastation on the faces of his family. The confusion of his children, the soul crushing weight of responsibility that struck his wife Miranda. The months and years that passed gave Darren perspective, helped him appreciate the humanity of people in the wrong place at the wrong time. More than that though, everyone fell in love with Amara. Frequent visits to Walter Reed, to Homeland Security, they all watched her grow up and learn and take such a vital interest in her dad's recovery. It was difficult not to admire her.

Darren switches to his message app and selects Amara's name. "How is recovery going?" he asked her.

She responds immediately, "Good. Barely feel a thing."

"Liar."

"Nothing I can't handle."

"It would not hurt your career to return to work a day or two earlier than planned. Wolves are circling."

"I'll be there tomorrow."

Darren couldn't help but smile and added an emoji to indicate such. "Tomorrow's Saturday, genius. Wednesday will be more than sufficient. Maybe Tuesday. Anyway, rest up."

"K."

With a sigh, Darren leans against the wall, scrolls through his contacts, and finds 'Chief-of-Staff.' He fires off a quick message, wondering how many favors he can burn through before he damages their friendship. "Hey Joe, I need a favor regarding Amara James."

There is no immediate response.

Twelve hours pass and Darren straightens his desk in preparation for Monday. The office is simple, small, filled with way too many paper files. With no windows for his office to take up space, the famous *Times* photo of Innovo Pharmaceutical lying in rubble hangs center wall facing his desk. The first of many attacks that catapulted Millennial to global prominence. Each documented attack gets a place of dishonor around that photo, and the 490 First Street attack is the newest frame to be hung.

His phone buzzes: a response from Joe Dorner. "My days are numbered, dude."

"No, they're not. *Presidents may come and go, and all that remains is Joe.* Everyone loves you."

"I wish I had your optimism. So, again?"

"Sorry. But I still need this." Darren is starving but resists leaving as he waits for a response.

It comes a moment later, "You sure she's worth protecting?"

This time it's Darren that pauses. "Amara is a work in progress. I'll straighten her out."

"It's fixed. Go home."

Chapter 9

An armed agent opens the door for me, and I walk into the courtroom. It smells like paint, but I can't tell what has been painted. It's the same, worn crappy tan and brown that has seen a thousand careers die since the last time it got a coat.

I pass Agent Everett Zingg, who makes contact with me for as long as he dares, widening his eyes and gave me the slightest of shrugs, but what that means I have no clue. I know Everett testified in front of the panel, but I don't know what questions they asked or how he answered them. Everett would never screw me intentionally, but I knew from my past meeting with OIG that words could be twisted around to suit their agenda.

A set of thigh-high swinging doors split the room in two, and I push past them to sit at a table on the right side. The left table is empty, which I suppose I should be thankful for. Above me sit three Assistant Secretaries from Homeland Defense Criminal Investigative Division. The two on the ends each have laptops open and are ready to notate. The middle agent taps her pen on a tablet of paper and looks about the room for others to settle in.

Only ten months ago, these were members of the Office of Inspector General, a sort of Internal Affairs department. But while their rolls and ranks remain the same, the department has changed names due to the Homeland Liberty Act.

Homeland Security became organized as a branch of the military and renamed Homeland *Defense* after dozens of high-profile incidents occurred and from a wide range of enemies. State sponsored terrorist attacks, infrastructure targeting, paramilitary Cartel forces, and a host of opposing homegrown groups who hate the government just a smidge more than they hate each other. The detonation of 490 First Street building was the straw the broke the camel's back.

Behind me sits Supervisory Agent Darren Franciscus with a tablet and stylus. He's quiet and rigid, which he warned me would be the case. Two rows behind Darren sits Assistant Secretary Tyesha Keownes and three others who I do not recognize. They may not even be Homeland Defense from the quick look I got of their ID badges. I have never spoken with her, but Keownes' photo hangs in the hallway right next to Joe Dorner's on the way to our cube farm, a reminder of who is next in the chain.

"The officer will secure the room," the center figure speaks into the microphone. The men on either side of her share her rank, but she clearly holds seniority. Her name isn't readable from this distance. She has no nameplate, and she never introduces herself. The information in this hearing will be decidedly one-way. I hear the door open, the armed officer steps out, and then the door click shut. When it does, she continues, "Special Agent Amara James, please stand and raise your right hand."

I do, almost tipping my chair in the process. I clumsily set it on all fours and clear my throat.

"Do you swear that the testimony you shall give in the case now in hearing shall be the truth, the whole truth, and nothing but the truth?"

"I do."

She picks up a file, reads through it with her lips silently moving. When complete, the Assistant Secretary begins to recite the instructions before her. "This panel has been convened with the understanding that, in its transition format, you may be referred to a military court martial under the Homeland Liberty Act, if indeed such a referral is warranted. And while you have not yet taken an oath under the Uniform Code of Military Justice, your oath given to the Department of Homeland Security is recognized as legally binding in disciplinary cases under the aforementioned Homeland Liberty Act. Do you acknowledge and agree to the terms set forth by this panel, waiving all other rights and privileges?"

"I do."

"Please sit, Agent." When I do, I hear a bench squeaking behind me, probably Darren.

The three officers take their time, passing documents to each other. I turn to look at Darren, but he only nods ever so slightly in the direction of the panel and I snap my head back into position.

"Let the record show that all members of the panel are cleared to hear top secret testimony. In addition, members of the gallery are cleared by the Department of Homeland Defense to witness top secret testimony.

"Special Agent Amara James, this panel requests detailed information regarding the incident taking place on October 13. This panel has before it case number one-zero-four-six-eight-seven-bravo, authored by you. Are you familiar with this case file?"

"I am."

"And can you explain to this panel how you came to be involved in this case?"

"I can."

She stares at me. It takes me a moment to realize she wants me to actually speak, and I feel my stomach tighten.

"Oh, sorry. Yes, the case..."

Chapter 10

It was nine months after we found the Millennial crypt, after they almost killed me and Iván, when we got our next break. The information came from the newest member of our team, and it was this noob that set us on the path.

Millennial terrorist members have eluded capture for years, starting with the destruction of Innovo Pharmaceutical. At that time, my father was looking into losses from the pharmacokinetic department. A half dozen individuals came up on his radar, and he dug into their activities on the Innovo campus in Paramus, New Jersey. Along with his partner David Tsai, they brought a half dozen individuals in for questioning. Unfortunately, what they thought was industrial espionage turned out to be something far more sinister. Far more deadly.

Since then, eight incidents had been attributed to Millennial, some quietly, some stating publicly that their aim was to halt humanity's march toward an event called *singularity*. An artificial general intelligence lab bombed. The corporate headquarters for Global Business Machines incinerated. A billionaire who funded cloning experiments bound and suffocated with a bag taped over his head. Another FBI agent set on fire in front of his family. And when they claimed credit, they ended each statement with the following message: *"We are vigilant. We are eternal. We are coming for you. We are Millennial."*

This group was far from being the Luddite extremists originally anticipated, though. We knew that the original terrorists at Innovo included members of the scientific community, people of education. Sophisticated, organized, tech savvy. They developed a drug that could slow the human metabolism to a crawl, an innovation that to this day couldn't be duplicated or corrected.

My own run-in with them, with their proposition to me and the subsequent First Street bombing, showed they employed counter-surveillance technology. These were not CCTV jammers or de-authers or infrared projectors, although it appears those were used as backups. Studious Stanley and his gunman partner employed camera benders or "egg scramblers" as they came to be known, a new disruption tech that started in Hollywood to enhance the privacy of movie stars. This device, worn on the person, would emit a signal to garble their image, even if the camera was a thousand meters away. It was so advanced that Congress tried to outlaw it (as if people who committed murderous atrocities would obey such laws). The Supreme Court eventually sided with privacy advocates, thus protecting the interests of actors, research companies, conspiracy nut jobs, and terrorists. That's okay. We still had them on a hundred other charges, if we could just find them. But that was the problem: finding them.

Geo-fencing generated no leads on cell phones used at or near the restaurant where I met Studious Stanley. NSA data generated nothing but end-ends. DNA swabs taken from the restaurant gave us four thousand samples and zero results. Even traditional investigative techniques such as sketch artist renderings and witness interviews fell far short of expectations.

But one technology, an advanced volatile chemical detection library, came through for us a few weeks back. The AI applied to it was responsible for taking samples from terrorist bombings across the country and comparing them against each other. The goal, like DNA libraries, was to tie incidents together that may not have been credited.

Darren called me into his office one night when we were both working late. He gave me the worn speech about how it was important to have a social life, I called him out for choosing his career over his marriage, he pointed out that he didn't like his ex-wife anyway, and then we would talk shop. This night in particular, I met our newest department member.

"I'd like you to meet ALEI," Darren offered, turning his screen so I could share the view. "Or, more formally, Artificial Law Enforcement Intelligence."

On the screen was a text interface with a camera window to the right showing nothing except a woman's unmoving face. "Amara, say hello to your new best friend."

I rolled my eyes and grinned. "Hello, my new best friend," I said aloud.

"I'm sorry, but I don't understand that command," the image spoke.

Darren shook his head and scolded me. "Don't be like that. She's still learning. Try again."

"Hello, ALEI," I greeted the AI.

"Hello there. With whom am I speaking?"

"This is Special Agent Amara James."

"Hello, Agent James. May I ask for your fingerprint authentication please?"

I ran my finger over the reader, received a red light and a squelching noise, ran it again, and got my green passing light.

"Great! It's nice to finally meet you, Agent James. Would you like to run a speech print so that you may access my features quicker?"

"No thanks. Somebody could spoof my voice and conduct nefarious activities in my name." I said it mostly for my own amusement and because it would annoy Darren. I was surprised when ALEI responded.

"Not to worry, Agent James. I employ a synthetic speech detector which will preclude that as a possibility."

Darren gave me a snarky look as if to say *she put you in your place!*

"Oh really, ALEI?"

"Yes, really."

"What countermeasures do you employ for your synthetic speech detection?"

"I employ an amalgam of spectral features consisting of multi-band cepstral and 4-D predictive coefficients, and enhanced spectral analysis for signal clarity. This fusion allows me to differentiate between genuine organic speech and synthetic speech. I am also constantly evaluating CVVS files to communicate more effectively, and if any user were to deviate from assigned vectors, a two-step authentication would be used."

"I have one of these in my kitchen, got it on sale for four million dollars less," I snarked.

"I think you'll like her," he glossed over my sarcasm and continued. "The voice interface is superficial, fondant on the cake. The real power is in the AI. High resolution scripting tiles, on-the-fly updates to analysis... ALEI can out-think anyone or anything else our government has."

"Which means our government didn't make it."

"Damn straight. GBE contracted." Global Business Enhancements was an offshoot of IBM years back. GBE stayed out of politics and filled the gaps other tech companies felt inclined to leave alone.

"Okay, I'm impressed."

"Really?"

"Really. I didn't think you would know anything about fondant."

Darren eyerolled me.

"I just don't believe we have the money for an upgrade like this."

"Homeland Liberty Act has opened up a much larger budget for us. CIA and DOD use a similar model, but this one is tailored specifically for us. We beat out FBI for the prototype."

"ALEI, remind me tomorrow to run a speech print for you," I said.

The AI responded warmly, "Of course."

As I stood up to go, Darren held up one finger, "That's not what I brought you in here for though."

I feigned childish excitement, "There's more? It's like Christmas *and* a fucking birthday!"

"You jest, but..." He cleared his throat and directed his speech to the computer. "ALEI, please show me the report we reviewed ten minutes ago."

ALEI responded, "I'm sorry, I don't understand."

Darren grumbled. "ALEI, show me the last report on chemical detection matching from today."

"Got it," ALEI's avatar quickly vanished and was replaced with two separate file images. "The chemical detection library match for records CB4061ZE and FD5041DE show a 96.2% relationship. It is highly likely that these samples are related."

I tapped on the screen to expand the first file. The names of the victims, perpetrators, as well as the date and location were known to everyone in Washington DC. "This is the Stephanie Bartles bombing. The Bukum Yilani Crime Syndicate was responsible for this."

"Yup," Darren said. "And look what it matched with..."

I minimized the file and went to the second one. I looked to him with shock. "This can't be..."

"It is."

"This is the 490 First Street bombing. This is Millennial."

"I told you ALEI was going to be your best friend."

Chapter 11

The next day, we set out on an expedition to uncover their relationship. ALEI's insight into linking two of the world's worst terrorist organizations by the bomb materials used floored us all. Iván questioned the data, not in an attempt to show off, but because he legitimately didn't understand.

"Why is 96.2% a match?" he asked. "Why not 99%?"

"It's because..." my voice trailed off as my ignorance bubbled to the surface. "That's actually a really good question."

We found out that ALEI's creators arbitrarily picked the 96% threshold as a match because another AI fed data to the software design team based on web searches, who then assumed that was a scientific standardized number. They never bothered to confer with an explosives expert, or Homeland Defense, or anyone, to discuss why a static match would be a bad idea. Contamination of samples, or the site already having other chemicals that might interact with explosives, or the age of the explosives used, or modification to the devices, or the materials the explosives discharged through. All of these factors and more meant ALEI was about to pin our eyes open.

"ALEI, display all matches from the database at a relationship of 90% or higher to sample FD5041DE."

Top of the list was once again the First Street bombing sample relating at 96.2% to the DC Trade Center bombing. This was Bukum Yilani's introduction to the United States. How they coaxed Stephanie Bartles into the lobby we still didn't know, but we knew the threats that came after from these human traffickers would never be taken lightly again.

Besides the DC Trade Center, only one additional record manifested on the screen. This sample, taken seven years ago, came from an office in Seattle run by Global Business Enhancements. Millennial had taken credit for this publicly, so connecting it to the destruction of 490 First Street only solidified that Millennial perpetrated the crime. Some folks actually doubted it, such as conspiracy theorists who blamed the government for the bombing to usher in the suspension of posse comitatus. If only they knew it was my exuberant chase of a suspect that prompted the destruction of the Millennial crypt and the entire building.

Iván and I exchanged glances, and I could tell he didn't understand the implications. I tapped on the screen, "You get how big of a deal this is?"

"Yeah," he said, with as much confidence as a middle schooler, "We can confirm that was a Millennial crypt we found."

"Yes, but it's more. It doesn't matter if Bukum Yilani supplied the explosives to Millennial or the other way around. We now know their relationship goes back at least seven years."

Iván couldn't have appreciated the implications of such a long-term relationship. Bukum Yilani Crime Syndicate wasn't a well-known operator in the US seven years ago. Sure, they were big, but not international big.

Before we took our findings to Darren, however, I wanted to test the limits of this new database. I bypassed the ALEI interface, opting for the reporting tools instead. I did the same thing ALEI did, selecting the First Street bombing sample and brought the relationship percentage down to 85%. Then 80%. Then 75%. Nothing.

At 70%, the database kicked out one more record: a meth house explosion in Stamford, Connecticut six months ago. I was perplexed why this event even made it into the terrorism database—nothing about it indicated anything other than drugs.

"Do you know anything about this? You're from up that way."

"Nah, I was in training in Virginia at the time. But Stamford has lots of meth coming out of it. That shit was always coming down into the Bronx."

I raised an eyebrow. "Did you really just blame Stamford for sullying New York?"

He cracked a smile, "Hey, don't go beating up my city! New Yorkers are the best people you'll ever meet."

"Yeah, yeah, you all wear fucking halos. Can you start pulling everything you can on this Stamford explosion?"

"Sure."

"I mean everything." I stood up, grabbed my phone, and locked my station.

Iván slathered on even more of his New York accent than he normally let out, "Okay! I got it. You say 'everything,' I get you *everything*. I'll write a novel about it. They'll make it into a series. You'll see it on all the
services. It'll carry all the award shows..."

"You're an idiot."

He had a comeback of some type, but I was already walking away, shaking my head and suppressing a smile as I headed for Darren's office.

Chapter 12

The leading Assistant Secretary puts up her hand to stop by testimony, makes a series of notes, then leans over and confers off-mic with her two companions. The break gives everyone in the room an opportunity to adjust, and soon the quiet is filled with a series of bench creaks, throats clearing, whispers, pen tapping, a single small burp. I turn around to look at Darren Franciscus who holds up one hand in an 'okay' symbol. I exhale a long breath.

The lead Assistant Secretary re-centers herself on the microphone in front of her and begins tapping her pen again. "Agent James," she begins, "You mentioned that you directed Agent Fagundes to research the Stamford explosion, to get you 'everything' as you put it. And yet this directive was predicated on the idea that an explosion with a matching relationship of seventy percent was enough of a link to the First Street bombing—"

"Seventy-four point two percent, Assistant Secretary."

"You stated seventy earlier."

"Well, I set the threshold in five percent increments, so when I dropped to seventy-five percent, ALEI wasn't able to register that record. She was only able to glean it—"

"I understand," she cuts me off. "Thank you for the clarification.

"You're welcome." I try to smile, but the look I'm getting is not one of appreciation.

"And Agent James, allow me to clarify something. ALEI is an 'it', not a 'she'."

"Yes, uh, yes, of course Assistant Secretary."

Tap. Tap. Tap. It feels as if she is tapping on my forehead. "Agent Fagundes followed your instructions, I assume?"

"Yes. Yes, he did."

"And what did he find in this attempt to get 'everything?'"

"Agent Fagundes reviewed Stamford PD's report, and that witnesses they interviewed heard two or three explosions, depending on the account. It was the series of explosions that prompted Stamford PD to sample and submit the explosion to the Federal database in the first place."

For the first time, the Assistant Secretary on the left speaks up, "And yet subsequent investigations conducted by Stamford's lead detective and the Stamford Fire Marshal determined that the explosion or explosions were the result of 'gas appliances in adjacent rooms,' did they not?"

"Those reports were inaccurate," I immediately regret answering so quickly.

"And how do you know that?" the one on the right asks this time.

"Because they didn't have the chemical analysis, Assistant Secretary. They could not have known what caused the secondary and tertiary explosions."

Lefty hits me again. "So, they lied on their report?"

"I don't know if they lied or not," I answer, my voice cracking as I did. "I only know that without the chemical analysis, they could not have known."

"Do *you* think they lied?" Center asks me.

I stop and instinctively turn to look at Darren, but Center presses her mouth against the microphone and startles me into facing forward again. "This question is for you, Agent James. Not for your supervisor. Do *you*, Agent James, believe the detective lied on his report?"

I clear my throat and lean into my mic. "I think he phoned it in, Assistant Secretary. It is my belief when they had a drug house with drug paraphernalia that was as much as they needed to know. They other explosions were... Were... I can't think of the word right now."

"So, you believed these other explosions were in fact explosives or explosive materials that shared a..." Righty reads along with what must be text from my report, "A 'common source to the bomb material detonated at 490 First Street, Washington, DC.' Is that still your belief?"

"Yes."

Center cuts in quickly. "And this caused Agent Fagundes to investigate the lease holder of the building? A Mister McCormick who, according to the police report you just poopooed, was exonerated from all wrongdoing."

"Agent Fagundes did not investigate Mister McCormick. I did. It was Agent Fagundes' opinion that I was pointing things in the wrong direction."

"And yet you did a deep dive into Mister McCormick anyway."

"I did."

"Including a FISA warrant application that was denied by the court."

"That is correct."

"And still you pressed on, with multiple open-source searches, most of which have not been properly cited, that eventually yielded a property in Newark, New Jersey that was involved in a human trafficking arrest four years ago, in which Mister McCormick wasn't even the owner."

"Actually, he was," I counter, reading through my notes. "He purchased the property from Randon Enterprises, a shell corporation whose holders were under indictment for their involvement in human trafficking at that property. It was his purchase of that property that gave them cashflow and allowed them to mount a legal defense."

Lefty raises an eyebrow at my last comment and actually laughs. "Agent James, you do understand how flimsy of a case that is, right? A judge or jury would easily see this as a man who purchases properties in areas some might consider suspicious for the simple motive of turning a profit. Even your own report shows he holds dozens of properties that fall into high crime areas. Being a property owner where there is crime is not a crime, Agent James."

"I- I- yes, I am aware, Assistant Secretary. But—"

"*But* you did not end your investigation even there. You employed ALEI to perform a search function it was never programmed for—nor authorized to conduct, did you not?"

The nausea starts to kick in, but if I don't see this through, I could be facing criminal charges... *Military* criminal charges.

I nod, but the lead Assistant Secretary reminds me I need to answer verbally. "Yes."

"What did you instruct ALEI to do?" Center asks.

"I submitted a request to Global Business

Enhancements to integrate ALEI with multiple databases nationwide."

"And you submitted this with the approval of Assistant Secretary Keownes?"

"No."

"Your supervisor?"

"No."

"Did you involve anybody else?"

"No. I- I- I just did it on my own."

"And which databases did you integrate?"

The words cling to the inside of my mouth.

"Agent James, please answer the question. Which additional databases did you instruct GBE to integrate."

"All- all of them," I whisper into the mic. "But it worked! Once ALEI was integrated, it allowed her—*it*—to analyze the databases I provided her—I mean *it!*—I provided *it*, ALEI, with access to data relating to human trafficking incidents on the Eastern Seaboard. I then gave it access to all the properties currently and previously owned by Mister McCormick. From there, I asked it to crunch the data geographically."

"And what did you find?" Center asks.

"I found what appeared to be two major centers of human trafficking, Assistant Secretary. One, inactive for the last several years, centered around a property owned by McCormick. Once sold, the activity stopped. The other is currently—or I should say *was*— active, with more than three dozen incidents falling within two miles of Antonio's Pizzeria in Philadelphia, PA. Antonio's was a business owned by McCormick, along with the building itself, which also included a motel and a tobacco shop, all owned by McCormick."

"And based on this lead, you requested a surveillance team on a pizza shop?"

"In fairness, we were focused on the hotel, but the pizzeria ended up being... Well, it was where things drifted."

"Once Supervisor Franciscus authorized this surveillance, what happened after?"

I opened my mouth. "Chaos."

Chapter 13

The city of brotherly love existed as a dichotomy of income and privilege. Much like Washington, DC, Philadelphia could transform from historical to fancy, exclusive to deadly with a single turn down a side street. Poverty often breeds desperation, and regular people suffocated under the weight of a hundred life variables over which they had no control and a hundred more they chose to ignore.

Our surveillance van couldn't be more camouflaged in such a place: gray primer sides, an orange door legitimately from a junkyard, tinted windows that violated city ordinance, and exactly one hubcap. When opening the back doors, a beaded curtain would part to reveal a trashy velvet curtain: beyond that, our surveillance equipment, weapons rack, fold up cot, and food stores. The department bolted half-inch anchors every two feet to the floor in the event we needed to secure a prisoner, but the only thing those anchors had managed to do so far was bruise my knees as I shifted in the back of the van.

I looked around outside via a covert camera—one of eight—attached to the top of the van. Cracked sidewalks, cracked windows hiding behind iron bars, cracked people scrounging to survive in an urban war zone. My father and mother used to take me to Philadelphia when I was a child, but never to this area. No Liberty Bell, no Independence Hall, no Franklin Center where you could walk through a human heart or mint a coin or converse with a hologram of Benjamin Franklin. This place existed as a wholly different city that my parents used to drive through with the windows up and the doors locked.

We followed the protocols of double redundancy for our surveillance. I requested Everett Zingg, but not only because he is my best friend. We communicate well with each other having gone through training together, and he was the only one in our department to shoot a perfect score at the range with all three weapons. I was good, but he was the best. If anything went south, I knew he would be the best trigger man. Iván Fagundes asked to come for field experience, and the boss thought it a good idea... All under the watchful eye of Special Agent Grazelli who led our team.

I knew why Darren made Grazelli our fourth. As a career agent with more years in the field than our supervisor, he'd be invaluable in using the surveillance to teach us. But Grazelli was also the one who was there when I went a little rogue during the First Street bombing. He would be watching me closely, and Darren knew it.

Darren assigned a second team on the other side of the block where the alleys fed out away from the hotel and pizzeria and smoke shop. We did our homework, we knew those apartments to be HUD housing, and probably not involved. And since Team 2 was on the far side, they would be the best ones to deploy drones if need be.

We were taught in training that surveillance is 99.9% boredom and 0.1% adrenaline. It wasn't my first surveillance, but I mentally prepared for long runs with no bathroom breaks, fatty burgers, and caffeine injections from a variety of beverages.

Grazelli knelt next to me studying the display screen, shifting repeatedly until he found the least uncomfortable position. He pointed through the side of the van like I possessed Supergirl x-ray vision and said, "Okay, you see the skinny guy with the pants way up above his chest?"

He referenced a man close to stick figure status with frizzy hair, flip-flops, and a thick bifter he rolled between his fingers. Every time he took a drag, he closed his eyes and shook his head like it was the tastiest joint he ever rolled. "Yeah, that's a new fashion thing."

"That's not fashion, that's a ball sack waiting to get crushed. So, see how he's just lighting up and chilling in front of the pizzeria?"

"Sure."

"Watch him. Even odds says he's a lookout. Not sure what he's looking out for, but he's looking."

"Okay, what am I watching for?"

Grazelli turned around, grabbed a jar of mixed nuts from the webbing on the van wall and, with a mouth full of walnuts and pecans, dispensed his wisdom. "Lookouts can be operating solo or in teams. If he's in a team, there might be a hand signal, gang symbols usually, a twist of a hat, or even him getting up and walking away. Be prepared for a long surveillance on this mutt..."

I watched our Skinny-man snub his bifter between his fingers and stand up to greet a shorter man in a delivery uniform—big handshake, small man-hug, a lot of talking and looking over their shoulders. Then both turned in one direction as a third man stepped from a white rental van I hadn't even noticed. The handshakes continued, only this time with a roll of cash that I would have missed had I blinked. Soon a white box appeared from the van and made its way into Skinny-man's possession.

"Hey, Grazelli," I asked slowly, eyes trained on the scene unfolding, "What does it mean when a lookout guy meets with two strangers in a delivery van and then hands them a wad the size of a soup can in exchange for a box?"

"You fucking with me, Amara?"

"No sir."

Iván and Everett, both banking some down time in the front of the van, overheard us through the speaker and wanted in on the intel. After speaking over each other a few times, I chirped the comm. "Not sure what we're looking at. Maybe we just witnessed pepperoni being delivered." *Really expensive pepperoni.*

Chaos is never released in easily digestible amounts. Were it so, order would absorb it, consume it, bury it beneath its placid surface. Chaos always comes in waves of reactions, pool balls striking one another in ways that are impossible to predict in the instant of their release. Moments like a train derailment, or a satellite collision, or rioters clashing with a police line.

Or in this case, a pigeon.

Ten minutes prior, Team 2 launched a didi-drone to hover over our area, give them a set of eyes beyond what fed from our cameras. These didis were tiny, maybe the size of a soccer ball. They were fast, quiet, reliable, and expensive. But anyone looking at them from a distance wouldn't see them as anything other than simply a kid's drone.

Parking enforcement came by and began writing a ticket when our agent hurriedly waved him off, eventually offering to move the van to a free spot without a meter. He couldn't flash credentials with so many eyes around, and it was too late to contact the city to push the parking enforcement out of the area. As our number two van moved up and down the street, the didi-drone did exactly what it was instructed to do: hover directly above the sidewalk, peering down at the pizzeria foot traffic. They recorded Skinny-man hanging out by himself, the van arriving, the driver and passenger stepping out to greet him, the money exchange, the passenger retrieving the white box and handing it to Skinny-man.

The box hand-off was the last thing our didi-drone recorded. Typically, a proximity detector would have kicked in and the drone given instructions to automatically evade an incoming object. We never did figure out why, but a pigeon decided to take that moment to collide with one of the drone propellers, driving the poor bird into the chassis and sending the machine and beast into a death spiral to the ground. Feather-covered plastic debris landed at the feet of Skinny-man, who looked down, looked up, looked around, and then looked directly at our van.

"You gotta be fucking kidding me!" the voice came over the comm. James Stenitz, one of our Team 2 agents, said, "Team 1, we've got a situation—"

Grazelli responded watching our one suspect kick at the debris and feathers, "Got it, drone down. Stand by, let's see if we're made. He's eyeballing our van."

"We're hosed," Everett mumbled from the front of the van.

"How's that?" Grazelli said.

"Because I know what's printed on the bottom of those drones."

Skinny-man picked up the drone, a cautious balance act of grabbing the drone while not dropping the white package, all made more challenging by whatever he had been smoking. He inspected the bottom of the broken drone, rubbed it with his thumb, looked up one more time at our van, and sprinted into the hotel. The duo from the delivery van could not have known the didi was marked with 'Property of DHS.' They probably didn't even know a drone fell from the sky. All they knew was their contact was running, and they jumped into their own van and peeled away.

"Arms and armor!" Grazelli shouted, "We're going in! Team 2, this is Team 1. Block off the alleyway and proceed to the hotel." He made a call to Darren Franciscus that was stunted with comments about workforce, carelessness, mission critical roles, all in a matter of twenty seconds. All the while, it was a scramble to grab our vests and gear, four adults squirming and bumping, thrusting our arms into our vests, smacking and bumbling into each other.

"Ow! Fucker!" I snapped at Everett.

"What?" he asked, securing the bulletproof vest tightly to his chest.

"You punched me in the boob!"

"Your boob will grow back. Let's go people!" Grazelli popped the back doors open and parted the curtain for us.

All four of us exited the van, vests on and weapons drawn. We sped past the pizzeria and toward the hotel main door. People on the streets fell into two categories: sprinters and videographers. Sprinters may have been involved, but most likely had no desire to be caught up in a mess. The videographers were ready to show our mishaps and misdeeds to the world.

"Two by two! Two by two!" Grazelli called out. "Double redundancy! Team Two, this is Team One at the front!"

We stacked up against each other at the hotel main entrance, a pair of worn wooden doors resting ajar. Iván took rear guard and could feel Grazelli's body heat through my shirt. Stenitz responded over the comm, "Team One, Team Two at the back, breaching now! Go! Go! Go! DHS! *Don't move....!*" They were in, and I listened for those two seconds with a clenched jaw before Grazelli performed the same actions.

"DHS! Don't move! We are here to serve a warrant! Don't move!" We technically did have a warrant for searching the entire building, but this was a recon mission first, with assets set to expire after four days. We never wanted to execute the warrant in the blind with only eight agents, especially after observing the building for only an hour.

As soon as we entered the lobby, I stepped right and Everett stepped left, scanning for anything—humans, pets, drones, bots—that might bring us harm. Grazelli screamed at the desk clerk who stood with his hands up behind a bulletproof glass enclosure at the front counter. Eyes wide, fingers splayed, he opened the door to the counter area and then hopped back with his hands up. Grazelli zip tied him, brought him out to the middle of the lobby, and positioned him on the floor. I could hear Grazelli talking in low tones to the guy as he patted him comfortingly on the shoulder.

"Staircase and corridor!" Everett called out his view from across the lobby.

"Elevator!" I shouted. Somebody duct-taped a cardboard sign to the doors that looked older than the elevator. "It's out of order. Clear!"

"Team Two, this is Team One, we have a clear lobby," Grazelli said into his earpiece. "Position?"

Stenitz responded. "Team Two moving down corridor, heading your direction."

Everett dropped his pistol into low-guard position so our own people could see his face and the bright DHS logo on his vest, not be greeted by a gun barrel pointed straight at them. From my angle I couldn't see our approaching agents, and Everett disappeared down the hallway with Grazelli behind him.

"Amara, you're on steps," he said over the comm.

I moved into a shielded position by the handrail. Back turned to everything, trusting everyone, seeing nothing, listening to it all play out over the open line. Above me I could hear people scrambling, yelling, shushing, opening and closing doors. An occasional shadow or eyeball would come into view and I would shout up, "DHS! We are serving a warrant! Get down and remain on the ground with hands visible!"

I can't remember how many times I repeated that phrase in Spanish and English and Cantonese as my attention split between listening to Everett and the team clearing the first floor. I could hear shouting, zip ties, a language I did not understand, furniture toppling, and several iterations of "Clear!" and "Secured!" Less than a minute passed since we stormed in here, but it felt like anyone on the second floor could get away out a window, onto the roof, or some other escape.

Grazelli pulled me to the side and took the point position, Everett shoulder-to-shoulder with him as Stenitz identified our presence once more. He was rubbing elbows with me in the rear, a booming voice much louder than somebody his size had business having. When I yelled, it sounded like I was scolding grandchildren from the kitchen. When Stenitz yelled, you could feel the vibration in the air.

We double-timed it up the steps, eyes in every direction so we didn't get caught off guard with a bat or a bullet. The upstairs corridor split in opposite directions from the staircase, ending in large boarded up windows. I noticed three women on the ground in cheap miniskirts, quivering and crying with their hands up and stealing glances at us from underneath the poor lighting. As we approached, Stenitz leaned down and secured their hands behind their backs, eliciting a cry from each of them. Once secured, Grazelli and I paired off to take the hallway in one direction, while Stenitz and Everett pushed down the other.

One agent on the back door. Two agents guarding the first-floor corridor and everyone zip-tied in their rooms. Iván on the front door. Stenitz and Everett moving away from us.

Our thinning numbers approached the first door, Stenitz announced our presence for the umpteenth time, and Grazelli slammed the door wide as Everett and I moved in, guns forward. Not a soul to be found, but the room... One half lay covered in plastic tarps tacked to every surface. Bright LEDs beamed onto a massage table draped in clean white towels. Off to the side a series of medical devices lay scattered on a stainless-steel tray, including a large metallic syringe that would terrify me if I saw it in a doctor's office. Here, its presence seemed incongruous with everything about the hotel.

The cherry on top was the computer station next to the massage table. Body scans covered the screens, text running alongside them in characters that weren't quite Latin but weren't Cyrillic either. Cables snaked out of the computer and fed into large shiny plastic clamshells with rounded interiors.

"What the fuck..." I whispered to myself.

"Stay focused." Grazelli patted me on the shoulder and gave me a reassuring look.

Room one cleared.

Out the door, down the hall, rapped on the next door with the same announcement, four more women cowered in the corner with their hands up. Filthy walls, filthy beds, filthy faces. As I zip tied one of them, I realized even with her sunken eyes and disheveled hair she couldn't have been older than fifteen. I looked at the others. Lost teenage souls caught up in a living nightmare. Four girls crowded into a room with a burned box spring and a mattress on the floor. Soiled clothes scattered in wads, underneath pizza boxes, wrapped around soda bottles, mired with stains. The room stank of body odor and marijuana. And we left them there, zip-tied on that repulsive floor, to finish the job.

Out the door, down the hall, rapped on the next door with the same announcement—only this time the door didn't give way. Grazelli used his body as a siege weapon, splintering the door jamb as we pivoted and moved forward in a tight formation. In front of us a heavy wooden table seemed to hover in the air, propped on its side, moving quickly toward us. I heard the pop-pop-pop of a pistol, but only noticed a single handgun snaking out and firing in our direction after the first hit.

Grazelli fell backward, letting out a gasp. Training said I should take cover and return fire, but instead I slipped back against the doorway, cringing and ducking as if I could somehow evade the rounds flying past me. Stenitz got hit next, his body spun around and fell to the ground as a second gun rang out from the other side of the encroaching furniture barrier. Everett dropped to one knee and fired repeatedly into the table, and I watched it splinter and crack and spit shards of lacquered wood everywhere with each round. However, the perps behind the table seemed unaffected.

The comm became a chatter of activity. One of the agents below called out "Shots fired!" multiple times, or multiple agents called it out at the same time.

The table smashed into Everett, bowling him over, then tipped and tilted and swung downward, landing on Grazelli and Stenitz. I stepped back, tripped, and fell backward into the hallway. Rolling to the side, my martial arts training kicked in and I slapped the ground hard with my free hand to break the fall. I watched three people step from behind the table—two of them armed—all moving in a blur. Two pair of boots and one set of flip-flops stampeded over me, catching my arm, stomach, groin, and neck. I tried to aim my pistol up at anybody, but one last boot and the weight of a human being on the side of my head ended all hope of that.

"Agents down! Suspects on the move! I repeat—"

Stenitz's voice powered through both the comm and the walls of the hotel, "Two vest strikes! I repeat two vest strikes! Apprehend suspects!"

He called for the others to reinforce from the stairwell, and the chatter grew thick with incoherence. A dozen more people poured from unsearched rooms, and rather than being trampled again, I crawled on my hands and knees, dove sideways into the room that housed the teenagers, and managed to escape further injury by inches. This low to the ground, the smell of a thousand deviant sexual acts wafted from the carpet, and my left hand came back grimy and moist. The girls were still there, writhing and crying.

I scampered to my knees and looked about, noticing a draft from the window. It wasn't open when we first came through though. Then I saw the hand holding onto the sill...

"Stop! DHS!" I yelled, arms straight out, gun pointed at the window, as I stumbled to my feet. The hands vanished. I holstered my pistol and looked down to see Skinny-man bouncing off the pizzeria sign, falling backward, and then smacking the back of his head on the sidewalk. The white box lay on the sidewalk next to him, no doubt tossed out the window ahead of his descent. I grabbed the window frame, swung my legs outside, and jumped onto the sign. Rather than break in half or break my fall, the sign split the difference and bent downward at a forty-five degree angle. Both my legs went out in an upside down 'V' shape as I landed on my chest. I heard my palms squeak against the aluminum top, my buckle scratching train tracks down the sign as I slid and fell.

My heels struck first, body lost balance to momentum, and then my butt cushioned the rest of my descent to street level. Out of the corner of my eye, Skinny-man had tucked the white box under his arm and limped into the pizzeria. I grunted into the comm as I wobbled to my feet, "Amara in pursuit of suspect with white box! On foot going in pizza place! Request immediate backup!"

I drew my pistol once again, took a guarded position, and pushed the door open. Two men in a corner booth already had their hands up and crab-walked along the edge of the restaurant, eyes on me, shuffling to the relative safety of the front entrance and the outside world.

It was a quick step to the opening in the counter, sweeping for movement. A swinging door separated the counter area from the kitchen, but the edge had caught on a flip-flop which acted as an unintentional doorstop. Voices carried from the back, Spanish, probably South American, Ecuadorian? I only caught the tail end of a warning that somebody was coming. That *I* was coming.

"DHS! Down on the ground! Down on the ground! Now!" Skinny-man stood between two men in flour covered aprons, a single flip-flop on his right foot and the white box in his hands. The three men shrank carefully to the tile floor, with Skinny-man kneeling and leaning on the cardboard package he'd carried everywhere.

"You! Slide that box over here and get on your face! Do it! Do it now!"

"Amara, hold your position!" I heard Grazelli's voice.

I answered, "Amara holding. Need—"

Then I began flying, flailing, falling, failing to keep track of anything except the wind being knocked out of me.

Chapter 14

When we reviewed the surveillance cameras later, we would know that she came around from the alleyway, and rather than flee for safety, she came back into the pizzeria. Maybe it was to help her friends, maybe it was to recover the box. Either way, Kacela Fantine introduced herself to me with a powerful kick to the back, launching me toward the men who I had ordered to lay on the ground. My sudden change to a horizontal orientation may have actually beaten them to the floor. When my eyes stopped rotating in my skull, I could see them actually getting to their feet already, scrambling away like roaches.

The cooks sailed out the side door leading to the alleyway, colliding with a Team 2 agent and flinging him into the brick wall and out of sight. Skinny-man dove for the white box, grappling it like a fumbled football as he slid through spilled olive oil and vegetable toppings.

"You come at us, bitch?" I heard her hate, heard the church bells of a dozen pizza trays toppling and clanging against the floor and each other as she flings a small rolling island aside. A lanky, towering woman rendered even taller by my position on the floor. Dark skin and tight-fitting jeans, vest shirt that showed off muscular arms and tattoos in bright colors. It was the first time I actually saw my assailant, and she was far too close for me to do anything but react.

"DHS! Don't move!" I shouted, floundering to bring my firearm to bear.

Her hand shot out in a blink, grabbed the pistol, and twisted it backward. My finger accidentally squeezed the trigger, but that round never came close to her. It connected with a pizza oven door, leaving a spidered hole in the thick glass. The webbing of her hand caught on the register as both of us struggled for the weapon.

I planted my legs, spun in place, and drove a solid knee to the back of her thigh. She should have dropped, or lost balance, or even buckled a little. Instead, she pivoted with a speed I'd never seen before, knelt on my chest, and drove punch after punch into my face, all whilst twisting the pistol forward and down. Leverage and pure strength pried my gun from my grip a degree at a time. A second more and I would be disarmed. Two seconds and my brains would be scattered across the pizzeria.

I let go of the pistol, flipped my body, and punched her in the jaw. The strike distracted her enough for me to get a better grip on my gun, first with one hand and then with the other, all while twisting my body to block her other arm. The maneuver worked, and soon I had my whole body wrapped around her arm. With a violent pressure, it became my turn to bend her wrist back. The pistol gave way, which provided this woman with the opportunity to snake her arm out from its hold.

I turned and she punched me repeatedly in the neck, rapid strikes that triggered ganglion nerves and shocked my entire body. With a leap, she was on her feet, took the time to half-step and stomp my face. Her heel caught a gap between my teeth and I could taste the filthy streets between the treads of her boot. Floundering, eyes glassy, all focus on halting a size 12 from being jammed down my throat. My pistol was barely in my grip. I was unable to get my finger to the trigger, blinded by panic.

I flipped onto my stomach, shielding my face, my neck, shielding everything this bitch had already hammered. I tried to curl up, but her weight flattened me into the floor. Then she stepped off my back for just a moment. I barely glanced to catch her launching a full snap kick that sent me gliding further along the tile.

Before I could turn around, she grabbed the box and launched herself out the open side door. Skinny-man followed—barefoot this time—right behind her. The agent who originally came to back me up—who had been bowled over by the cooks—managed to get to his feet just in time to be slammed into the alleyway wall again.

Scrambling, slipping on pizza trays, I still managed to get to my feet and follow down the alley after them. The comm was still on open transmission and I called out position, direction, description, huffing and puffing through what felt like a loose tooth. Everett radioed back this time that he would intercept at the end of the alley, and my excitement grew knowing the two of them were about to be trapped.

The woman and man broke past the plane of the buildings and out on the street. No Everett, no other agent to assist. I heard footfalls behind me and realized Everett had gone to the wrong end of the alleyway.

"Shit! Suspects are now on Forrester Street heading south, still on foot!"

"Correction," Everett broke in. "Suspects northbound on Renaissance Avenue on foot! Everett and Amara in pursuit, request vehicle backup!"

We broke out of the alley and caught sight of our prey. As we ran, I realized I also had become disoriented leaving the pizzeria. I called for backup to the wrong side of the alley, allowing them to escape. But now it wasn't just me. Chatter flew and now another two agents were in pursuit in the Team 2 van... The noose began to tighten.

The perps spotted the van right away as it sped up Renaissance Ave and took the opportunity to duck into a three-story building. As we drew closer, the sign came into view: Happy Days Daycare. I split off from Everett, down the side street, and to the backside of the building. Everett and the other two agents arrived in the front before I could get to the back and called out to wait for instructions. Grazelli should have answered, but instead Stenitz ordered us to standby.

I did my best to control my breathing, checked my service pistol, and approached the side door. I tapped the doorknob and verified it as locked, and did my best to listen. Furniture moving around, kids screaming, and then adults screaming. Screaming to get away from the kids, to leave them alone.

"Permission to breach," Everett called out from his position. "We got screams from inside."

The door flew open in front of my face and my pistol barrel leveled on the face of a young woman, tears in her eyes, four children behind her. She let out a gasp, but I pulled my weapon back and hushed her, encouraging her to the main street. As she did, I wedged my body in the open door and held there. Seconds drew out in an unnatural perversion of time, and the sound of broken glass and yelling from within became an irresistible tug to move inside.

"Go!" Stenitz shouted. He mentioned something about local law enforcement on the way, but I was already in, sweeping through the daycare kitchen, squishing dino bites and tater tots into the linoleum. Above me I could hear our other agents sprinting up a set of steps as they pursued the woman who attacked me.

I found a door ajar. Whining and crying and a meek voice whispering into a phone asking for help. I peeked inside, saw the white box, saw blood smeared across its logo, saw a woman hiding behind an overturned table, holding a child whose light green shirt now bled to crimson.

"Please hurry," she whimpered, "he's hurt really bad and now he's got another kid."

I stepped into the room, pistol up at eye level, body pressed forward, and found Skinny-man with a toddler wiggling in his arm while he held a kitchen knife straight out. His eyes darted about but kept his focus on a glass window in the door across from him.

"Don't come near me!" he shouted. "I'll kill him!"

"He's got a knife to a kid here," Everett called over the comm, presumably from the other side of the door.

"Standby," Stenitz responded.

"He's bleeding a lot," the young woman pleaded over the phone, "you've got to get us out of here..."

I looked at the little boy and the blood pooling beneath him, looked at Skinny-man with a fresh unharmed kid tucked into his armpit.

"E, open the door," I whispered.

"We've got to standby," he answered.

"E, open the door now. I'm on the side door. Be loud."

Eyes focused forward, a mere ten feet away, I waited to see if my friend would follow orders or listen to me.

The door swung open and banged against a folding table. Skinny-man instinctively pointed his knife in the direction of the noise, the child dropping a bit in his grip. I leaned mere inches to the right, lined the barrel of my weapon with his head, exhaled, and squeezed.

Chapter 15

The panel of Assistant Secretaries confer with covered mics and stolen glances in my direction. My pits are soaked and I swear there's a strange odor that is coming from me, like a gland excretion from a trapped animal. Note to self: get better deodorant in Leavenworth Prison.

The center Assistant Secretary uncovers her mic and begins speaking. "Agent James, thank you for your patience. As we wrap this up, I have a few more questions."

"Of course, Assistant Secretary."

"You mentioned in your testimony that Agent Zingg is by far the better marksman. If that's the case, why did you take the shot?"

"It was a matter of distance, Assistant Secretary. I was closer. That and I was sure I could make the shot without hitting the child."

"And what did you find in the white box once you recovered it?"

"The box was empty, except for a packing slip. The paper showed the contents were from Bokan Labs, nano technology called Sublime."

"Where did the contents go?"

"We think that Kacela Fantine, the woman we later identified as my assailant, took the contents and escaped via the rooftop."

"Your report doesn't indicate what Sublime does. Do you have any new information that you can bring to the attention of this panel?"

I shook my head and said, "Only speculation. Bokan Labs indicated that Sublime is used as a nanotech alternative to traditional anesthesia. We suspect that they were injecting girls and boys with the nanobots to knock them out, transport them, rape them. The list of possible horrible things is long, but we can't confirm anything as of now. But we continue to investigate."

"This panel is in recess. Agent James, you are dismissed."

As I walk out, Darren Franciscus gives me the tiniest tilt of his head, a gesture that I think indicates that he has no clue what will happen—and neither do I.

Chapter 16

Orev Yitzhak bats the agent's punch aside and slides the knife edge of his own palm against the man's chin. It's a reach as the DHS agent is a solid foot taller than him, but Orev plants his heel and stretches upward. The assailant's head goes back, his weight shifts, and Orev's other hand rests on the man's shoulder. He discerns the split-second change in direction. He manipulates the man's new movement vector. Even with this giant twisting and swinging for Orev's head, gravity and momentum have betrayed the assault. Orev lands an elbow to ribs, connects with armor, but pounds him twice more before the agent's body collapses into the mat with an echoing thud.

Reaching back, Orev grabs the knife, draws it from its plastic shield, and plunges it into the man's thigh mere inches from his groin. A red patch appears in the fabric and grows with each successive plunge of the blade. The action doesn't halt the DHS agent, however, who rolls over and stumbles to his feet.

"Stop!" Orev puts his empty hand up. The agent immediately complies, but his eyes say the wound is deep. Orev turns and faces the class. "Okay, what did Agent Binting do wrong?"

"Fuck with you," someone quips. A couple chuckles follow.

"True. What else though?"

"Didn't block."

Orev confirms, thick Hebrew accent clinging to each syllable, "He didn't block. He put everything into an offensive move, assuming that his big boy size was going to overwhelm me. Now he has red ink all over his pants."

Agent Binting dismisses himself from the mat and joins the others against the wall. Conciliatory pats on the back are met with him frowning and shrugging. Many point out the slash and stab marks on their own clothing.

"Things for your body to learn: defense and offense are simultaneous. Size is important but not everything. But what else? The fight does not end when you hit the ground. He did nothing to protect his legs. Now he is bleeding to death, and armor did nothing. You see now?"

Iván raises his hand.

Orev waves it down. "This isn't the kindergarten. Speak."

"Okay, well, he didn't have a knife like you did."

Orev laughs, flipping the plastic blade in a dance through the air. "Yes, my fearful ink knife. You all hate this, yes? You walk out of my class with red legs, red necks, red balls. But you go out there and the pieces of shit who you fight will not care if you have no knife. No gun. They have a knife. They have a gun. They have friends. They have a chain or wire or razor or stick. We don't train for fair in here. We train so that when you fight some dirty abortion, you aren't covered in your own red. Humiliation will be the least of your worries. Okay?"

Iván nods, looks over at Amara who is sporting a big red stain along her rib cage, and then looks back at the instructor.

"Besides, I stab him after he's down. That's about as fair as you get from me. Other questions? Other complaining that I'm not fair? Okay, get out. I need to refill my knife and stab the next class."

Iván climbs out of his squat and unbuckles his armor, relieved as the binds are released and his chest breathes free. He acknowledges the need for training in gear, but the sweat and the discomfort are still enough to trigger his desire to flee to the shower.

Everett appears, his own gear already doffed and buckled into a handy bundle to carry. "That was a painful session."

"No shit," Iván coughs in response. "My head is rattled from hitting the mat a hundred times."

"At least you didn't get red."

Iván gives himself a once over and grimaces. "I wish he did. I wasn't even worthy of stabbing. He just beat me like I was a toddler. So *embarazada*."

Everett burst out in a laugh.

"What?"

His teammate's eyes grow wider, "*Embarazada?* That's hilarious, dude. Keep it up and you're going to teach all these other agents bad Spanish though."

Iván laughs nervously, "Yeah, gotta avoid that. They'll all be *embarazada* too."

The comment is enough to bring Everett to stitches, "Oh, that's an image." A couple others glance over, curious about the punchline they missed, but not curious enough to approach and find out. When Everett finally calms himself, he gets a good look at Iván's abashed expression. "Oh, wait a sec. You didn't know... You actually think... You don't know Spanish!"

With a quick step, Iván closes the space between himself and Everett. "Shh, don't say it out loud."

"Oh man! I'm sorry. I just figured this whole time, you're Puerto Rican, you're from New York, you are always talking to Amara in Spanish."

"Can you keep it down?"

"What? No big deal. You think everyone is multilingual around here?"

Iván shushes his friend, "Everyone is. And I'm supposed to be. I might have... I might have exaggerated my Spanish skills on my application."

"Oh," Everett responds, then his eyes go wider. He softens his tone, lowers his volume. "Ohh, shit. Yeah, that's a problem, dude. You need to do some language classes."

"I know. I've been doing a little."

"You thought you were *embarazada*? Better do more than a little or your gonna say *qué pena* in the unemployment line."

"*Qué pena?*"

"It means your embarrassed, and more importantly, not pregnant."

"You wanna help me?"

"I can help a little, but my secondary is French. I've picked up a lot from the boss and from Amara, but I'm not that good."

"Who speaks French?"

"Uh, the French do? Half of Africa. The Swiss. A third of Europe..."

"I've never met a soul who speaks French."

"Says the guy who's monolingual."

Iván's critique ends there. "So, you think Amara could help me?"

They both look over at Amara James as she lands elbow after elbow into the punching bag in the corner. Sweat pouring off her, grunts and calls and curses occasion the blows. The red ink in her tan shirt is already drooping through the fabric and bleeding into her camouflage fatigues.

Everett calls out, "Hey, A! You coming? We're going for drinks!"

She barely glances over her shoulder, shakes her head, and goes back to pummeling whoever she's imagined to be in the space occupied by the punching bag.

"That means no." Everett turns and walks away.

"No shit." Iván follows. "I don't think suspension agrees with her."

"Understatement. But it's that Kacela Fantine woman that has Amara all pissy."

"Why? Didn't they just arrest her?"

"Yeah, but Amara took a few blows, almost got killed by that psycho bitch. If you haven't figured out, Amara holds a grudge. You know she's an aikido black belt, right? She can hold her own against our pen wielding nut job Krav trainer here. I've never beaten her in a sparring match, and I outweigh her by fifty pounds. But she goes out in the field, gets stomped by Fantine. Now she's in Yitzhak's class three times a day, five days a week. I mean, she's on suspension, what else is she going to do, right?"

"Yeah, but... Did you miss the part where Fantine got arrested on Friday?"

"She smells blood, dude. And God help the asshole who she gets a hold of next."

Chapter 17

Sitting in the SCIF began as an exercise in educating myself on Millennial's activities. Parsing the interview for clues relating to contacts, motivations, organizational structure, anything that could shed light on their activity. It devolved into a preoccupation over my father's assault. Watching each motion of Bruchmuller, listening to each inflection, wishing each time the video would change, alter my course through history.

My dad must have seen his suspect with his hand in his pocket or witnessed some type of motion that clued him in. "Dr. Bruchmuller, were you just using your phone?"

"No, not at all."

"Are you sure?"

"Are you accusing me of lying?"

A long break took place in which my dad moved off-screen, settling into his chair, texting David Tsai as to the whereabouts of their missing suspect. All the while the doctor stared straight ahead.

He cleared his throat. "Should we wait for Mr. Tsai to return before we continue?"

My dad quipped, "Nah, I like to put my feet up."

Bruchmuller let out a small laugh, pasted on a polite smile. "Well, let us continue then."

The questions that followed were all related to Innovo. All of them were vetted as solid questions and all related to the losses from the company. Bruchmuller answered them grudgingly, legalistically, carefully. His attempts to distract the interview met with my father's admonitions.

"I'm giving you an opportunity to tell me your side of the story, but if you aren't interested, I am sure the authorities will be fascinated with what's been going on here."

"You haven't contacted the authorities?" Bruchmuller raised a lone eyebrow.

"No, I have not contacted the authorities. That's not how we operate. Innovo has a policy of discussing these matters first with employees. Even when there has been some sort of wrongdoing, we'd prefer to avoid the bad press. It hurts the price of our stock, you see."

"That's very comforting," he said slowly.

Each time I watched the video, my stomach tightened at this moment. Through the lens of history, I watched my father's oversight unfold. The clue was so obvious as to what would follow that I would grow angry with him for not seeing the telltale signs, not hearing the warning in the doctor's voice. Martin James, an expert interviewer, should have known, should have stopped, should have left the room and called the police, and then none of my life would have been my life and we'd be a family again. Instead, I would mentally scream at the screen for the twentieth time, thirtieth time, fortieth time, for my dad to stop.

"Does Director Thomason know you are accusing a senior researcher of the company of stealing?"

"Director Thomason is fully briefed on this case and has complete confidence in our investigation."

"I don't like where you are taking this, Mr. James."

"I'd like to see your phone, if you don't mind, Doctor."

"I think I do mind. I don't see how it is relevant."

"How well do you know Albert Vies, Doctor?"

"I want to speak with my attorney."

My father hesitated at this moment as if he was weighing his choices. So foolish. Private security, police interview—it made no difference. When somebody lawyered up, you stopped. Instead of following policy and ending the interview, he asked one more question. A question about an experiment conducted in the PK lab.

"Tell me about the rat."

Such a simple question. Five words that immobilized Dr. Dieterich Bruchmuller for five seconds. Then a blur of motion followed, the doctor rushing forward, moving off-camera and knocking my father backward with a grunt. A glimpse of a shoulder, two frames of video showing Bruchmuller's snarling face, the sound of a kick and the wind being knocked out of my dad.

And then the camera itself was in motion, the device becoming a bludgeoning weapon that swung down repeatedly into my father's skull, cracking the lens, bruising his face, breaking the mechanism, and then going dark. The audio still fed up into the cloud though.

The opening of the door.

The whispering of voices.

The shuffling of footsteps.

The sliding of my father's body across the interview room floor.

Then nothing.

And I would again be me. Here. Now. With no place to go but forward. My only solace is that in about a week I will be distracted by another, more important puzzle. My father will be synchronized after nine years from his chemo-preservative state. Once he's able to interact with us, he will be offered a cure, and I will have to convince him to not take it, even if it means losing another decade of his life.

Chapter 18

The house in Beacon, Pennsylvania felt like a museum each time I visited. Occasionally a new exhibit would make its way into our home—a new interface to communicate with our father, or a new security drone to secure his presence in this secluded country landscape. But ultimately, my father's existence moved at such a slow pace that there was no need to acknowledge it as moving forward at all.

Tonight, the house has more visitors than usual. Although they've been invited, I wouldn't call them welcome. Walter Reed Medical Center brought their team and their equipment to manage my father's condition, to somehow convince his body's cells to operate at a normal pace. To do that, they need to speed them up 4000 times, a feat that Innovo has been unable to accomplish.

Innovo Pharmaceutical was supposed to send Lenny Chari, one of their specialists who developed an antidote called Dambra-44. Nine years ago, Lenny administered the Dambra which worked for several hours, but it ultimately failed and my father slipped back into a chemopreservative state. Despite their best efforts, Lenny and his team had not been able to improve on Dambra-44, and so when the Walter Reed team developed a new cure, everyone could tell Lenny was deflated. Now, almost a decade later, he had planned to return to assist in the case of an emergency, but a storm leaving Charlotte delayed the plane. He finally landed in Philly and asked if we would wait, but the process to synchronize my father was already underway. There is no stopping this ship from leaving port.

I walk into the sitting room where my father spent the last decade, find his chair empty, electrodes and earbuds neatly laid out on a metal tray. It always smelled of plastic in here, and today is no different. I hear the door open, and I look up to see Mike Gandry waving me over.

"He's already in the lab with your sister and the Walter Reed doctors," he says, giving me a handshake. "The only one from Innovo is Randy, can't remember his last name. He's a lawyer though. Never met him before."

"Yeah, Lenny's on his way, should be here soon."

Mike had been a part of our family's life for years now, living part-time in the guest room, conducting tests on behalf of Innovo that had to be done by a professional. I knew he was seeing a guy in Philadelphia and that the relationship was on edge because of Mike's job here, but he never wavered in his dedication to us, not even when our mother walked out. Bella might be good company, but she had her own life and often left Mike alone 'house sitting' while she and Keith went out.

"Do you want me to make some coffee?"

"You've done more than enough."

"I know. But I'm hoping this is the end of my assignment here. For your family's sake."

I force a smile.

Mike disappears into the kitchen while I stride out the side door and across the yard to the lab. Originally built by Innovo as a sterile environment, they eventually allowed it to slip into a general-purpose medical room once we learned that infections were ineffective at attacking chemo-preserved cells. Thanks to Millennial's forced injections, my father had become immune to disease—a benefit we were sure he would give up to have a regular life back.

Bella turns and gives me a brief hug when I walk in, reminds me to hug her back. She's decorated in a white Spring dress, hair curled and down, like she is ready for a date night. She makes me feel so under-dressed in suspenders and with my hair pulled back tight to hide the fact I haven't washed it today.

Maggie Gonzales comes to see me next, grabbing me roughly and turning my head to the left and right, as if she is inspecting a head of cattle.

"Amara!" she starts. "You made it! Cutting it close, aren't you? What's this? Why the new bruises?"

"Not so new," I clarify, gently pushing her hands down. "Met somebody who didn't like me is all."

Bella breaks in, "Wait... Who? Why? Where do you have bruises?" Now both of them are prodding me, and I have to swat them away.

"Back off, mother hens! Don't you have another patient to attend to?"

I point at my father who is reclined in the hospital bed and surrounded by magnetic emitters, micro-arrays, and two state-of-the-art Barinq-3000 surgical robotic arms. Our dad is the reason for the season, and despite everyone being familial and loving, the reality is that these very same people who have come here to 'cure' him are really using him as an experiment. My cursory look into Maggie

Gonzales' data clued me in months ago, but since then I'd gotten no additional insight from Maggie or Dr. Nikonov or anyone else on the team.

Though as badly as I have wanted to make this my top focus, my cases at DHD kept me narrowly focused. The goal to capture Millennial and find their antidotes remains paramount to all other considerations. Perhaps it was ignorance on my part to think that Walter Reed would give up, or that I would find out more before they decided to implement their treatment, but it doesn't matter. The day is now, and I could find no clear evidence to stop them.

"So, are we really doing this?" I ask the room. It stops all conversation, and all magnetizes everyone's eyeballs to rest on me.

Dr. Nikonov tilts his head back in an attempt to hide his eye roll. "Amara, we've sent all the data to Innovo and to you. You've had it for months and said nothing. Why this now?"

"The Diox-9 you're using to synchronize my father back does not have the most consistent delivery. I don't know why we can't use Innovo's Dambra-44. We know that works." I hadn't expected to bring this up, but I couldn't bring up the parallel testing I spied on Maggie's tablet, the testing that showed my father was a lab rat for some other beneficiary.

"If we use the Dambra-44 and the procedure fails, it could be another decade before his numbers bottom out again. Do you really want to wait that long to find a fix?"

My father's body begins to move faster. We watch as his limbs twitch, a dog chasing squirrels through his dream, but my father is awake. The twitching increases in frequency and—more importantly—speed. But it's spastic, disturbing, possibly an indicator of pain.

"Are we looking at a seizure here?" Mike asks Maggie.

"Looks like it," she frowns, leaning over him and gently caressing his arm. "This wasn't one of the anticipated side effects, but I'm not surprised."

Another tech speaks up from the back, "Acute radiation encephalopathy?"

"Not at these doses. But it could be related."

"Suggested treatment?"

Maggie leans down, grabs his trembling hand and puts it against her face. "Give him a moment."

The involuntary movements shake the room to silence, all eyes in a state of observation as my father's spasms increase, then abate to infrequent tics of his fingers.

Bella and I hold hands, her grip soft and warm, my grip clammy. "It's okay," she assures anyone who listens, but the target is clearly herself.

His finger twitches are replaced with curls, and then his arms bending upward toward his face. Movements like this are uncommon as his chemopreservation means holding his arms up for even one second is equivalent to a normal person holding their arms up for over an hour. Gravity takes no breaks, and so we always support his limbs. Now, however, he is synchronizing and moving in a way...

My sister pushes past me and runs to my father's bedside. These are not slow-motion finger twitches or gravity forcing his limbs to flop. At first, he looks like he's reached up to adjust the goggles, but soon it's obvious he's struggling to get them off his head. The saline sprayer is designed to moisten his open eyes when awake and syncing forward, when they're open for over five hours in between blinks that take twenty-two minutes. Now the goggles are dousing his eyelids.

Mike Gandry removes the goggles and dabs my father's eyes as if he were a preemie in a NICU. I watch his pupils contract, dart, and focus on my sister's form hovering over him.

"Wake up, Dad," Bella soothes. "Your body is synced back finally. You're in real time."

His lips move, nothing but a hiss escapes. He tries clearing his throat but even that fails. Maggie hands a bottle to my sister who places the tip in his mouth and squeezes. The concoction, a spray of water, oil, and citric acid, wets his mouth and brings smiles to everyone when we see the reflexive move of his Adam's apple.

He paws at the bottle, then manages to grip it and serve himself. I look over at Nikonov and the others, and I see nothing but optimistic smiles. It's difficult to parse their reaction, as they would be happy regardless of their intentions. And yet I find a modicum of solace.

He practices making noises and clearing his throat. It takes another ten minutes, but then he croaks out his first word in years, "Hey, Baby Bella."

"Hi, Dad."

"Bella. Don't you look so pretty! And is that my big kid back there?"

My heart thumps when he looks to me, oh-so-familiar eyes filled with incredible disconnect. I take a few steps forward and squeeze his calf. "Hi, Daddy," I say softly. "Welcome back."

He takes another sip and replies, "So, where's your mom?"

Bella turns and looks at me uncomfortably as the conversation across the room stops. Bella turns back to him and pats his chest. "She couldn't make it, Dad."

"But where is she?"

"Let's talk about Mom later. We're on a tight schedule."

"Okay..." his voice trails off. "Can you at least tell me what year it is?"

Bella and I had prepared for this conversation for months, focusing on the concepts of easing into the truth and how psychology of grief worked. Now, face-to-face with him, it feels like we're dangling the truth just out of his grasp.

"You've been asleep for almost nine years. You're just past the thirteenth anniversary of the Innovo bombing."

"Are you sure?" his voice cracks.

Bella squeezes his hand, "Dad, it's okay, just—"

"Nine years?"

"Dad, we don't have a lot of time. This team is from Walter Reed, and they have a plan for fixing you permanently."

Dr. Nikonov approaches and introduces himself, stepping in front of me and extending a hand toward my father. "I'm working with the Department of Homeland Defense on this initiative, and we're all quite excited to be able to put an end to this nonsense."

Despite Nikonov's grating tone, my father appears to break from the spiraling doom. "Sounds good to me, Doc. What's the process?"

Dr. Nikonov hesitates slightly before continuing. "We used a derivative of the Dambra treatment to sync you back. It just means you've been brought up to speed, no pun intended. Anyway, the new treatment is 100 percent chemical. We call it Diox-9. It means no more radiation treatments to work in concert with your syncing."

"Hell, I didn't even know there was radiation involved in the first place. So Diox-9, huh? What happened to Diox-1 through 8?"

"I wouldn't worry about those."

The subterfuge about a second patient concerns me greatly, but now Dr. Nikonov's dismissive attitude is too much   for   me. "Diox-2, 4, and 6 were all failures," I say. "Diox-5 and Diox-7 almost killed you. Diox-8 they never even administered, since the tests showed it would cause instantaneous death. Oh, I forgot, Diox-1 actually turned the cell sample they tested it on into plastic."

"Holy crap," my father shouts. "Are you trying to kill me?"

"If we wanted to kill you, we would have subjected you to thirteen years of romance novels," Maggie Gonzales tosses out, her back turned to everyone. With her silly comment, my father turns toward her and softens. It sounds like an inside joke, one that I'm not privy to.

"Hey, Doc," he says, "Long time no see."

"I wish I could say the same thing," she replies. "I've been staring at your mug for all this time. Will you just synchronize already and get this over with?"

"Well, ma'am, I would, but where else am I going to find a job that pays me to sit on my ass for a decade?"

There were a couple of chuckles around the room as Maggie embraces my father. "I don't know if you know this, but Amara has been helping us find a cure for you ever since we first met."

"Miranda told me last time I was, I was, you know . . ."

"Synced?"

"Okay, synced. Anyway, Miranda mentioned that Amara was quite involved."

My face flushes a bit, remembering my 'contributions' to saving my father. Wildly out of my depth, I spent my teenage years reading medical research papers that I couldn't possibly understand. Maggie actually tutored me on many occasions, spending hours on calls while she worked in the lab. The only time she lost her patience with me was when I turned down a full scholarship to Georgetown Medical, along with an internship at Walter Reed that she sponsored.

"Hey, I tried to help too," Bella says.

I roll my eyes. "Oh please. Your big idea was giving Daddy lots and lots of coffee to speed him up."

"You wanted to stick him in a microwave!"

"That was a joke! But since Dambra kinda does that, it turns out I'm a genius."

"It's not anything like that," Maggie assures my father. "Martin, let's talk about your condition on a very basic level. Whatever material you were injected with reprogrammed your DNA to fool your cells into operating at a fraction of their normal speed. Ever since, we've been trying to make your body work how it's supposed to. Innovo has been trying to create an antidote, but the longest they've been able to keep you synced is less than a day.

"Our team originally tried synthetic catecholamine to jump-start you—something akin to Bella's idea of pumping you full of coffee, but on a chromosomal level. As you might recall, that almost killed you and only worked for less than two hours. Diox-9 is a derivative of the Dambra-44 treatment that Innovo developed, but we fully recognize it's a temporary solution at best. We synced you this time so you could give us permission to try step two of a treatment we've developed."

"Go on," he says.

"We have a way of tricking your body into producing fully synced cells that will function normally, but there will be some complications. We'd like to implant your body with nanobots that will penetrate your forward-syncing cells and make them operate faster."

"Why does that sound terrifying?"

"It shouldn't. Nanobots have been around for a while. They're essentially super, super small robots that can be directed with a high degree of precision. While this new series of nanos is still experimental, they show a lot of promise in treating cancer and other genetic disorders. The process could take many years as some cells reproduce slowly, while others don't reproduce at all. The good news is that if it works, you could live a reasonably comfortable life—"

"Tell him the bad news, Maggie," I interject.

Doctor Gonzales shifts in her seat. "Martin, you would be held in sync with this nanotreatment, and we feel comfortable that it will work. The bad news is that the nanobots require their own special field that they absolutely must remain inside. Since your brain and nerve cells won't replicate on the scale we need, they need to be regularly adjusted by the nanos. Without that field, part of your body will age normally while the rest of you will sync forward. It could mean paralysis for you . . . or worse."

"Couldn't you just shut the whole thing down? Like, if they aren't working properly and it becomes a worst-case scenario, can't you just turn them off?"

Maggie glances at Dr. Nikonov. "Maybe. I can't guarantee that, though. Your cells may forward sync asymmetrically—that's a fancy way of saying that bad things could happen."

"It doesn't sound good. So how would this field work?"

"You would have to remain in a tightly controlled environment with very little moving around, since the field needs to adjust to your movements accurately."

"You'll be bedridden, Daddy. You'll be stuck in here for as long as you live."

Bella angrily steps in front of me. "Shut up! He doesn't know all his choices! How do you expect him to make a decision if you don't tell him everything?"

"He's not stupid—"

Our father clapped his hands together, "Hey! Hey! Hey! Stop it!"

"Martin, nobody is hiding anything," Dr. Gonzales reassures him. "In time, we might be able to get the field to grow, but we're dealing with technology that is untested. What Bella is talking about is how your body reacts to the syncing. Since you were first injected, your body has been struggling to slow down as much as it can. Every time we've put you through a procedure to speed you back up, your cells stubbornly revert back. But each treatment meddles with the rate at which your body decelerates, which means each time it takes longer for your cell speed to bottom out. And since we don't want to kill you, we have to wait longer each time we try a new cure. If we don't do this nanotreatment now, it could be another ten, maybe twenty, years."

The lawyer suddenly speaks up. "Martin James, my name is Randy Lindale, and I represent Innovo in these dealings." He hands our father a datapad. "This letter declares that Innovo Industries has not signed off on the nanotreatment designed by the US government. Our original agreement with the federal government of the United States regarding your treatment stipulates that Innovo can neither block treatment nor advise you not to take treatment offered by any federal institution. We can only tell you that research conducted by Innovo has not been able to vouch for any claims of viability for this procedure. You should also know that you are not required to take any treatment from any institution, ours or the government's. Furthermore—"

"Okay, I've got it," our father waves him off. "Let me talk with my family."

When the room is soon empty save for the three of us, I say, "You should know there is no consensus on how your condition should be handled, not even within the Walter Reed group. That alone is worrying me."

He shrugs. "Well, it doesn't mean it's a bad idea either though, right?"

"Daddy, you can't do this treatment. They aren't ready. I know it sounds like they are ready, but the Walter Reed doctors aren't considering a lot of variables. It's not worth the risk."

Bella waves me off, "Dad, do you really want to stay like this? How many times can you do this? What do you think you're going to do when Innovo loses interest in you completely? We don't even know when or if this drug will wear off. At least Dr. Gonzales is offering you a chance to live with us. Please, Dad, just do it—"

"No! Don't do it—Bella is wrong! They're all wrong!"

"Screw you! What makes you so smart?"

I'm feeling an urge to flatten her, but instead I look our father dead in the eyes. "Daddy, you have to trust me. It isn't hard to read between the lines. Innovo doesn't even believe it will work."

"How can you say that? What makes you the expert?"

"Because Maggie's lying."

"How can you say that? She's been taking care of Dad for—"

"She's lying, Bella! Sorry if I don't trust every living soul like you do, but she's lying to us. How you can be so gullible all the time."

"So, Ms. Secret Agent gets a badge and has all the answers?" Bella picks up an empty plastic vial and hurls it right at my head.

"Stop this!" our father yells, then gathers himself. "Bella, let me ask Amara some questions. I listened to what you had to say, now let me talk to Amara alone for five minutes."

"Dad—"

"Please, Bella. Just five minutes."

"But you're taking her side—"

"I'm not. I'm trying to hear both sides."

"Fine," she snaps. "I hope you're still synced after five minutes." Bella grabs the purse I bought her two years ago and storms out of the lab.

Chapter 19

The modified ECG chimes delicately, indicating his heart rate is up. For my father, that's a novel experience. The loud chimes on the terminal are reserved for his heart rate dropping, a strong indicator that his condition is slipping back to its poisoned ways.

I expect him to dig right into my Walter Reed concerns, but instead he points at my badge. Of all the discussions to have at this moment, this is one of two I don't wish to have.

"Is there something you want to show me?" he asks in a low voice.

I rotate my hip to show him my badge and sidearm.

"Who are you working for?"

"Homeland Defense. It used to be called the Department of Homeland Security, but things got reorg'd with the uptick in IEDs being set off in shopping malls. It's a national police force dealing with terrorism, interstate gangs, and whatnot."

"You were majoring in bioengineering and computer forensics last time we spoke. And on a full scholarship to boot! What happened to your education?"

"I finished it, Daddy. You saw my graduation pictures."

"Yes, but I didn't think you were going to just end your education. You've got a tremendous mind, Amara. Why wouldn't you push into what you're good at?"

"What makes you think I'm not good at investigations? You're a great investigator, and I am way smarter than you." I'm hoping to lighten the mood, but he's having none of it.

"Sweetie, I do investigations—or at least did them—for a living because it's the only thing I've ever been good at: it doesn't mean you have to. You could be doing so much more. Certainly making a hell of a lot more money than I did. It seems like you're selling yourself short."

I start picking at my cuticles. "You know, most people just said 'congratulations.'"

He sighs. "I'm proud of how well you've done for yourself, but I just don't understand your career choice—dealing with terrorists? And in the field, no less?"

"How did you know I was a field agent?"

"I know the look. Jesus, Amara, I wanted to become a field agent before you were born. But I got lucky, and budget sequesters ended up with me getting canned. It was the best thing that happened to me. Do you know how dangerous the job you've signed up for is?"

Did I know? Gee, I've only been blown up, beaten down, shot at. "I know how to handle myself, Daddy. I'm not a little girl anymore."

"True, but have things gotten better in the country over the last thirteen years? From the news articles you pumped across the screen to me, I'd say they look a heck of a lot worse. That fancy pistol you're packing isn't going to do you a bit of good when your car gets T-boned by a truck, or a bomb goes off in your building, or they set your sister on fire because you were poking around too much."

He couldn't have known about Millennial's proclivity for dousing people in kerosene, but the imagery isn't lost on me. "It's not like Innovo did anything to protect you from being attacked. Somebody's got to stand up to these people!"

"Somebody, yes. But not you."

"Why not?"

"Because you're my child."

"Why are you being like this?" I can't even look at him now, and I feel a tear escaping down my face. "I thought you would be proud of me."

It's quiet for a bit.

"Sweetheart, I am proud of you. I am, honestly. I'm just worried about you in this line of work. How can I not be?"

"Can we...can we drop it, Daddy? Just . . . drop it. Let's talk about your treatment, okay?"

He rubs his face in his hands, takes a deep breath, and does his best to act as if the previous two minutes never happened. "So. What makes you think Dr. Gonzales is hiding something?"

I share what I know about Walter Reed testing his blood samples against somebody else's and how his samples were always tested first, and how Maggie never bothered to disclose any of it to me.

"And Bella doesn't know?" he asks.

I shake my head.

He nods and asks me to get my sister. I step outside and wave to Bella through the kitchen window. She neither waves back nor smiles, and when she silently walks past me, she even angles her shoulders away so she doesn't even catch me in her peripheral vision. Mike and one of the other Walter Reed technicians step into the lab right behind her: why, I don't know.

I step away from the lab and the house and soon the darkness of the countryside wraps around me, with a band of stars so bright it feels like I've been transported to a different world. In DC, I can barely see the Big Dipper because of the light pollution. Out here, I can barely see the constellations through the myriad blazing suns that burn above us.

Somebody yells angrily in the lab, breaking me from my stargazing. With a spin, I turn back.

It's my father's voice. "Get out! Out! Out! Out!" A metal tray clatters. Mike and the other tech scamper out the door. Bella exits next, balled fists and cursing under her breath. She glances my way and then turns away.

I saddle up shoulder-to-shoulder and we face opposite directions. "I told you not to say anything about Mom, and you did it anyway."

"He kept asking. What was I supposed to say?"

"You lie to him," I answer flatly.

"Well now he hates me. Are you happy?"

"No. Because now he's going to take the treatment. And it's going to kill him. And then I'm going to hate you."

Chapter 20

Miranda—our mother—moved back to New Jersey once Bella turned eighteen, having served her sentence of country living and staying dedicated to our father for 'too long.' Even prior to the Innovo attack, she had always been hard on us...on me, anyway. After my father's condition grew more defined, the reality of waiting for a cure, waiting for a discovery twisted her focus.

She resented my father for being a victim of a terrorist attack. She resented the government for hiding us away from the people who could return at any moment to kill us. She resented Innovo for giving us a home that was secure and money to live on. She resented me for remaining dedicated to our family when the easy thing to do was give up. She resented Bella for not giving into the poison she fed to split us from our father, from each other. She resented herself for staying in a marriage that she committed to years before. Once the obligation of being a parent expired, Miranda abandoned us all.

Now, even standing outside, I could hear her voice over the vidcall. It cut through the lab, crushing my father as he realized his marriage was over. I knew Bella would play the part of peacemaker, attempting to justify and forgive and explain, but Miranda's voice hammered away, breaking my father's spirit with one realization after another.

When the call is over, Bella informs everyone that our father will be taking the nanotreatment after all. Dr. Nikonov looks satisfied: now he'll have a set of data to perfect this treatment for whoever else has been injected with Millennial's mystery drug.

I walk into the lab as a razor buzzes away a circular patch in the back of Daddy's head, little tufts of dignity scattering on the chair and floor. Dr. Gonzales is hovering near him with a tablet, admonishing him for not relaxing as a room full of scientists prepare to experiment on him with untested technology. He actually apologizes to her. For the first time I see my father as weak, and Miranda did this to him. It wasn't enough for her to abandon us. She had to destroy whatever willpower he still had.

Dr. Nikonov directs his staff to adjust the emitters while Maggie inclines herself to working on her tablet, calling instructions to her assistant to fill several large syringes from a clear plastic barrel with a central blade agitating the viscous liquid into swirling eddies. Bella is trying keep our father calm by sharing news about the world and Keith, with neither topic helping keep his heart rate down.

"Hold this," Maggie tells me, dropping the tablet into my hands. She rotates the surgical arms into position behind our father. I start mentally tallying rough costs of the equipment, testing, personnel, and so on. I conclude that this is a budget sink, and there is no way they've gotten approved for any of this without there being solid review of what they've done.

Maggie inspects the syringe for bubbles before fitting it into the robotic arm.

Our dad chuckles nervously. "You're not going to stick that in my legs, are you?"

"No, of course not," she said with a smile. "We're injecting it into your brain."

"Dr. Gonzales," he said, "why is it that Dr. Bruchmuller only injected me in my arms and legs, and now you are going to shove a four-inch needle into my brain?"

"We don't know," Maggie responded. "Nobody does. I can't be sure if I told you before, but your condition should be medically impossible. Of course, almost everything in this lab was impossible thirty years ago. It's only a matter of time before we figure out what you were injected with. Until then, we inject your brain."

"If this doesn't work, what happens to the nanos? Could they damage me?"

"No. We could direct them to move out of your body, turn off, or even break apart on command. Until we start the treatment of reprogramming your cells, you'll be very much yourself. However, once your cells start replicating in sync, there is going to come a point when we won't be able to shut off the nanos. Powering down at that point could be bad."

"Bad? What exactly do you mean by bad?"

"Well, computer models say we can nanosaturate your nervous system in about three days. Your body may sync forward by then, so we're prepared to monitor your cell generation rate across your body. We'll do our best to target any failing organs with massive nano injections."

His previous spark of hope doesn't dim with these questions. I knew these details from our conversation at Walter Reed, and they seem like reasonable preparations and well thought out precautions. Only one aspect troubled me: the second set of data left unmentioned by Dr. Gonzales.

Maggie's tablet lets out a chime in my hand followed by a burp, then another, then another. Instinctively I glance at the screen which shows a 'Connected' message followed by a 'Disconnect', then repeats. I try to mention it to Maggie but she's in deep dialog with my father as she connects a variety of sensors to him... The source of the alarms.

I'm feeling for the volume buttons on the side when I see the data Maggie must have been working through when I got here. A typical spreadsheet, lots of numbers, but the cells are highlighted in an odd pattern, three lines and a circle:

N O.

If I click anywhere on the screen, the highlighted selection will disappear and everything will look normal. This is not a coincidence, or a cutesy message, or a random cell clicking doodle. When I try to make eye contact with her, Maggie turns her back to me. Nikonov is looking straight at me. I smile politely, nervously. My father is deeply ingrained into their conversation as he batters her with what-ifs.

The preparations are completed, and Nikonov moves quickly to get the procedure started, reaching for a tray full of needles near dad's intravenous line. Maggie Gonzales still has her back turned to me, but the only one that matters is my father who drums his fingers on his thighs and flexes his toes.

He finally glances my way. I steal a look at the tablet then and I mouth the word "No" slowly. I dare not hold the tablet up, because it will reveal Maggie is behind the message. Instead, I press it to my chest and hold my gaze.

"Maybe this isn't such a good idea," escapes my father's mouth.

"You'll be fine, Mr. James," says Dr. Nikonov.

My dad puts his hand up, his voice growing confident. "Hold up."

Nikonov forces a smile. "Martin, relax. You're in good hands. We'll take care of you." He reaches up and positions the needle near the feed, but now that my dad's declined the procedure, that's all I need to protect him and—presumably—Maggie.

I grab Dr. Nikonov's wrist and lock it forward. He squirms in my grip as the needle drops out of his hand and into my free one. "My father said hold up!" With three fingers, I apply just enough pressure to the joint to drive Dr. Nikonov to his knees.

He grimaces while maneuvering to attempt fleeing the pain. "What the hell is wrong with you? This is just a sedative, you crazy bitch!"

"My father said he doesn't want the treatment," I enunciate slowly.

Bella stands up. "Amara, let him go! He's just trying to help!"

"You've made your point," Maggie snaps, "let him go!"

The other assistants are yelling too, a situation well outside their comfort zone.

They've all been lying. They let things get to the point where my father is nothing more than a lab rat to them. And while there's no way Nikonov made this decision in a vacuum, he's the one at my mercy, and I want to hurt him.

Dr. Maggie Gonzales picks up a plastic tray and whacks it on the metal bed rail repeatedly like a gavel. Startled, I let go of Nikonov.

"Amara, what has gotten into you?" Maggie shouts, stepping into my space and helping Dr. Nikonov to his feet. "Have you lost your mind?"

My dad answers. "She's just trying to take care of me, and I changed my mind: that's all. I don't want to go through with the procedure."

Bella storms past me. "This is all your fault!"

Dr. Gonzales sets the tray down and gently puts her hand on me. "Martin, what's wrong? why the sudden change?"

Dad glances at me so briefly I have no time to provide a facial cue, but somehow, clever duck that my dad is, he gets it. He puts on a smile. "Hey, Doc, don't take it personally. I want to be sure about this procedure, and I'm not. That's all. I just think that between you and the other doctors at Innovo, you'll have a permanent cure figured out in no time."

Maggie's shoulders slump a little as she rubs my dad's shoulder. It's a long moment of awkwardness in the room as she and Nikonov whisper so very quietly to each other. She turns to my father and say, "Martin, it's your decision, and I respect it. We'll do the best we can, okay?"

"Thanks, Doc."

Dr. Nikonov walks over cautiously and pats him on the leg. "Sorry I didn't listen to you, Martin. No hard feelings I hope?"

"No hard feelings," my father returns, a courteous southern response that I knew meant 'you're dead to me.'

The Walter Reed team—save Maggie—huddles tightly with almost-whispers and over-the-shoulder glances at me.

Maggie is at my father's feet, removing the sensor straps that she put in place minutes ago. The tablet squelches with each snap undone, and I hand it to her, unsure of what I can say—or should say.

Maggie keeps her head down and chats with her patient, still pushing the nanotreatment and all its merits right up to the removal of the last sensor.

"Dr. Gonzales, we need to have a meeting off-site. All of us. Now." Dr. Nikonov stands arms folded, gazing at the lot of us.

Maggie starts to protest, "Somebody should stay back to—"

"Now," he repeats.

Maggie almost responds in kind, but then deflates and looks at my father, brushing one hand gently against his cheek. The hand becomes a wave and she says, "Good-bye, Martin. I hope you'll see me soon."

He nods and says, "Me too, Doc. Watch over the girls for me, will you?"

Maggie looks at me as she passes. "I'm not sure they need watching over anymore."

With that, they all funnel out of the room. Bella runs to dad's side to plead her case. Randy immediately jumps on his next phone call. I look into Mike's eyes and it is apparent he is the only one here who truly understands how bad the situation has degenerated.

"You have to go get them," he tells me.

"I know," I say, trotting out of the lab.

"I have no training on the Diox-9."

"I know!"

The SUV has already pulled away, whisking Maggie Gonzales away along with the Walter Reed team. Only Dr.

Nikonov remains in his rental car, lights on, aiming down the driveway. I step in front of the vehicle.

"You have to go back in there!"

Nikonov cracks his window. "We're coming back, Ms. James. Now get out of the way."

"You can have your meeting in the house, Doctor. And we don't know how to handle the Diox-9."

"The Diox-9 will probably last two days. Now move!" He inched the car closer to me, but I stood my ground... Kinda. I felt my feet angling to the right, positioning to jump. His car lurched again. "Amara, get the hell out of the way!"

"You can't leave him here unattended! Something could go wrong!"

He rolled his window down further. "We have to discuss research matters that are not secure here. We'll be back in a few hours."

"No! You can't—" my plea is interrupted by him bringing the car so close that it's touching my leg, "—hey! Just use the house for your meeting!"

"It's top secret."

"I have TS clearance."

"It's need-to-know."

"Walter Reed granted me access to all lab work relating to my father."

"Not anymore."

My gut drops into my shoes. I step to the driver's side to get closer and Nikonov starts to pull away. I grab onto the window as he slowly accelerates the car down the driveway. "What do you mean? What the hell are you saying? Stop the car!"

"Let go!"

I'm running now, holding onto the window as I hear the electric motor push the glass up in a rather one-sided game of chicken with my fingers. I give up and Nikonov hits the gas, launching gravel and dust into my face.

The taillights of the SUV and car disappear and reappear and disappear again from behind the hills, shrinking into two pair of evil red eyes that finally wink out of existence. The sides of my head hurt, and it takes me a moment to realize I'm pulling knots of my own hair in opposite directions.

I dial Nikonov and unsurprisingly it goes straight to voicemail. I try Maggie next. Her phone rings, but she never picks up. I try the emergency contact at Walter Reed, and here I get an immediate answer. The woman (I think her name is Ping) asks me for my ID number and reason for the call. I start to explain I need the research team back at the lab. Ping places me on hold for a minute, two minutes, three. The sunset loses its orange streaks and fades to dusty blue. When Ping finally returns, all she tells me is that the team is scheduled to return to the lab in one to two hours.

I ask her to try Nikonov again, but she deflects my requests and tells me to call her if there are any signs of problems with my father. When I try to ask another question, the connection goes dead.

A text to Maggie. Another. And another. Nikonov next. Twenty texts go unanswered. I call Lenny Chari from Innovo, but a voicemail response brings no solace.

"What did I just do?"

Returning to the house, I see our father dressed in regular clothes and walking arm-in-arm with Bella out of the lab. We had kept the clothes vacuum stored, to be opened when he is healed and ready to live normally again. We sometimes spoke about opening them signifying a new chapter in all our lives.

I glared at Bella. "What the fuck are you doing?"

My father waved at me, "Watch the language. I told her I want to walk around. I know I only have a day or two, but I want to stretch my legs."

"We don't know you have two days, Daddy. We don't know anything. You need to get back in the lab and into your gown."

"Amara, he looks fine," my sister says. "Look, he's up and walking and the house is right here. Let him be."

"Daddy, please—"

He stops me and asks me about my car, and about my service pistol, about my job. I end up locking arms with him, taking short steps to keep him as close to the house as possible. He does everything he can to delve into my work, but now I don't feel like answering: not because I'm angry, but because I didn't know what to tell him. How do I explain being courted by terrorists? Destroying an entire building? Gunfights, human trafficking, and investigative panels that saw me suspended for weeks? How do I explain to my dad—who saw me last in middle school—that every choice I've made to save his life has resulted in abject failure?

I opt for an easy deflection, telling him what they report in the news. Essentially, a lot of nothing. My hospitalization and eardrum replacement are conveniently missing from my tales, and Bella thankfully does nothing to fill in the blanks. A call from Darren Franciscus allows me to step away and—hopefully—put some attention on Bella's life.

"Hey, what's up?" I ask, putting enough distance between them and me as to not be able to eavesdrop.

"Your creds at Walter Reed are suspended. Just came across my desk. Everything okay?"

I sighed. "It's a misunderstanding, is all. I'll get it cleared up."

"I know this is your family we're talking about, so if you need me to get involved, I'll swing the bat."

"Thank you."

"No problem. How's everything else going there?"

"It could be better."

"Is he okay though?"

"Yeah, I think so. We're not expecting any change."

"Well, that's too bad."

"Yeah."

"We'll redouble our efforts when you get back."

"Thank you."

"Did you give him the note?"

"Not yet."

I hang up and turn around to rejoin my dad and sister only to find them farther down the driveway. Catching up with them is easy, but the distance from the house is making me increasingly uncomfortable. Bella and our father ignore my concerns, however, and he tells me he wants to feel the cold and breathe the fresh air. Yes, his condition when syncing forward is like being trapped sensory deprivation chamber, and this small touch of real life is the first contact he's had with life in almost a decade. I try to sympathize, but all I can think is having him uncomfortable is far better than having him dead.

"My supervisor is dedicating our entire department to finding Millennial," I tell him. "We've figured out the crypts they told you about when they took you. They're hideouts for Millennial members. They put them in buildings. They slip in, take the drug and wait until they're ready to come out. Six months or six years later.

"That's bizarre. I figured they were in cemeteries or something."

"That's what everyone thought, but..." I stop short of explaining that our first encounter almost resulted in my death.

"I figured they were using them to help sick family members, not as safe houses."

"It's both, we think. These people use the drug they injected you with to skip forward, hoping we'll give up on finding them. But we're going to. We're going to crack open one of those crypts, and... Don't worry, Daddy. We're going to get them."

"I hope you're right, kiddo. I would be a liar if I told you living like this has been pleasant. It sounds like your supervisor is just as motivated as you are."

"Just about. In fact, he asked me to give you something." I reach into my pocket and pull out a small folded white card, handing it to him in the encroaching darkness. One of the garage lights gives him just enough opportunity to read it.

13 people at Innovo lost their lives on my watch. I don't intend to lose a 14th. Stay strong, Mr. James. I promise I'll keep her safe.
~Darren Franciscus
PS: You were right about the illnesses.

Twilight clings desperately to every pebble, every leaf, every square centimeter on our faces. My father glances from me to the paper. "The last time I saw him, you know, after the attack, he promised he'd fix things. I just didn't think that meant... Well, he's not putting you on assignments where you can get hurt, is he?"

"I'm behind a desk, Daddy," I tell him, "Mostly."

Bella doesn't contradict me, but his expression moves from one type of worry to another. I give my sister a look and she takes the cue.

"I've been dating this guy, Keith Heffley."

"How old?" he asks, finally distracted.

"Not much older," she says.

"Six years older," I interject.

"He's a real gentleman, Dad. You would like him! He's handsome, and funny—"

"A redneck, barely employed, lives with his parents—" I continue to add to the fire.

"—and is really good at fixing things. Oh, and you should see him with his dog."

"It's not even his dog. It's his parent's dog..."

"You can just tell he's going to be a good dad . . ."

"You know he's dumber than a stump, right?"

"So sorry that Keith doesn't have an education. Some people can't afford to go off to school you know."

"There's no amount of schooling to fix that boy."

Our father freezes and teeters like a statue without a pedestal. Thank God we're holding onto him, but his limbs have gone waxy and he's not a light man. It's an effort to keep him from hitting the ground. Just before he goes horizontal, he puts his foot out to regain his balance.

"Dad, what's wrong?" Bella asks.

"I'm fine." He steadies himself. "Nope, I think I'm starting to slow down again..."

I called the lab and Mike answered. "Prep the lab and call the Walter Reed emergency line. Dad is syncing forward early. Get Randy to bring the car down the driveway and pick us up."

"He's on the phone—"

"I don't give a shit who he's talking to. Tell him to get the car down here now!" I turn my anger to Bella, "I told you it was a bad idea to bring him down this far!"

"I'm sorry!" she responds, more with anger than remorse.

We droop his arms around our shoulders and strain together up the driveway. The gentle incline multiplies our difficulties with the added weight of a grown man, and Bella slips out of her flip-flops for the third time.

"Why can't I feel my feet?" dad asks.

Each time dad previously synced forward, his whole body triggered simultaneously, with every cell slowing its metabolic rate to about 1/4000th of normalcy, a chemopreservative state that was a miracle of science designed by the world's worst terrorist organization. "I think it's the Diox-9 Walter Reed administered. Something about it is causing you to synchronize asymmetrically. I told them this could happen!"

He stops talking. He stops breathing. I see the panic in his eyes as he starts flailing and clinging to Bella like a drowning victim draws a lifeguard under the waves.

"What do we do? What do we do? Oh my God! Dad! Dad! Just breathe!" Bella is in full panic, trying to lay him down, but the house is still two hundred feet away.

"We need to keep him moving and get to the lab!"

Headlights appear. Randy stops, jumps out of the car and opens the back door.

"Throw him in!" I order, "Hurry! He can't breathe!"

My father's twisting body is tossed into the backseat with no regard for comfort or injury and Bella and I pile in, practically on top of him. Randy throws it in reverse and flies the car back up to the house. I tell him to drop us as close to the lab as possible, and Randy comes through down to the letter, running the car into the bushes outside the lab window.

Mike opens the lab door and all four of us grab dad's spasming body and haul him out. His lungs or his heart must be slowing while the rest of him starves for oxygen. I'm sure everyone is thinking the nanotreatment might have prevented this. Maybe. And maybe they're right. Maybe in my attempt save my father, I've killed him.

Dad suddenly gasps loudly and we drop him in a startle in front of the hospital bed. Randy backs up into one of the readout stands and fells it like a tree.

"Dad!" Bella shouts, "you can breathe!"

"You dropped me!" he squeezes out between deep breaths.

Mike grabs him by the armpit, "Let's get him back in the bed. Amara? Where's our support?"

I had already banged out a flurry of text messages to Dr. Nikonov and Dr. Gonzales while waiting for Ping to pick up on the emergency line. The line rang twelve times before she picked up.

"Amara, the team is already on its way back. They should be back at your location in twenty minutes." Her tone is painfully even, and I want to throttle her for not sharing our desperation.

"Twenty? They left twenty minutes ago! I texted them ten minutes ago."

"There's a lot going on, Amara. They probably—"

"Screw you and your excuses, Ping! You knew he was going through the Diox-9 procedure months ago. Somebody should have stayed here to help Mike out in case things went to hell, which they have!"

"Maybe you should have let us do our job then."

"Tāmāde, tiānxià suǒyǒu derén dōu gāi sǐ!"

"What did you just say?"

"You heard me." I'd been practicing my Mandarin for just such an occasion, and clearly it's intelligible enough for Ping to be offended. The click from the phone tells me I can add her to the bridges I'm burning tonight.

When I turn around, Mike has already repasted two dozen sensors onto my dad's skin.

"It's starting agai—" my dad's voice cut short from underneath the mask, then he sways back and forth, terror in his eyes.

"It's his diaphragm," Mike says, looking at the readout. "And chest too. His core muscles are out of sync. They can't pull air in."

Alarms blare over Bella's crying and the squeaking of the metal frame bed. My dad's arms start to flail as his body burns through the oxygen in his bloodstream. We dragged him from the dark driveway just to suffocate him under bright LED lights. Mike yells at Randy to hold his legs and Bella to hold his arms.

"Amara, get the BVM! The purple mask, get it!"

I hand it to him and places it over my dad's face and squeezes the air into his lungs. I watch his chest rise and his muscles relax as we feed his cells moment by moment.

"Amara, push on his chest and abdomen. We need to breathe for him."

I do as he says. "For how long?"

"Until I can get my head wrapped around what to do."

"Mike, we can't keep this up."

"I know."

"It could be his heart next time."

"I know."

"What are we going to do then?"

"We, uh, we . . . I don't know. Gimme a minute to think!"

"We don't have a minute, Mike!"

The lab screens flickered with calls, and Bella jumped up to answer both. On the left, Nikonov and Maggie crowded together on the screen, bouncing in the back seat of whichever vehicle they managed to meet in. Lenny Chari's face comes into view on the right, a shot from inside his rental car as he focused on the road in front of him.

"Hi everyone," Lenny begins. "I got the message that Martin is in trouble. I'm ten minutes out. What's his status?"

"Asynchronous abdominal syncing," Mike responds. We're breathing for him, but the Diox-9 is wearing off unpredictably."

"Administer a second dose," Dr. Nikonov says. "It will stabilize his system."

Lenny cuts in. "We can't dose him over and over. He's going to sync forward at some point, and you could kill him after the second dose—definitely after the third."

"But it would give us time to administer the nanos. Those would stabilize Martin's nervous system, which is what I suspect has gone asymmetrical. Not his muscles."

I can't keep craning my neck to look up at the screens and I'm forced to yell at my dad's bellybutton. "Even if you had time to administer your brainchild, the Diox-9 will wear off too fast."

"We had the wrong dosage, that's all."

I shake my head. "The drug is not fading uniformly. Any solution that involves the Diox-9 is going to kill him."

"We can use the Dambra 44," Lenny offers. "We know it works. There's a stable dosage in the lab's cold storage from four months ago."

"Amara, the Dambra will mean not syncing him again for *years*," Dr Gonzales warns. "And it's possible that the combination of Diox-9 and Dambra-44 would cause an adverse reaction," Dr. Gonzales warns. "Nobody bothered to test for any harmful drug interaction, at least on our end."

I strain to look over my shoulder at the screen, "Nothing? Not one DDI evaluation? What the actual fuck...?"

My father begins tensing again, pulling, then kicks erratically. No new alarms had gone off, but something inside is slowing down. Blood cells? Endocrine system? Brain cells? It doesn't matter though. We can't keep breathing for him, and the equipment we have here was never designed to assist with his respiration.

"What do we do?" Mike asks.

"Inject him now."

"They're saying we shouldn't."

I run to the refrigerator, grab the Dambra 44 doses, and drop them into Mike's hand. "Do it, Mike! He's dying."

By the time the injections are complete, my father's thrashing has him falling somewhere between a seizure and demonic possession. What damage is done when your cells can't even agree how fast to move, or when to produce autocrine signals? I can only imagine the microscopic chaos of his body deteriorating one horrifying system at a time until, a minute later, he finally stops moving altogether.

Chapter 21

The lab is lit by a single table lamp in the corner and the faint glow from the instruments. The alarms have fallen silent. Bella sleeps in a chair, cheeks streaked with eye makeup. Mike is hunched asleep on the counter, a stack of binders for a pillow.

Dr. Nikonov, Maggie Gonzales, and their entourage have come and gone, vanished into the kitchen perhaps. Even Lenny Chari from Innovo finally made it to the party just as our father's condition bottomed out. All the 'what ifs,' 'maybes,' and 'not quites' are expended. all that's left is me with a datapad working out what happens next.

When he finally wakes up, the first thing he notices is the crash cart next to the bed with the paddles dangling against the plastic cart. I snap my fingers in front of him and watch his pupils contract and focus.

"Daddy? Can you hear me?"

"What happened?" he whispers.

"Your body went into shock. It's fighting to go back into chemopreservation. The antidotes are like poison to your cells—too much and they'll kill you. We managed to bring you back, but it was close."

"Thanks for saving my life. Again." A glance at Bella and he asks, "What time is it?"

I pointed at the clock.

"Four AM? You've got to be exhausted."

"I'm working on some numbers, trying to figure something out."

"Can't it wait?"

"Not really. I'm calculating how much time you have before you sync forward."

"Oh," he says. "So...?"

"Not much, Daddy. Even if I am off on my numbers, you won't make it to sunrise. I'm sorry."

He tries to hide his grimace. "Those numbers tell you how long before you're able to get me back to normal?"

"No, but we've figured your body is building an immunity to the antidotes. It's not just the Diox-9 we can't use, but the Dambra-44 won't work for more than an hour next time we sync you back. It means we have to come up with something new, or there is no point in bringing you back at all..."

I hold up a pair of Absorb-wear, explain that he should put them on now or have to deal with the consequences. The thought of being catheterized for years is enough for any man to relent to wearing these ridiculous looking spandex shorts. I turn around, give him what little dignity he can maintain, and turn back when I hear him settle into the bed.

We look at each other for a while, neither sure of how to process what happened this evening. He finally puts on a dad face, a resignation of types that make me 9 years old again.

"Amara, this isn't your fault—you know that, right? I am so grateful to have you as my daughter. So grateful for both you and your sister. But you can't let it eat you up like this. It's not healthy. It's going to ruin your life."

"I'm fine, Daddy, honestly."

"Are you?" he presses. "Are you really happy with your choices? I mean, if I had never gotten myself into this mess, do you think you would have ever chosen this career path?"

"I don't know. Maybe? Probably not."

"What would you have chosen then?"

For a moment I dig through my mind to find something I want, something that makes me want to live for me. "I mean, this is reality, and I can't change it. I've got a job to do now and a house, a sister, and a dad who are counting on me. I can't afford to screw around finding myself."

"I'm afraid to ask if you have any friends."

"I have a few close friends. I'm not a social butterfly like some people."

"Amara, if you're happy, then you won't get any complaints from me. I just want to be sure that you're sure. You're my big kid, and I worry."

"There's nothing to worry about. Trust me, okay?"

"I'll trust you on this." There is a pause in the conversation, and then he annunciates each word deliberately, "Amara, I'm very proud of the woman you've become. It was wrong for me to demean your choices."

"It's okay, Daddy. I understand why you said what you said."

"Are we okay?"

"Yeah." I look over at my sister. "Should I wake up Bella?"

"Not yet. I need to talk to you about something important."

I adjust myself in the seat, pull closer, hold his clammy hand in mine. He reaches out and pushes my bangs out of my eyes and back behind her ear like he used to do.

"Amara, this isn't the easiest topic, but I want to talk to you about your mother."

My recoil is unintended but happens, nonetheless.

He leans closer to me. "Please, just listen. I miss your ma a lot. I miss her more than you know. From my viewpoint, she walked out in the middle of our marriage, hours ago. But as much as it hurts me to say it, your mother has every right to a happy life. She isn't perfect, and she isn't as strong as I would have hoped, but I think your sister is right: she hung in there as long as she could. Regardless of what happened between your ma and me, you shouldn't alienate her like you have. Or call her names or kick her out of this house."

I separate from him completely. "She walked out on you, Daddy! She left us here so she could 'have a life'! Why would I want somebody so selfish anywhere near me after she turned her back on her own family? After she left us to take care of you? So, her wedding vows mean nothing to her? You didn't see Bella and me run away from our responsibilities! She disgusts me!"

"Amara, that's not fair. Nobody should have to go through what your mom and you kids have had to go through. You've been so strong when it comes to dealing with my condition. Don't you think you can be strong enough to find some forgiveness in your heart for your mother? This is the woman who carried you, birthed you, who stood watch over you when you were sick in the hospital, who helped you with your homework and fed you and loved you—loves you—with her whole heart."

"Where's all that forgiveness for your own mother when she walked out on you?" The comment is a deep cut, but I can't stop myself. "Pretty sure there's a whole other side to this family I've never known."

"Not fair, Amara." I watch his eyes grow glassy.

"Look around, Daddy. Life isn't dealing us a solid hand. 'Fair' doesn't play anymore."

He swallows hard. "This whole situation has given me a new perspective on how I've handled problems with my own ma. How about this: we both make some changes. Can you call your mom? Just one call? Maybe it will be the first step for you two to begin reconciling—"

Bella groans, waking up to the sounds of our hushed dispute, her eyes still heavy from exhaustion. I feel like I'm going to have a panic attack and escape to the lab door.

He calls out, "Where are you going?"

"I love you, Daddy. But Mom… Leaving us… I just can't let it go."

Chapter 22

'Special Agent, Department of Homeland Security.' I take one last look at my old credentials and toss the leather binding on the desk. The administrator hands me a similar set of credentials: 'Private Agent Amara James.' It's a new title, and the old logo is replaced with the Department of Homeland Defense shield and crossed swords. The new title strikes me as unwieldy—but carries much more serious implications than tongue twisting.

I head to the armory to pick up my new service pistol, another change I am not looking forward to after rocking every single qualification for the last thirty months.

Everett shoulder bumps me. "Hey killer, welcome back!"

"Too soon," I groan.

"What? He'd just got done stabbing a toddler."

"He was high."

"Like it makes a difference? Screw him. One less degenerate in the world." He sees me turn away. "You okay?"

"That was, you know..."

I still see him. His head flinging backward, his skull emptying out, his life force spraying all over the kid he threatened to kill. And only twenty years separated hostage from human trafficker. For all I know, his mom used to drop him off at Happy Days Day Care.

Everett puts his hand on my shoulder. "I saw. But there's more of them out there. Better him than somebody's kid."

"True."

"You know I'm with you."

"Yeah."

"Seriously, right to the end."

We stop in the hallway, my gaze fixed on him in study. "Oh my God, that was so seriously corny!"

Everett rolls his eyes, "I hate you so much right now."

I snort.

"Okay, you need to shut up."

"I will shut up... *Right to the end.*"

He ignores my mocking, pivots the conversation away from anything personal. "You know they caught Kacela Fantine?"

"No! Who?"

Everett plasters on a fake smile, "The transfer. Wadsworth."

I knew that name. It belonged to the man that cuffed me in my own building, who treated me like a suicide bomber and lied about me in his report. "Don't tell me that."

"He's supposed to be a beast. Maybe he'll end up on our team... Awkward!"

It's my turn to change the subject. "Get your new creds?"

Everett's demeanor shifts, and he pulls the leather case from his back pocket and scowls at it. "Yeah. Private Agent Everett Zingg. And my picture is awful. She wouldn't take a different one either."

"*That's* the part that upsets you?"

"Well, the suspension of *habeas corpus* is a close second. How are we supposed to be law enforcement and military at the same time? But yeah, mostly it's my picture. I look like Sammy the Talking Semicolon."

As we move through the crowded hallway, the familiar presence of Special Agent Franciscus forms ahead, a trajectory that will unavoidably intersect with us. His stride is usually more casual than the young recruits around him: he's a civilian law enforcement agent to the core, and the military regimen unable to gain a foothold in his demeanor. Today is different. Darren Franciscus parts uniforms and suits alike and inserts himself between Everett and me.

Everett smiles widely, "Hey Darren, I was on my way to see you."

"Go away."

Everett wisely reads Darren Franciscus's tone and extricates himself from the group, turning down the nearest hallway.

Franciscus points to the elevators at the end of the corridor and makes a beeline.

I smirk, struggling to keep up without running. "You know you scare him, right?"

"He's on a Counter-Terrorist task force. If I scare him, he's in the wrong job."

"So... What's the hurry?"

"We have a meeting. Decision has been made on the Philadelphia operation. We're heading up to see Major Keownes now."

"What did they decide?"

"I know nothing."

"So Assistant Secretary is now a rank of Major?"

"I think. Some of them. I don't know."

"You really don't know anything, do you?"

"I know you're a throbbing pain in my ass, Amara. That's my current knowledge base."

As we move through the hallways, I get nods from some of the agents, people with whom my contact has been limited to range time, interdepartmental briefings, tech training. They know about my kill. Their chin bobs in my direction are symbolic of approval. My taking a life is a rite of passage that allows me further access to the 'in' of the dynamic that lives and grows and changes all around me. I make no assertion I am indispensable—no organelle within this complex cell, one in which my removal would cause it to fail. There are no vital parts here, a fact that I've been tutored on as of late. But if stealing a life from one bad guy means I have more chances to save my father, I'll line them up like steel range targets.

The plaque on her office already reads the rank change of Major Keownes. Meanwhile, half of us don't understand the military ranking system and the other half don't know their own rank. With posse comitatus suspended, classes run throughout the day explaining our rights and the ease in which we may now operate. Support material reads differently, however, and the list of restrictions under which we are to operate is a quagmire. We no longer need warrants, but we can't operate without orders from a superior, and those ranking officers must gain authorization to act from a military panel specializing in law. We're told they are not judges, yet all of them are former judges. Our existence is a series of looping questions, and I can't even begin to decipher any of it until my suspension ends.

"Private James, Lieutenant Franciscus, come in," Keownes gestures to the chairs.

I smile awkwardly and follow Darren's lead of silence.

Upon her desk is a tablet, and imaged in the center sits the seal for Homeland Defense Criminal Investigative Division. It's upside down, but I can read the word 'Disposition' followed by a case number longer than the seal is wide. The Major has spoken to me on exactly one occasion, and that was just prior to the hearing. She carries a demeanor of control, a tone that packages her visitors into perfectly predictable boxes and slides them along whichever career conveyor belt she deems fit.

"Private James," she begins, "Before we get to the findings of the CID, I want to review a concern of mine. Can you tell me what the department policy is on double-redundancy?"

"Yes, Ma'am. It's to prevent loss of life—"

"What is the policy, Private?"

"Well, it says where there's one there's two. And—"

"And where there's two there's four!" She finishes for me, her voice raised to levels that could be heard by anyone passing by the office. "And yet, you decided to jump out a window to pursue a suspect and whip a bullet past a child's head..."

"But—"

"And prior to that, you chased down a terrorist and blew up a building..."

"I don't think that's a fair—"

"And yet everyone around you has rallied to your defense despite you putting lives in danger—"

"I think that's enough," Darren is the one interrupting now. The Major is taken aback by his interjection, but quickly regains her composure and gestures to us both.

"The lieutenant has proved my point," her smugness oozes from her now. "Why do you think this is, Private James? I'd really like to know."

Darren is stepping on my foot. No: he's grinding his foot into the top of my shoe, a gesture kept concealed from Keownes by the angle of the desk. It is purposeful and painful and without subtlety.

"I... I couldn't say, Major," I answer.

Taciturn glares at each of us illuminate that while my actions are being judged, Darren and I pilot the same boat. She sighs, breaks plane and thumbs through the tablet to a specific page and recites, "'...Amara James acted with bravery and dedication, and displayed a degree of character above and beyond the call of duty. It is the judgment of this tribunal that she be afforded the rank of Corporal and be returned to duty immediately to a role commensurate with her skills.' There's more but I think it's obvious you've impressed a few people."

Major Keownes stands up and extends a reticent handshake. "Congratulations, Corporal."

My face is smiling without permission as I extend my hand to meet hers. "Thank you, Major."

The handshake is firm and does not disengage, the seconds ticking by and sucking the joy from the moment. "It's time to start impressing me now. Am I clear, Corporal?"

"As a bell," I copy a phrase Darren is fond of, but my delivery is not nearly as confident.

Drinks flow at Kelly's, my hand sticky from slaps on the back shaking the grapefruit juice from my glass. I don't enjoy beer—I'm a wine girl on most occasions—but I put on a show when out with the department by drinking tequila. Everybody respects a tequila drinker, and nobody is checking to see if the paloma has been ordered light. Still, Grazelli stumbling past me and jettisoning a wave from his mug ensures my pants will smell like Coors for the remainder of the evening.

Hastings demands I trade shots with him as we celebrate our promotions on the same day. Shen and Bó manage to distract him with flushed faces and Mandarin drinking songs and I'm two more deep for the night. I steal a swig of Everett's pricey merlot: turn up my nose. Maybe it's beyond my humble tastes, maybe the bottom shelf tequila has stripped my taste buds of whatever meager refinement E has managed to help me develop. Iván's handing me another paloma while holding onto its twin. This drink isn't a camel and the tequila is strong, but its smooth and tastes like Don Julio and it goes down fast.

Across the room I see my krav trainer Orev Yitzhak hanging his head into his beer while his hands do most of the talking. The mollifying gestures of his companions carry sincerity; their sideways glances indicate the conversation is a buzz kill. I've snaked my way to check on him, but I'm intercepted by Mitch who's overjoyed to bestow his supervisory knowledge.

"Here's the thing," he reaches out and snaps one of my suspenders, "You can try to be their friend all you want, and that's fine. But at some point, you're gonna need to put your foot up their ass. So, somebody starts testing you..." He pulls back on my suspender belt again, only this time I gently grab his hand and bend it downward, locking the wrist and tangling his fingers up in the elastic.

"I get it," I force a smile. "It's good analogy."

"Right?" he chuckles.

"Very clever teaching tool, Mitch. Thanks for the painful visual."

"One more thing, though?"

I sigh and give him the cue to continue.

"Can I have my fucking hand back before you snap it off?"

I immediately let go and he swivels his hand as if he's concerned it's been loosened and will fall off. "I'm so sorry, just reacting."

"No, no! Don't apologize to anybody about taking care of yourself. Especially from some half-juiced douche whose dispensing barroom wisdom."

Iván appears by my side asking if everything is okay, and it takes several repetitions from Mitch and me to cut through the cacophony and growing inebriation of the swarm. Weiss is at the bar talking shit to a pair of FBI agents while Hastings does his best to separate them. One of the Feds calls him 'Gestapo' and Weiss reaches for his tie and the room is now setting down drinks and beelining to mitigate or aggravate, depending on how high they'd blow on their BAC.

Mitch's chair is now filled with the hulking presence of Iván who clinks his glass against mine and says, "Salud."

I watch the Feds puffing their way to the exit, expelled by the glares and calls from a dozen DHD agents. I look back at him and smile, "I didn't take you for a grapefruit guy."

He sips his drink, his face twists, he smiles back. "The tequila almost makes it tolerable."

I laugh and call him ridiculous while watching Weiss storm out the door to pursue the FBI agents. Hastings and Darren chase after and I shake my head.

He points at me. "I was wondering if you could help me with something important."

"Sure."

"It's confidential."

"Okay."

"It's really personal too."

"Is it a mole? I can't do moles, and you gotta keep your pants on."

"No, it's not a mole. What the hell?"

"Just spit it out! Nobody can hear you in here. I can barely hear me."

"I need help with my Spanish. I might have lied when I got hired."

"I was wondering about that. I figured you for a *pocho*, but didn't think you'd be ballsy enough to fake it to get a job."

"Well, that's me, all balls."

"Please never say that again."

"Fine. But can you help me? On the sly?"

I raise my glass, "*Brindo por no te despidan*."

He raises an eyebrow.

"Here's to you not getting fired."

Chapter 23

Forming my team took all of five days. Private Agent Everett 'E' Zingg came on board as a given. Known for over a year, he was my real drinking buddy and a perfect friend. Reserved, lovely, never a prying word. E was neither uncaring nor indifferent: he sensed my reservation and stayed in zones of conversation he knew we could navigate together.

The two of us welcomed Iván 'I' Fagundes next, who seemed to take Darren's initial orders to protect me like an oath from a sworn knight. I have no illusions that I can hold my own regardless of situation... Agents with that mindset end up set on fire. Iván cares about me, trusts me enough to put his career in my hands. I owe him more than my Spanish tutelage; securing him to my team while I am on the upswing is the least I can do. I only hope I don't get him killed in the process.

Weiss didn't know it, but he was my second choice. Unfortunately, his chances went out the door of Kelly's with him when he punched an FBI agent in the back of the head.

Demoted and suspended without pay for striking a Federal Agent, he would be waiting for a review board for a long time. Last I heard, he was still waiting. When I talked to him after the incident, his only regret was "that FBI fucker made bail" before he could. Might have dodged a bullet with his elimination, come to think of it.

Darren Franciscus took the liberty of filling the fourth member of my team, and we waited impatiently for personnel to clear Orev 'O' Yitzhak from his own suspension after he broke a student's nose and jaw. I wasn't there when it happened, but everyone knew about his trouble by the time they closed Kelly's that morning. Classroom exercises often get out of hand, but it's almost always student-on-student issues. When a new recruit wouldn't take no for an answer, Orev put him in his place. Again, and again, and again. Calls from the classroom told the kid to stay down, but each time his pride dragged him to his feet. Major Keownes wanted Orev shipped back to Israel. Darren begged for him to join us because "he's a bad ass." I personally had my concerns adding him, only because bossing around my former instructor after he's tossed me all over the mat for three hours a day seemed unrealistic. And yet Orev was—and is—a good soldier first. He follows orders, he offers solutions, he doesn't whine.

With our double-redundancy standard satisfied, it took only four weeks for us to build a case and raid an Abu Sayyaf cell in Richmond. Foreign Terrorist Organizations (FTOs) were becoming less of a problem with posse comitatus suspended, but they still popped up and distracted us from the mission of finding Millennial. One of their fighters, Omar Jajurie, a foot taller and outweighing me by seventy pounds, thought he could take me close up. Even stuck me with a knife when he failed to out-muscle me with a flurry of punches. It cost me thirty stitches and three weeks of down time, but I came out on the better end of that trade... I didn't even recall the details during my initial debriefing, the conflict moved so fast. But when they wheeled him into his arraignment, nausea struck me from the influx of memories.

I now know fighting a man is an occupational risk I'm prepared for. But I continue to train, harder, meaner. My aikido soke sees the changes in my style, compliments me in class while warning me quietly to exercise restraint with the other students. Even though he's no longer a combat trainer for DHD, Orev teaches me on the side to fight dirty, devious maneuvers to incapacitate and murder. The next time I see Kacela Fantine, there will be nothing left of her but a stain on the ground. And I will do everything I can to find her again.

Corporal Brett Wadsworth transferred from Federal Protection Service to DHD Terrorism Division, eager to make a name for himself with his quick actions. I knew him as the asshat who cuffed me in our lobby for suspicion of being a suicide bomber. Everyone else knew him as the agent that caught Kacela Fantine after the day care attack, and ultimately as the agent who stuffed his gun muzzle in a kid's mouth to uncover her location. The whole debacle occurred weeks before our switch to DHD, a blip on the calendar, an impulsive move that, had he waited for *posse comitatus* to expire, Fantine would have appeared before a military court and have remained in custody. Instead, a permissive judge with an ax to grind against Congress, released that monster back into the world, leaving the rest of us to choke on Wadsworth's poisoned fruit.

Still, we are doing our homework, lining up ducks to knock them down, desperate to hold onto our one lead for

Millennial: their explosive provider, Bukum Yilani. Leads relating to their use of the Sublime nanotreatment solidify, and we verge on the break we need. This is the inopportune moment when Darren decides to knock on the edge of my cubicle and send my whole fucking world into a spiral.

He waves me to follow, and now I'm cutting off coworkers in the hallway just to catch up. "Darren, I'm—"

"Better get your Ls and Ts in order, Corporal. It's Lieutenant Supervisor now, and while I could give two shits what you call me, we're headed for a meeting where I need you to be by the book."

"Okay, *L. and T.*, whose ass do you need me to wax before we get back to Millennial?"

"There is no more 'we' on Millennial. You've been reassigned."

"Me or my team?"

"You. Only you."

"Who the f--"

Darren stops suddenly and looks me dead in the eye. "You will follow me, you will get your new orders, and you will not mouth off. Understand?"

"I absolutely don't understand! You promised me I would be in your department, and a year later I'm pulled?"

"I know."

As he guides me into the elevator, he casts a solid glare at a young agent that tells him that the ride to the seventh floor is meant for only two. "You are still Counter-Terrorism, but they want you on the Cartel Alliance. You were hand selected by somebody way high. I had no choice in the matter—"

"But—"

"Listen, Amara. I can't do anything about your transfer, but if you do a good job, I will try to pull you back onto Millennial. I need time though."

I lower my volume. "There has to be something you can do. My dad almost died, and the only antidote that won't kill him isn't working the way it should anymore. We need find another crypt. We need to find Millennial."

The doors open and we're moving down a hallway I've never been in. I glance out the window, never having climbed this high in the GSA building before. Gone are the crowds of fatigues and recruits, the fresh faces filled with wonder and confusion. Here the suits abound and push chess piece folders across a board spanning the length and breadth of the building.

"Amara, we're flipping over rocks and coming up empty. We thought the Millennial crypts would be in graveyards and then you find one in a federal building. That opens our investigation from a scant 140,000 acres to the whole fucking United States.

"Then you make contact with somebody who claims to be Millennial—"

"*Claims?* Are you siding with CID now?"

"*Puñeta!* You know I'm not." He's stopped me in the hall now that the foot traffic has thinned. "But the team ran down every lead dealing with the Ag Department on that thumb drive to their conclusion. The men you saw used advanced tech to cover video captures of their faces. We subpoenaed four-hundred phones, reviewed over a hundred CCTV shots, interviewed eighty-two people. Those guys who claimed to be Millennial aren't ghosts, we know they exist, but we're dead ending."

"Bukum Yilani? That's not a dead end."

"No," he wipes his finger underneath his nostrils. "No, that's definitely something, but the BY investigation has to run everything through the State Department because of Türkiye, and that leads us here."

"Here where?"

"Here where?" A glimmer of a smile appears. "What are you? A fucking caveman?"

"Neanderthal, thank you."

He puts his hands together almost in prayer. "We're going into a meeting with big-bigs. State requested you specifically on this investigation. We're scratching backs here. *Hoy por ti, mañana por mi.*"

Chapter 24

We walk in silence to a numerated conference room. A pack of ties, lots of bald heads, older women packaged into unflattering pantsuits. Handshakes and greetings abound and I have already forgotten every single name.

"Ah, you're Amara," one of them greets. "I'm Lucas. Please, get comfortable and we'll catch you up."

Darren and I shuffle to a pair of open chairs. The order everyone sits in doesn't seem related to rank or department affiliation, but I feel relief in Darren sitting beside me.

"I thought it was all about the L's and the T's," I mutter.

"Shut it."

The baldest of them all speaks. "Thanks for meeting at short notice. Everyone should have the briefing packet delivered to their tablets by now? Everyone? Good. We've been directed by State to McAllen, Texas for full operations, but the governor has blocked those moves as you all know. Terror threat level is currently at... Orange right now, Lucas?"

The dark-haired, middle-aged man who greeted me raises his hand. "State recognizes we are effectively at a red threat level given our newest intel."

Baldest man continues. "CNC has reliable intel that the Cartel Alliance is assisting Chinese Nationals in smuggling a dirty bomb across the border. If you scroll to section, uhm, 4B, in your packet, you will see the NSA SAT data showing the target in grid 1015-0936 at roughly 2300 hours last night. Lucas Machado will be reviewing that with us. Go ahead."

Lieutenant Supervisor Lucas Machado stands, touches the tablet to the wallscreen, and the image is transferred in all its fuzzy glory for we assembled to scrutinize. "Thanks, Bailey. At 2308 hours, a radioactive signature was detected and recorded for roughly one minute. We believe this was caused by the bomb being transferred from one shielded case to another. Possibly something more portable to facilitate its transportation across the border. Isotopic fingerprint is still pending, but preliminary findings point to it being one of ours."

I scan the room for any reaction. There is none. *Am I the only one who doesn't know what's going on?* I look to Darren for any hints, but he is staring directly ahead. My shock must be visible, as Lucas's eyes come to rest on me.

"Not well publicized, but we've had four dozen broken arrows since Hiroshima," he explains. "Most of them are ancient history and a matter of public record. The core of the weapon we're dealing with right now is thought to date back to the 1960s. Go ahead and scroll to section 4E..."

My eyes scan the data, a trivial synopsis of what should be one of the most terrifying events in history. December 5, 1965, the crew of the aircraft carrier U.S.S. Ticonderoga watch in horror as one of their planes rolls out of the hangar and into 16,000 feet of icy death.

Lieutenant Douglas M. Webster: gone.

Skyhawk attack plane: gone.

950-kilogram nuclear bomb: gone.

The how's and when's of this weapon's loss are baffling enough without discussing its recovery, and yet two senior voices drill down with questions to which there are no answers.

Lucas continues his breakdown of the targets and their radioactive cargo. Experienced faces in the room go still with each detail lending all too much reality to a once theoretical concern.

"Are we talking about a fissionable weapon here, Lucas?" another baldy asks. Kenson? Kenden?

"Yes, my question exactly," a red-haired pantsuit cuts in. "Are we talking mass destruction or mass disruption?"

"We don't know. What we do believe is that they possess the uranium from the broken arrow event. If employed as a radiological dispersal device, the explosion would be conventional, followed by a cloud of radioactive fallout that would be nonlethal to most people in the short term. Long term no way to predict. The panic, however, would shut down any major city in the U.S."

"And if it's fully weaponized?" the same woman asks.

Lucas Machado clears his throat. "Ma'am, if that happens, assuming they have been able to recover eighty percent of the lost uranium 235, we could be looking at losses in the hundreds of thousands. Depending upon the target."

Discussion breaks out into groups on possible targets, delivery mechanisms, law enforcement deployment, contingency plans. When Lucas completes the briefing, I look up to find my name prominently listed at the top of the action plan.

"Corporal Agent Amara James will be liaison with Captain Hank Taylor of the Texas Rangers who is lead on this investigation. We will assemble our team and follow the Corporal here as we transition the case from the Rangers to DHD." Lucas Machado nods toward me, which directs every eye in the room at me.

The briefing room becomes as quiet as a morgue, and the weight of a thousand cumulative years of experience crushes my flagging confidence. I feel the perspiration drip from my armpits and a tickle at the base of my ponytail feels like a beetle scraping along my scalp. The gentleman across from me (Wallace, according to the conversation) is smacking his lips and making his jowls jiggle as he stares. There's no placing his expression. Resentment? Curiosity? Absent-mindedness? I wonder what Wallace would do if I took the stylus from this tablet and vigorously scraped at my head. *That's right, Wallace. It feels really good to scratch it. Right. There.*

"Corporal Agent James is one of our up-n-comers who is fluent in Cantonese and Spanish," Darren says, and my body expels a long sigh while I make an ejaculatory prayer.

Wallace taps on the table with his thick fingers. "You're the one that took the shot on the daycare killer."

I return with a curt nod. "The Bukum Yilani terrorist. Yes, Sir."

He is indifferent to my correction. "Pretty ballsy move too while he was holding a kid. Is it true you did a head shot on a quick draw?"

I still see the perp's head snapping back, body falling backward, blood spraying the poor kid in his arms. "No, Sir. My service pistol was already drawn."

The rumor mill made me a legend, and this almost pornographic interest in me ending somebody's life might have been the only thing that saved me during the subsequent CID panel. I wonder if Wallace here would be as impressed if he knew I threw up after splattering the perp's brains on the arts and crafts table.

"Amara James is exactly who we need on vanguard," Lucas Machado says. "Darren is pissed I'm taking her, but we need her more."

Subdued chuckles make the rounds. I hear whispered questions— undoubtedly about me. I should be proud, but each mumbled word shrinks my confidence incrementally.

The meeting adjourns. Darren shakes hands with Lieutenant Supervisor Lucas Machado, gives me no more than a glance, and walks to the elevators. And with that, I've been re-homed. No moving photos from my cube, no saying goodbye to my team or anyone in my department.

"So, you're Texas bound. You ready to get dirty?" Lucas asks with an experienced smile.

"Are you?"

He hands me a sealed briefing package and shrugs. "Hell no. I hate Texas. Besides, I'll be running ops from here. There's a lot of moving parts."

"Who else is on my team?"

"Nobody," he drops the word with a blunt thud. "Governor Hollister is refusing to allow Feds to run full scale operations within the Texas border ever since the President suspended posse comitatus. He's threatened to arrest anyone not explicitly authorized."

"That's insane."

"It is, but elected officials don't have to pass psych evals."

"Didn't the Red Wave come through El Paso?" The Red Wave was a name the media gave to the string of FTO attacks that struck over the last year. While we focused on Millennial, the rest of the country struggled with abductions, bombings, murders. Some of the events went unclaimed and most unlinked; this gave conspiracy theorists plenty of room to run through their sanitarium chat rooms to claim government involvement.

"The border blame game goes back decades, and now we have a political showdown between our Commander-in-Chief and Governor Hollister. And we can't afford to start shooting each other when there's a bomb coming across the border."

"Of course, Sir. But I don't know what I'm doing."

"The governor approved one liaison from DHD. *One*. And you're not running the investigation. You're helping the Texas Rangers and reporting back to me so that we can lend support as needed." He points at me as move down the hall at a brisk pace. "I know this is not where you want to be, and I wish we had time to get to know each other better, but we are counting on you to play this sharp and to follow orders."

I want to refuse the order and resign. "You can count on me."

We arrive at a set of doors marked 'ROOF ACCESS' and it occurs to me I'm leaving the building from here. "Lieutenant Machado? I need my laptop. My keys, my jacket, my charger, my purse..."

"Already loaded in a duffle along with fatigues, your service pistol, ammo, toiletries, and an envelope of cash for expenses. Buy what we forgot from the commissary and save the receipts. You can send for other effects if absolutely necessary. Hope you don't have pets or plants!"

The helipad is empty, but the deafening drone of rotors combined with the shadow overhead tells me not for long. As the helicopter settles onto the tarmac, Lucas snaps his fingers in front of my face to catch my attention, yelling over the whirling blades.

"Last thing! Hank Taylor and the Texas Rangers! Don't assume they are friends!"

"Hey! You can't just drop a bomb on me like that!"

"Poor choice of words, Corporal!"

Chapter 25

I shoulder my duffle, don my sunglasses to a blazing Texas sky, and step off the Lockheed transport with two guardsmen bound for separate duties. Supposedly. Everyone is top secret clearance level. Everyone is need-to-know. Everyone is compartmentalized. They give me a polite wave and head to a uniformed officer waiting for them.

A man approaches me wearing a pressed white collared button-down, khaki pants, and an olive tie that clashes with his Stetson hat. His right hand extends, like he's been prepping his handshake since San Antonio. He has silver hair and skin matching the leather on his boots.

"Corporal Agent Amara James," he calls out slowly, enunciating the awkward new title. "I'm Hank Taylor. Welcome to McAllen. I'll be bringing you to the Op Center. May I take your bag?"

I hand the duffle to him. "Thank you. I appreciate you meeting me, although I'm surprised to see you here. I could have called a car."

"Oh no! Governor Hollister called me personally and told me to extend every courtesy to our DHD brethren.

Besides, we need you for the Cantonese translations, and I can think of no better use of my time than to brief you on the drive there."

His smile is genuine and there is a twinkle in his eye—playful, but paternal. I match his brisk pace and finds myself in the back of an air-conditioned SUV with smoked windows. Hank hangs his hat on a hook in the back of the console and rummages through a satchel full of folders.

"I reviewed the 10F briefing on the way here," I tell him, glad to be ahead of the game.

"Good. Here are 10G, H, and I." He dumps the folders on the seat between them, each one prominently marked 'Top Secret'.

So much for being ahead. "Want to give me the short version?"

"That is the short version."

"Shorter?"

"I thought you were a speed reader. Heard you were faster than a babysitter's boyfriend when the car pulls up."

A laugh charges out of me before I can stop it.

"Never heard that one?"

"Yeah, but my dad used to say stuff like that when I was growing up."

"My kind of guy. He's still around I hope?"

Hank doesn't know. Nobody knows. Just how the government wants it kept. Martin James is a state fucking secret. "Yeah, he's still around. But forensics is my specialty, actually."

"Forensics. Speed reading. Same thing." Hank grins, perhaps sensing he's upset me. "Even so, let's see what you can do with this."

I unwind the thread on the partitioned folder for 10I and looks over the printout. The source is redacted, so either the NSA mined the intel or somebody on the inside funneled it to DHD.

It's an email from Xiàoliăn Logistics to Siemprelopez Brokers, a customs firm on the Mexican-U.S. border. Xiàoliăn is a shell company NSA ferreted out two years ago, and Siemprelopez is one of many corporations caught up in the Cartel Alliance's bid for nation-state status. I already know the latter from the previous intel, but the former is new, and the Cantonese correspondence is translated into English on the following page.

I scan the Chinese characters, then read the English translation, then back again. "What the hell?"

"Something wrong with the translation?"

"No. I mean, yes. The translation is shit. But that's fine. I don't need it. It's the chengyu they've used."

"Chengyu?"

"Proverbs. Little lessons summed up in four characters. They have tremendous cultural meaning. Anyway, you normally see them in Mandarin, but this..."

"What does it mean?" Hank asks.

I shake my head.

I am not prepared for Texas. The Ops Center is decorated in mounted boar heads and looks like the love child of a computer lab and a hunting lodge. The usual vending machines are replaced with folding tables covered in casserole dishes of shoo fly pie and brownies. The refrigerator has a case of long neck beer bottles labeled "Off Duty Only!"

Texas Rangers are a different breed as well. Their genuine smiles, their quiet temperaments, the courtesy that seems to extend beyond their professional demeanor and into their personal interactions. It all runs in sharp contrast to East Coasters with their colorful range of unhappiness. When a question is asked, Hank suggests instead of directs, and the women and men in his command take no affront if opinions differ. One of the greener Rangers calls him "Pops" and often a somber conversation is eclipsed by mild chuckles. We have something like this in our small department, but it is a social enclave that isolates itself. After only a few hours here, there is no doubt in my mind these Texans would welcome anyone in with open arms.

In a rare moment of friction, another of the Rangers makes a comment about DHD not trusting them to do the job right. I haven't been named, but the comment is clearly meant as a jab.

"And with dumbasses like you dragging us down, Mike, who could blame them?" Hank says. The retort brings all negative commentary about my presence to an end. I try to make eye contact with Hank, but he is eyes deep in a computer screen.

Evening closes in. The translations are complete and I rub my temples, stretching my stiffness away. I look about the room. Twelve eyes fixed on six monitors watching five men move two crates.

"You're doing a fine job," Hank whispers. He is standing behind me, left hand wrapped around a microwaved burrito.

"I haven't done anything," I whisper back, frowning.

"You worked out the translation kinks and you're keeping as cool as a cucumber. I hope the rest of the DHD agents are as good as you. Although I doubt they will be," Hank adds a wink and starts to walk off.

"Hank?"

"Yes?"

"Thank you."

Chapter 26

How's it going, Corporal Agent Amara James?

Just dandy, Lieutenant Supervisor Lucas Machado of the Department of Homeland Defense.

Yeah, yeah, I get it. So how goes it?

I thought you got my updates?

I did. I want to know what you really think is going on.

I included my comments. The chengyu refer to betrayal, specifically to breaking faith.

And?

And it sounds like they are happy about this. Something is being communicated here in the subtext.

You suggested a false flag in your commentary.

Yes, but I'm not certain.

Because it's in Cantonese instead of Mandarin?

Yes.

What did Hank say about that?

I didn't offer my thoughts to him. I figured—

Good. It's better to keep these ideas between us. We'll funnel information down to the Rangers through proper channels if need be.

If need be?

Just in case. Is that going to be a problem?

No, it's just that he's leading the investigation into a dirty bomb—

We don't know what kind of bomb it is yet, Corporal.

Yes, sorry. But don't you think he should have every resource we have? He's on our side.

You sure about that?

Is... is there something else going on I should know about? I don't understand why we would withhold information from our own people.

And yet you withheld information from them.

Because you—

Let's keep this under wraps for now, okay?

Yes, Sir. And Sir? Is there any word about sending more DHD personnel? This is a lot.

The White House has been in touch with the Governor's Office all day long. I think we'll get some assistance to you soon though.

Okay. Thanks.

Keep up the good work.

Chapter 27

The Op Center is quiet and dim. I can hear Douglas—not Doug, as I was explicitly told—talking quietly into his cell to who must be his wife about the late hours he is working. As he paces behind me. He's older, around Hank's age, and seems like he's known Hank from before they worked together. On one of his passes, he tosses a baseball cap on the desk that reads JAFO. It's an old joke, but I give him a courteous laugh and set it aside.

When Douglas is done with his call, he places an envelope on my workstation. It's marked with evidentiary tape and bulges with potential. He scans the barcode and has me put my thumb print to the screen to complete the chain of custody.

He departs, leaving me alone with a cell phone, a thumb drive, and a file as thick as a book. I page through the paper trail and realize they've printed out the entire data log from the sim card. Another dead tree. I toss it aside and push the thumb drive into my computer.

The cell phone was recovered early in the Texas Rangers operation and contains an encrypted message opened with an app called "LuCyph3r," a common enough and legal way to encrypt and send information. Not exactly the most secure way to send a message now that quantum encryption breakers have arrived, but good enough.

Publicly accessible cartage instructions being encrypted and sent to a burner phone makes it suspect by its very nature. I dig. Get up. Drink coffee. Dig more. Rinse and repeat as necessary. Buried in the Cantonese shipping instructions for football bobble heads is a reference to a purchase order that exists nowhere else in the documentation: 27172385.

The number is out of place, but the next purchase order is dashed, and the "-99424739" provides the big reveal. I pull out my phone and plug the numbers into my map application. Nothing. I stare at it for a bit, then flip the order of the numbers and drop a decimal point in each.

GPS coordinates on the U.S.-Mexico border register.

*   *

It is eighteen hours since the plane landed and I'm holding my HK pistol at the ready. The chill of a desert morning is on my flushed neck as I try to tune out a coyote screaming from behind the shrubs as it calls for a mate. The earpiece crackles and I can barely make out the voice of one of the Texas Rangers introduced to me prior. This is their operation, their calls, their catch. I'm just another fucking observer. But it's all a result of my digging, and now I find myself an invaluable lynch pin between DHD and the Rangers.

"Show me your hands!" The command is off in the distance. Machine gun fire follows, followed by the pop-pop-pops of M-47 rifles. Commands cross over the comm, and a pained cry comes from all too close to me.

I've been told to hold position until given the 'all clear', and after the run-in with Bukum Yilani, I am more than happy to take the back seat. Gunfire builds. The scream goes unattended. I don't know his name, but I recognize his voice even in the form of wails. I know I shouldn't be worried, but my brain keeps summoning Everett to my flank.

The screams continue and nobody is coming.

"Shit! Shit! Shit!" I take a deep breath and peek around the corner. A Ranger in body armor writhes in the alleyway in the back of the abandoned gas station. He clutches his leg, blood spurting from shredded fatigues.

I sprint toward him only to flatten myself to the ground when semi-automatic fire breaks through the air in bursts. I'm horizontal and eating gravel, my body pressed against the fallen Ranger. He catches a hail of rounds in his legs, neck, and arms. Blood spatters around me, concrete and asbestos clouds above me, and now I'm shrinking behind the man I abandoned cover to rescue.

The gun dusting my position stops. A moment between reloads or merely re-aiming? A wrong decision will be my last one. I hear small arms fire returning in earnest from the Rangers, and I realize this is my only chance to get to safety. I low-crawl through the pebbles, dragging the Ranger behind, my nails cracking and bending backward. When I reach the cinder block retaining wall, I check the motionless man for a pulse on his bloodied neck, only to pull my hand back in disappointment.

"-pect on the move! White box truck pulling out—" the comm chat is buried by a machine gun singing its deadly song. I shield my face as bits of building and roof are torn apart and thrown into the air. This is a 50-cal military grade killing machine that tears holes through the atmosphere and carries fear at six hundred rounds per minute. It is a sound unforgettable to anyone with even the smallest experience with it.

Whoever is firing is not aiming for me though. Without daring to look, I can hear it scything into different parts of the gas station, into metal, wood, glass, up in the air and deep into the ground. It doesn't matter though. This machine gun could cut me in half, and there is no hope of getting out of my position until somebody stops it.

My unspoken prayer is answered with a break in the swarm of lead being cast our way. Then another scream, this one quick and gutted, and then another. M-47s dominate the cacophony now and the friendly comm resumes.

"Go! Go! Go!" The chatter comes fast and I take staccato glances around the corner before stepping out. The Texas Rangers are scattered. Their targets are moving, and only now do I inch forward to get a better view.

A truck appears in a roar: a rush of white metal, diesel exhaust, heat, and proximity: if I purse my lips, I could kiss the truck's aluminum side.

I reach out and grab the handlebar on the back of the truck. Jerked sideways and up, my index finger accidentally squeezes the trigger on my HK. Grabbing onto this truck is as foolish as it gets, and I've already discharged my weapon and hit God only knows what—or who. All I know is the bullet vanishes into the chaos as my shoulder pulses in agony from the jerking momentum.

With my body swinging, I firm up my grip and stuff my boot into a gap in the steps beneath the bumper just as the truck's sharp turn wraps me around and face plants me into the vehicle's side.

Stars—nerves in my nose—blur my eyes and stun my brain. Another sharp turn in the opposite direction and I bank into the roll-up, a misshapen door swung wide open and hanging from fleshy hinges.

Eyes blurred by motion, tears, and dust, I watch the gas station shrink, the Texas Rangers chasing on foot in desperation. Another minute and they will be specks on the horizon—assuming I can maintain my grip for another minute. Already my fingers are weakening, my twisted foot wedged in the bumper step the only thing keeping me from becoming a human strawberry when I hit the pebbled road.

The truck shakes. I glimpse the driver's face in the side mirror, his visage twisted in fear and anger as he moves the steering wheel erratically. He's determined to dislodge me from my perch.

I wedge my second foot into the bumper step and use the added strength to squat down, my right arm fully extends up to the bottom of the handlebar. I wait for the driver to crank the wheel. Hand still gripping the HK, I fire four shots at the double rear tires beneath me. They all miss. Another wild sway of the truck and he nearly flings me to my death.

"Oh, *vete la chingada!*" With a purposeful swinging of my legs, I whip my body to the side and fire my weapon downward, this time hitting both tires.

The truck lurches and swings: brakes slam and tires slide. I'm pressed into the roll-up door. One more wild swing and the truck angles sideways. Swinging to the right, I fire my HK rapidly at the front tire. Each round seems to go wild, striking the door, the mirror, or nothing at all, but one finds its mark.

The truck pitches in the opposite direction and this time I'm incapable of holding on, flung into the air, pistol whipped skyward to direction unknown. I tuck my head into my arms and my muscles remember Aikido class as I roll like a rogue hubcap. For that split second, I realize that I should have struck the ground but haven't. The ground falls away underneath. A ditch. The tumble ends as I slap the earth hard with my left hand.

The truck is wailing as it slides down the road on its side, crying out a death song of rent metal and scraping stone. Laying below the plane of the road, I'm unable to do anything but listen to the truck skid into stillness.

Quiet descends, save for the ringing in my ears and the thump, thump, thump in my head. The pounding is replaced by footsteps and a car's engine roaring to life, and then the silhouettes of the Rangers appear above me. I close my eyes and say nothing, my mind finally catching up with the wild recklessness of what I've just done.

Chapter 28

I look in the bathroom mirror at my purpled back and bandaged neck, arms, and hands. How I escaped a concussion goes beyond good reflexes and falls into the realm of divine intervention. What I do know is that the pain from flesh wounds will be far eclipsed by the stiffness to follow in the morning. I can hear Hank Taylor talking on the phone, see him pacing in and out of view through the crack in the door. The phone calls have been relentless, and Hank is on his fourth identical conversation.

A lead-lined cargo container is all that is recovered from the truck. The information from the intercepted messages was either incorrect or old, and the bomb is nowhere to be found. Hank has taken the matter with amazing optimism, convinced we will catch up with the perpetrators and their deadly cargo. I can't tell if he is truly confident or placating the people on the other side of the conversations.

Hank goes quiet. "Amara, are you okay in there?"

"Yeah, I just can't get my shirt on without... I'll be just a minute."

"Are you decent?"

"Yes."

Hank slowly pushes the door open and sees me struggle with my sleeves. Everything is tender. He winces sympathetically, and with ginger fingertips, he lifts the fabric up over my wounded skin and into place.

"My daughter Nellie used to do motocross, but she was lazy about donning her gear. She was the only teenager I knew who had a skin graft before her sweet sixteen. Couldn't keep her off those damned bikes. Once her boyfriend taught her how to ride, that was it. I always worried I'd lose her to an accident."

"How old is she now?" I ask.

Hank switches sleeves and holds the shirt open for me to slip my other arm inside. There is a long silence, but I feel the pressure of the question inside my belly, begging to climb out. I know I shouldn't, that saying anything now is opening an old wound, but the question escapes, nonetheless.

"What happened to her?"

"A young undocumented gentleman came over the border—used to call them 'dreamers' back in the day—and took a liking to my Nellie. Pretty thing even though she was a tomboy. Turns out this 'dreamer' killed his entire family when he was fourteen. Took his sixth and final victim five years later here in Texas. Our government didn't bother to conduct any background on this 'dreamer', assuming anyone young and handsome couldn't possibly be capable of committing a heinous act."

"I'm so sorry, Hank."

*   *

Two men are in custody, and I don't have to travel far to see them either. Both lay in the ICU with tubes in their throats. The first is Emiliano Zapata Salazar, and after a quick search I find it's a name remembered as revolutionary in Mexico. Maybe it's an alias, maybe he's from a patriotic family. Either way he's playing with a radioactive death machine. The second is Pablo Saenz a.k.a. Pablo Saenz-Urias a.k.a. Paulo Santaya: career drug runner who joined the Cartel Alianza and became a lieutenant of ruthless renown. The file says he's retired; his presence in a truck that carried a WMD says otherwise.

When I stop by the ICU, the two perps are in one room under guard. Outside the door I see Jared 'Smitty' Smith whispering in hushed anger to his fellow Ranger, a woman I don't recognize from anywhere. It's a tone I haven't heard from anyone here, not even in the thick of the fight. Instead of rounding the corner, I stand there just out of sight, eavesdropping.

"...Fucking DHD tells us to stand down? While they sit two thousand miles away from the border..."

"...Maybe they'll start taking us seriously now..."

"...If this was headed for DC you know their fat asses would be carpet bombing the Cartel into extinction..."

"...Hank is playing this one right I think..."

"...He wouldn't flinch standing in front of a train..."

The conversation diminishes as I make myself visible, and Smitty's courteous smile and professionalism replace the rancor. They compliment me over my actions in the field and I give credit back to their real bravery of facing down heavy gunfire. It's from them I learn all the other suspects from the firefight are dead or have fled over the border. Two Rangers have been lost in the line of duty today. One more is expected to pass before sundown. Smitty also reports that forensics are mining the cell phones recovered from the gunfight and my language skills will be needed to decipher the messages.

"Good morning!" Bella's voice powers through my earbuds and forces my thumb to the volume control. I shift in the waiting room chair, waiting for Hank to finish his fourteenth call.

"Morning? It's four in the afternoon there."

"So? Where are you?"

"Mars, it feels like."

"What does that mean?"

"Nothing. Just been a day."

"I can tell. You sound beat up. Something happen?"

On my phone, I scroll through old emails, find one from Mary Kaczmarek in Human Resources labeled 'ICE file updates needed' and open it. "Yeah, I fell today. Hurt my back."

"How'd you do that?" she asks, cereal crunching through her words.

"Being stupid, that's all." I open the link and it takes me to a form labeled *In Case of Emergency*. I scan through the fields, verify Bella's contact information is accurate.

"And you call me the clumsy one. What's your day looking like?" I hear the slurp of coffee. Practically smell it wafting through the phone.

The next section labeled 'Secondary Contact' sits blank. For a moment I consider... I skip it and move on. "Working on some big files. Nothing worth explaining. Hey, do you still have my apartment key?"

"Yeah, it's on my key chain. Why?"

"I couldn't remember if I gave it to you is all." Tabbing through each field, I double my life insurance, maximize my accidental death and dismemberment payout. I designate an insane percentage to a dog shelter I follow online, but the rest goes to my sister. "What's Keith up to?"

"Are you sure you're okay?"

"Yeah. I'll be fine." Hank steps out from around the corner and saves me from lingering on the phone. "Listen, I've got to go. I'll message you later."

"Uhm, okay. Love you!"

"Love you too."

Back in forensics, I find an evidence bag on my desk with a sticky note that reads "Courtesy of your friendly neighborhood Texas Ranger." Inside is my HK pistol, now scuffed, gouged, and scratched from its fall from the box truck.

Douglas walks by and taps on the gun. "Hey, that pistol looks a lot like... you." He winks and keeps going.

"Yeah, yeah."

I open the register, inspect the pipe, and set it aside for a thorough cleaning later. My focus now is the translation that has already been conducted by computer. And in classic computer fashion, it falls far short of the gracefulness of the Cantonese language. The information is similar to the intelligence briefings they already have. A trail of breadcrumbs that leads from one target to the next.

The bomb is on the way to El Mezcital. Or already there. Or so the message says. Unlike the previous GPS coordinates, the messaging is overt and hurried. I won't share it with anyone here, but I'm as terrified about the prospect of the bomb getting to the Gulf as I am about the way the message is written. It's a fake. Undoubtedly, unequivocally, this message is a fraud written by a non-native speaker for duplicitous reasons.

Ferreting the Spanish is subtler, but the appearance of Dominican slang in a Mexican conversation only reinforces the suspicions I have about the evidence's authenticity. If the Cartel Alianza isn't involved, if Chinese arms dealers aren't involved, who is?

Hank Taylor and the Texas Rangers. Don't assume they are friends. These finds, these breadcrumbs, seem to be leading to where the bomb was, not where it is. Could Hank be feeding me misinformation? Keeping me busy? Telling me everything I need to be one step behind?

"How's it going?"

I jump away from the laptop, wincing as my muscles flexing trigger pain receptors across half my body. "Fuck! Hank! Why are you sneaking up on me?"

Hank chuckles. "I called out twice. You must have been deep in thought. Find something interesting?"

Is Lucas Machado onto something? "You mean, beyond confirmation that a nuclear bomb is on the way to the U.S.? No."

"What about those chengyu phrases?"

"Good pronunciation. Not sure yet. But I'll figure it out. You get anything on our terrorists in ICU?"

"Just idents. Saenz is a bad boy from the Cartels, but Salazar is definitely the interesting one. He's not Mexican at all. He's one of ours."

I swivel in my chair. "You mean an American?"

"Sorry. I meant one of *yours*." Hank hands me a tablet.

The name Emiliano Zapata Salazar snaked through the databases before landing a hit on the government roster. Originally from Mexico, Salazar qualified for citizenship and attended MIT. Shortly after graduation, he was recruited by the FBI, and there the trail ends with a 'Classified' marker from the State Department.

I click the request button on the bottom of the page. A small footnote appears in red. 'Request still pending.'

Hank slides a chair over and sits backwards, eyes square on me. "I know you don't work for us, but I've got a lot of people down here counting on me. I need an honest answer from you. Does this Salazar fella work for you?"

I'm back on my heels, suddenly compelled to respond. "I honestly don't know. I don't know anything about this. I didn't know anything about this case twelve hours before I met you. I didn't even want to be here. No offense."

"None taken. And your bosses never mentioned anyone working undercover?"

"Not at all."

Hank stares at me and accurately reads my consternation. "I'm only trying to figure out why they would send a rookie down here to do a handler's job." He adds, "No offense."

"I'm damn good at my job, Hank."

Hank stands and shoves his hands in his pockets.

"Hank, what's going on here?"

"My pa said 'never trust a man who shows up in the wrong place at the right time.' This Salazar character couldn't be in a more wrong place. You call your boss and see what he says. And I would take it as a kindness if you could expedite Salazar's mission specs to my desk, please. I'll push this from the Governor's office. If Homeland Defense has an operation going on here, we need to know about it. The last thing we need is to be shooting our own people."

After Hank leaves, I stare at the laptop. The work on the translations has now been further complicated by the Gordian knot Hank dropped in front of me.

Chapter 29

What's going on, Corporal Agent?

I would ask you the same thing, Lieutenant Supervisor.

What does that mean?

Salazar. The FBI agent who's lying in intensive care after our shoot out on the border.

He's not FBI.

Homeland Defense?

Corporal, I have no idea why Salazar is down there. He was assigned to Dallas—the Texan Separatists movement. Specifically, working their connection to law enforcement and, I hate to say it, to the Texas Rangers.

What?

This is all classified, Corporal. You will not breathe a word of this to Hank Taylor or anyone else for that matter.

But how did he end up on the Mexican border? With a cargo truck used to transport a dirty bomb? Why was he shooting at us?

Nobody has heard from him in two weeks, and then he ended up in your gun battle. That's all we know.

Do you think there's something else going on here?

What do you mean?

I don't—It sounds crazy even in my own head.

Speak your mind, Corporal.

A rogue element? In our own government?

You think somebody in our community wants the bomb inside the U.S.?

No, I—

Let's assume for a moment you're right, Amara. Who would benefit the most from a nuclear bomb being smuggled into the U.S. by the Cartel?

I guess the people who want tighter border restrictions. They would be able to say 'see we told you so' and everyone would rally behind them. But that's insane...

How's Hank Taylor been?

That's a weird segue.

You know he's dying, right?

What?

Lymphoma. Untreatable.

Why are you telling me this?

James Baldwin once said, 'The most dangerous creation of any society is the man who has nothing to lose.'

Chapter 30

The helicopter blades beat overhead, washing the Texas Rangers with a rhythmic bath of sound. The Stetson hats are gone again, replaced by combat helmets. The white button-down shirts are replaced with Kevlar vests and desert camo fatigues. The only aspect that differentiates soldiers and police are the shoulder patches displaying the lone star of Texas.

I sit directly across from Hank, occasionally making eye contact with the man I've grown both to admire and distrust. Most of the flight I work on laptop, parsing data from the Salazar cell phone. The screen bounces on my lap as the helicopter chops through turbulence.

A U.S. Coast guard sent word to Texan authorities that a narco submarine was running the coastline close to El Mezcital—lining up perfectly with the intel I've uncovered about the bomb. A cutter had been dispatched to intercept the sub, but two hours into the flight, no news reached them.

I tap Hank on the knee and point to my headphones. He holds up four fingers and dials in the channel. I switch to channel to '4' and hear the pop of a connection.

"Why haven't we heard anything from the Coast Guard yet?"

Hank shrugs, "It's over sixteen hundred miles of coast-line and there's maybe ten cutters available if we're lucky. Don't worry. AEWAC still has a beat on the sub. They can't offload anything without a special port or meeting up with another ship. Coast Guard cutter should catch up about thirty minutes before we arrive. You heard from your boss?"

"The DHD team should be boots down virtually the same time we arrive."

"Will Lucas Machado be there?"

It's the first time he has asked specifically about my boss. Something about the question unnerves me. "Doubt it. He hates the desert. He prefers to handle things from DC."

"And when that bomb goes off, I'm sure he'll be all heartbroken over the death of our citizenry down here at the border as he watches from his flatscreen."

"Maybe he finds it easier to coordinate with all the re-sources there?"

Hank can't hide his condescending smirk and stares at me. "Much easier to criticize from a distance than take re-sponsibility up close."

"I wouldn't say that. Lieutenant Machado is very intui-tive on things. He's been supportive—"

Hank waves me to stop. "You don't need to defend your boss. I get it. We just have different ways of doing things, that's all. Texas appreciates the tremendous support the Federal government has provided us thus far." His tone is polite and seasoned with insincerity.

W. Lawrence

I turn my attention back to my laptop and let my vision adjust to the bouncing of the ride. The phone calls from Salazar are limited to three numbers, all Dallas based. XG, the cell provider, traced the calls to what are most likely burner phones. There are a dozen other numbers in Salazar's directory that XG traced back to banks, check cashing services, restaurants. And not one was ever placed to any of them from his phone.

The photos taken are what you would expect from almost anyone's phone: drinking at the bar, holding a pretty girl in a selfie, close-up of a full color tat, a dog, another dog, the same dog, a fiery sunset worthy of capturing, a sixteen-ounce steak and a beer.

One more picture stands out: an address plaque with the letters HT. Mundane on anyone else's phone but a red flag here. Exif data populates for most of the pics and places them all in Dallas Fort Worth. The couple pictures are devoid of GPS coordinates. So are the dog pictures. It's all boring as hell and not at all the phone of a government undercover agent. Or maybe it is? How am I supposed to know? I'm on the job for a blip of time—I know nothing about how we do undercover stuff.

Obviously, anyone Salazar would be working for would question the average guy not having a cell phone. To fit in, you would want a phone that had photos on it, numbers in the directory, which looked used and got pulled out to play games when he was bored.

I stare at the address plaque. Normal addresses have numbers, or numbers followed by a single letter. I search for addresses but quickly give up. The nature of fuzzy searches makes this kind of query nearly impossible, not to mention there is no street name, no city, no zip code.

Maybe it's not an address at all? The exif data is missing on this one too, which means it was copied from someplace or removed on purpose. The picture is out of focus yet shiny. And there is something peculiar about the letters I can't put my finger on.

My phone buzzes, a text message from Bella asking if the pumps she's wearing in the pic make her calves look weird. They look great, and I'm jealous she can pull off wearing them. I wear heels and wobble around like a cartoon strand of spaghetti. I send her a thumbs up and return back to the laptop.

Bella's response is "So is that a thumbs up its weird or thumbs up you like them?" followed by a string of emojis.

I grit my teeth and type out, "Looks great. Working. GTG."

"Are you in DC?"

"GTG!"

I switch focus, scan through the list of apps and find the typical litany of distractions: word scrambles, killer birds, skateboard tricks, sudokus and puzzles, and more. The phone's hard drive shows fifty-three apps in all. All normal.

On a hunch, I look at the app account manager and sees fifty-four downloads: one app has been deleted. The digging doesn't take long, and the app reinstalls on my emulator. "Lucyph3r" appears on the menu.

I lean across the copter, tap on Douglas's knee, and point to his headset. Douglas obliges. "What can I do ya for?"

I enunciate each word, not wanting to repeat myself in the haze of noise surrounding them. "You know that cell phone that had the decrypted info? The one you gave me when I first got here? Where did that come from?"

"It was shared with us through a DHD contact. Frances Brambilla. Said it was to 'germinate an air of cooperation' or some crap like that."

"Who is Frances Brambilla?"

"No clue. Nobody here knows her."

I draw up the app used by the original cell phone and dive into the key registrar. The key is huge, but I only need look at the first eight digits. Salazar's app is next, and the key shows the same exact digits. Copy, paste, copy, paste. I line the keys up on my screen top and bottom and sees they are an exact match.

"Oh fuck." My expression isn't lost on Hank who taps me on knee. I ignore him. Instead, I flip my headset to a secure channel and place a call to Darren Franciscus. When the call goes to voice mail I call again. And again. And again.

My phone rings. "What the hell? I'm in a big meeting."

"Darren, I need you," I start, turning my head sideways toward the window so the others can't read my lips. "Something is fucked up here. I don't—"

"Okay, what's up?"

"Frances Brambilla. DHD. I need to know who she is and who she reports to."

"How did you know Frances?"

"I don't."

"She used to work for Lucas. She was killed in Dallas two weeks ago during ops. Whole thing was nuts. She's not even a field agent."

"Are you sure?"

"Yeah, his whole team took up a collection for her family. I put in a couple hundred bucks. Why?

"Where in Dallas?"

"I don't know. Is it important?"

"I need to know. You need to send it to me directly. No-body else. Now."

"Where are you going with this? Why aren't you talking to Lucas?"

"Something is wrong. I'm in the middle of something very wrong."

"What's happening? Do you want me to talk to Lucas?"

"No! Don't call him. I will. I will talk to him. Get me the location."

A long pause.

"Do you trust me?" I ask.

Another long pause. "More than anyone else I know."

"Then do this. Please."

I disconnect before Darren can ask me anything else and then pull up Salazar's phone data again. The request from the cell provider pinpoints his phone usage, and the app permissions thankfully show his location when they were used. A cluster of them all appear around Grapevine, Texas. A quick search places it a smidge north of DFW air-port.

Street View takes interminable seconds to load, but I find the warehouses where Salazar frequented two weeks prior. My finger becomes a car, racing around the streets that circumscribe the giant buildings, trying to find the view the picture was taken from.

Hank taps me again and I can see him waving to me in my peripheral vision. I can't ignore him forever, but I put up one finger, buying as much time as I can.

My phone vibrates and a message comes across from Darren. GRAPEVINE. WAREHOUSE. Within minutes, I have found a massive warehouse complex in the center of the Dallas Fort Worth metro area, with each warehouse given a two-letter address: AA, AB, AC, AD, and so on.

This is where Frances Brambilla was killed. This is where Salazar took the photo. When I look up at Hank, I consider using a private comm line, but instead I set my headset to ALL.

"Hank, we need to turn around."

"What's wrong?"

"The submarine is a decoy." I'm guessing, but my gut tells me time is of the essence. I also need to be able to put Hank on the hot plate.

"And how do you know this?"

"The bomb is in Dallas. In a warehouse. And if it isn't there, it will be."

"How do you—"

"The keys. The decryption keys from the phone Douglas got from Brambilla and Salazar's phone. They're the same."

Hank looks lost.

"These encryption keys are big prime numbers. If somebody sends an encrypted message one way, they give the recipient a key— this big number. When you multiply one against another that only the sender knows, it opens the message. They both have the same key. The chance that they would have the same key and be talking with different people is really, really low."

"So DHD gets a phone with this information on it and hands it off to us. This phone has data from somebody, we don't know who, and this somebody happens to be the same somebody that was sending information to Salazar?"

I nod.

"Any way we can track who sent the info?"

I bob my head. "Maybe. Encryption normally hides that. The quantum computer at Quantico is up and running, it could probably crack it. But it can't be a coincidence that information on a WMD went to two separate Federal agents."

While I'm not sure about Hank, a quick glance around the expressions in the copter tells me the Rangers are stunned by my revelation.

Hank looks around and sees his team staring at him. He realizes that their conversation has been heard by everyone and straightens up. "Who else knows about this?"

I hesitate. "I have a secure contact at DHD."

Hank stares at me for a moment. "You know, I've always had tremendous respect for our Coast Guard."

"What?"

Hank toggles the control to include the flight deck. "Captain Meekers, I need you to change your flight plan. Take us to DFW right away. Fastest available speed.

"Everyone, we have a change of plans. The Coast Guard will be taking charge of the submarine. DHD will rendezvous with their cutter and are more than capable of handling the situation."

The chatter crosses the helicopter at every angle. I switch to a secure channel and give Hank the GPS coordinates for the warehouses. We talk about Salazar's activity in Dallas, Frances Brambilla's death, and how she worked on Lucas Machado's team.

"You know, Amara," Hank begins, "Folk in Washington are not so happy with Texas and our independent way of life. Lawsuits filed against the Feds, border fights, budget issues. They call it a constitutional crisis. There have been rumblings here that DC would love nothing more than to blame the Texan Separatists for some horrible terrorist act. A 9-11 style action that would give the federal government reason to bring our state under their thumb."

"You think DHD is bringing the bomb into Dallas?"

"Who else would know that you studied Cantonese, that you papered on the chengyu, that you would find those hidden clues and have them lead us like breadcrumbs from one point to another? And, of course, leaving it all in the capable hands of the Rangers. What happens when a dirty bomb goes off and a hundred thousand people are sick from radioactive poisoning? Or worse if this is a nuclear device. Who will the media blame?"

The helicopter banks and sends my laptop to the floor, and when I pick it up the screen is cracked and pixelated. I'm dizzy with stress, hands trembling, and all I can do is rub my finger obsessively over the crack as if I had magical screen healing powers.

My phone vibrates again, this time a message from Lucas Machado. *Why have you diverted to Dallas? Report.*

I hold up the message and show it to Hank. "What do I do?"

Chapter 31

The sun sits high above the warehouse complex in Grapevine, Texas, beating everyone beneath it with shade-stealing indifference. The pop of small arms fire rings everywhere, punctuated by bellowed commands and muffled screams.

I hear Douglas calling for Smitty and me to clear the warehouse to their right, but stepping out of the cover feels like suicide. Somebody left six pallets of soil outside, perhaps abandoned when armed men and women began using the warehouse complex for war games. Regardless, they have managed to save our lives as automatic fire sinks into the bags, sending a cloud of hot manured earth into the air that rains down on us in a dark brown film.

"Can you see where they are?" Smitty yells to me.

"They're everywhere! Fuck! What do we do?" I understand for the first time the real reason for militarizing our department, and truly wish I had the soldierly skills needed to maneuver out of here. Instead, I crouch as low as I can, terrified a stray bullet will uncap my skull. Douglas is calling over the radio again, but his orders are drowned by a blaze of guns firing that rattles my cognition. Stepping to the left or right of this position will only land us in a coffin. I glance back the way we came, the only place not engulfed in violence.

"We've got to get the fuck out of here!" I grab Smitty by the arm and pulls on him, but he doesn't budge. Gunfire strikes the pallet again, only the angle has changed. Degrees of difference shrinking our filthy advantage of cover to nothing.

"We're being flanked," I yell. "We've gotta go back!"

"We're not leaving our position. Don't you run away, Amara!" Smitty looks angry, not understanding that our position is untenable.

"We're going to die here if we don't leave!"

As if by design, a machine gun rips the soil bags apart, inch by inch, digging their way through their thinning cover. I can no longer control myself and sprint back toward our original position. Hopefully the Rangers are still there. Hank. A command center. Something to protect me. I hear Smitty calling me a bitch and a coward and a cunt and now he's screaming for help but I can't look. Can't look back. The warehouse I run alongside is as long as a cruise ship and there is no cover anywhere. One bullet to the back and I'll fall and bleed to death on the burning hot pavement before anyone can rescue me.

The corner. I made it. I'm alone and safe and gasping at the heated air. Hank is nowhere. The Rangers are all missing. I grab my radio and try to break into the chatter, but everyone is avoiding the angel of death that rides every piece of lead fired. I look around the corner and see muzzle flash from a warehouse window, see what used to be Smitty now lying motionless. Looking down the rows of warehouses, I see nobody, hear nobody. All of the voices, all of the gunfire, is concentrated around Warehouse HT. I know I need to get back there, to help them, to find the bomb. I heard Spanish and English, and in Texas that doesn't mean a damned thing. I don't even know who I'm fighting.

We had found four dead police officers when the helicopter landed in the parking lot, and a Texas Ranger joined them in the afterlife the moment he touched solid ground. The helicopter was the next casualty. Eight of us managed to make it off before the engine bellowed smoke. The rest of the Rangers jumped as the pilot tried to take off—a liftoff cut short as the helicopter banked and sliced its rotors into a parked tractor trailer and collapsed into the cement.

I grab my cell phone and call Hank. Straight to voicemail. I call Douglas. No answer. I call Darren—an automated message returned saying he was unavailable.

"Shit! Shit! Fuck! Shit fuck!"

I look up at the warehouse plaque and see it reads RF, only the lettering is backward. It takes me a moment to realize I'm looking at a window, and the letters are reflecting from the building I've propped myself up against. When I look up, it reads FR. I turn back to the window. Salazar's photo was a reflection. The address plaque isn't HT.

I reload my pistol and keep it at the ready, then trot at a parallel from the firefight. FR, GR, HR, IR, JR. I run through the alphabet grid, looking both ways for friend or foe. Sirens in the distance. I can't tell how long until they arrive, and there's no time to wait, no time to consult. I keep running. RR, SR, TR. *Stop.*

The gunfire is still snapping and echoing between the warehouses. The heat is reflecting off their aluminum siding and slowly baking me as I move. I turn right and move up the alphabet now. TR, TQ, TP, TO. The fighting is fading to the sound of street level fireworks. My back is aching, and my shoulder throbbing on the inside and chaffing on the outside. No doubt the wounds from falling off the box truck at the border have reopened. My nerves have calmed, but only because the half mile I've run through this grid has exhausted my body's supply of adrenaline.

I see the TH warehouse ahead. Even with my goal in sight, I can only take exhausted steps, a pathetic skip here and there to maintain a pace above a walk. Then I see him. How he has not seen me is miracle.

Lucas Machado looks in every direction but mine and steps into the open door underneath the address plaque TH.

I run, although I cannot fathom where the energy to even move comes from. Fifty yards, forty, thirty. I hear a pop of pistol fire. Then nothing. I step cautiously into the building, but I don't know how careful I can be while panting like a dog and sweat stinging my eyes. There is a man on the ground lying in a pool of blood, Glock still in his hand. No need to check if he's alive with the crater in his face. I kneel down, peel the weapon from the dead man's stiff grip, check the ammo, and stuff the gun into my belt.

Bloody footprints lead to another door and into a warehouse filled with pallets stacked six feet high. The whole space of the building looks to be filled with nothing but pallets, and yet the fading bloody trail leads to a shoulder width space that forms a makeshift corridor. The blood has run out, and when met with an intersection, I turn left on a whim. Another intersection, and my right turn leads me to a wide-open area. Somebody has built these pallets into a wall to make the warehouse appear filled. Here in the center is what only could be the bomb.

It looks like a generator, perhaps four feet long and two feet wide. It sits covered in thick, dull colored metal plates hinged to the frame and it must weigh a ton. Two of the plates are swung upright, held open by metal props. The device is very much a dichotomy of technology, with an IOS-type screen duct-taped to a series of plastic beams, and a plastic key with a piece of yellow foam dangling from underneath that looks like it would open a locker at a waterslide park. Most telling however, is a large red rubber switch and an active digital countdown clock that reads four minutes and twelve seconds.

Lucas Machado steps from another concealed opening in the pallet maze, gun drawn but relaxed at his side as he walks briskly toward the bomb.

"Drop the gun!" I yell, my voice cracking and robbing me of all authority. I level the pistol at Lucas all the same.

He freezes, gun pointed away. He looks at me and his shoulders drop slightly as his free hand goes up. "Amara! Don't shoot! It's me, Lucas!"

I approach slowly, pistol never lowering.

"You had me scared for a second. I thought I was a dead man." Lucas wears a nervous smile that dissipates as I draw nearer. "Amara, don't you recognize me? Lucas Machado. Your boss. I sent you out here, remember?"

"I- I'm in charge here, Lieutenant. Lower your gun now!"

"Hey, don't you point that at me, Corporal! I am your superior officer, listen to me!"

"No! Drop *your* gun on the ground, Lieutenant, and back away slowly! Do it now!" I step forward, still distant enough that he can't grab me, but bringing lethal accuracy to my range. I glance at the digital counter on the device. Three minutes and fifteen seconds.

Lucas keeps the gun pointed away. "Corporal James, drop your pistol now! That is a direct order! Now do it or I'll have you brought up on charges!"

"The hell you will." Hank steps into the open area between the pallets. His revolver is pointed directly at Lucas. "Lucas Machado, you are under arrest. Put your pistol on the ground slowly and back away."

"Woah, now, everybody take it easy." Lucas sets his gun on the ground, takes two steps back, and puts his hands up. "Amara, you are making a big mistake. Hank Taylor is the one you should have your gun pointed at. He's the head of the Texas Separatist movement. He brought the bomb here."

I look at Hank then back at Lucas.

Hank scoffs, "That's nonsense! Amara, he's trying to mess with your mind."

"Amara, look at me," Lucas continues. "Hank Taylor is responsible for at least a dozen acts of conspiracy against the U.S. government and has been under investigation for the last two years. He's covered up the deaths of a dozen federal employees using his position—"

"Amara, secure that man—"

"—and plans to detonate that bomb as his final act before he dies! He's going to martyr himself. Amara, don't let him near that bomb!"

Hank has moved within twenty feet of the dirty bomb and holsters his weapon. "I'll get this taken care of. You get Machado out of here."

One minute, fifty-nine seconds.

"Amara! Don't let him touch it! I'm telling you he's going to set it off! There are seven million people living here. Seven million! Ask him who ordered Frances Brambilla killed! Ask him!"

"What is he talking about, Hank?"

Hanks continues toward the bomb, dismissing Lucas with a wave. "What a load of horse crap! She was my friend. Why would I have her killed?"

My brain clicks through the hundreds of bits of information I've had to swallow over these few days, and this one isn't going down easy. "Wait. Hank, you never said you knew Frances Brambilla."

Hank keeps walking, now within a body length of the bomb. I draw the pistol I took from the dead man with my left hand and point it at him. "Hank, just stop. Okay? Stop for a second."

Hank freezes, his fatherly tone returning. "Hey now, Amara. What are you doing there? You're not going to listen to this guy, are you?"

I look back and forth, sighting each pistol as I inch to a place equidistant from them both. The Glock is light in my left, the HK heavy in right, and the weight disparity is wearing on my fatigued body. "I'm not... I—I just need you both to back away so I can shut this thing off. Okay? Then we can sort this out."

Neither man is looking at me now, their gazes fixed upon each other, shouting vileness at each other. Lucas steps forward and my stance stiffens.

One minute, thirty seconds.

"Hey! No-no-no-no. Both of you just stop! I'm in charge here! I'm in charge now. Let me turn this thing off and we can all go talk or- or something. Okay?"

Hank leans in, "The time for talking is over."

I step forward again to ensure a head shot will not miss. "Hank, step back so I can turn it off!"

"You don't trust me..." Hank mutters.

"He's not going to turn it off, Amara," Lucas says calmly, inching his way to the bomb. "He's here on a one-way mission. He knows it, and you know it."

I step again, as close as I dare, aiming at Lucas's head. "Jesus Christ! Lieutenant! If you are on my side, stop getting closer to the bomb! Okay? We can all go home and do stuff... Not this... Okay? Just not." I can hear my speech turning to babble but can't control it.

"He's the one, Amara. He's the one that set you up as a patsy," Hank says. "All of us are patsies. It's a conspiracy to federalize every state in the union, and it starts right here."

Fifty-five seconds.

I feel the rise of bile in my throat and my arms quiver from holding the pistols out unsupported.

"Amara, I'm going to turn the bomb off real slow, okay?" Hank says.

I look at the timer, the key, and the big red switch that would flip if you blew on it. "No! Let me do it!" Let me do it, Hank. I'm your friend and I'll do it. I'll turn it off. I swear."

Machado bends low, his gun within reach.

"Lieutenant, stop!" I scream. I'm crying now. Actually crying. I'm a grown ass woman and a federal agent I can't control a fucking thing. My arms are failing. "Please, I'm begging you, stop!"

"I can't let you risk the future of our country, Amara," Lucas says. "You've sided with the enemy."

Hank leans in slow and steady.

Twenty-five seconds.

"No! Both of you! I can't—hold! Wait! You need to...Please! Please! Both of you! Please!"

Both men make tiny moves.

The most dangerous creation of any society is the man who has nothing to lose.

Never trust a man who shows up in the wrong place at the right time.

I squeeze both triggers.

I set the pistols on the ground, turn the key to the 'Off' position. The timer stops at fourteen seconds. There is a faint gyroscopic noise I hadn't noticed before: it spins down into silence. The warehouse is as quiet as a crypt.

Shuffling my feet is the best I can manage as I step around the bomb with the big red switch and the yellow key. I look at the bodies of Hank Taylor and Lucas Machado. My friend. My boss. My mentors. It's my knees that fail next as I drop to the ground between the two dead men and stare into the pallets. Snot drips from my nose and carries the shitty soil from my lip into my quivering mouth. Now I need to cry, to exorcise these last few moments from my body, but only breath escapes.

Chapter 32

Amara tugs the hospital gown off and stares at her bruised body in the mirror. She can't seem to look herself in the eye. She pulls her shirt over her head and winces. There is a stillness that comes with going through shock, as if only parts of the world exist and only parts of your body matter. She feels like she could remove her head and set it on the toilet seat and her arms and legs would move about fine on their own. The bruises only matter because her head says they hurt.

I wouldn't have to brush my hair anymore.

"Amara? You okay in there?" Darren calls from the door.

She remembers Hank asking the same thing when she was in this hospital only a few days ago. Her breath quickens and her chest heaves. *This is why I don't want my head attached.* The weeping billows out of her like a siren and Amara screams, screams and pulls at her hair and flails in circles, smashing into the walls and sink and toilet until the door opens and Darren grabs her by the shoulders and squeezes her. Everything is spinning and horrible.

"I killed them! I killed them!"

"You're gonna be okay."

Darren drags her out of the bathroom and to the hospital bed where she shakes with unfettered sobs.

In the hours that follow, Amara spells out to Darren all that transpired.

"And then I pulled the trigger. The triggers, I mean." Amara wipes her nose on her hand. "And that's it."

Darren sits quietly, staring out the window. "No."

"I swear, Darren. That's—"

"No. That's not what happened." Darren squares off his chair to hers and when he speaks it hovers just above a whisper. "You arrived and found Hank and Lucas dead—assailant or assailants unknown. You disarmed the bomb and saved untold numbers of American citizens from radioactive poisoning and death. That's what you did. And that's what is going in my report."

"But somebody brought that bomb here! Somebody in our government or from Texas and we need to know!"

"No. You need to follow my lead on this and never waver."

"Why? Why are you doing this? We need to know who—"

"No, we don't."

"*I* need to know!"

"No. If anyone knows you are wise to this conspiracy, you will be dead before week's end. DHD, Texan Separatists. No matter who was behind it, it will set off a civil war that will split this country in two."

"I can't keep this a secret!"

"You can and you will. You will tell nobody. You will never bring it up. You won't whisper about it. Don't even pray about it."

"I don't understand..." she weeps.

"I made a promise to your father to save him. And I can't keep that promise without your help. I need you alive, Amara. He needs you alive."

The past week blurs through Amara's mind. *I killed two men, and I have no idea who was lying to me. Maybe neither were lying. Maybe we're all patsies. Did I kill them for nothing?* She looks to Darren, his face buried in his phone. *Nothing is certain. Nothing is known. He's the only person I have ever been able to consistently trust.*

When Darren looks up, he lets out a long sigh. "The bomb was fissionable. Confirmed."

"Do they know who built it?"

Darren stares at her and they lock eyes. Amara wipes her cheeks with her palms and straightens herself up in the chair. She nods.

"So," Darren starts, "from the beginning. Tell me what happened."

Chapter 33

Saint Charles Borromeo Catholic Church maintains a modern appearance despite its age, the structure devoid of classic architectural signatures. Neither the ancient stone transepts of European churches nor the quaint abbey-like qualities of the warm churches of Americana are present in this building. It looks more like a Frank Lloyd Wright afterthought than a place of worship.

Amara approaches the confessional—one that has adopted tech savvy anonymity screens in lieu of the latticed openings of yon—and closes the wooden door—itself a departure from the norm. She waits there for the priest to step into his compartment, hears the latch engage, and waits for the dull gray confessional screen to turn a quiet blue.

"Forgive me Father, for I have sinned." She hangs on the comma in her sentence.

"How long has it been since your last confession?"

Although the screen she faces will mask both her sex and tone, converting her admissions into a neutered, homogenized, but pleasant artificial voice.

Amara momentarily considers lying. *Well, that would defeat the purpose of coming here.* "It's been a long time. I've... It's just been very busy at work." *There. That wasn't so bad.* She continues. "For these sins I accuse myself of... I lied to a lot of people. And...something else I don't even know I can say."

The confession has stepped out of its format early, but the priest is eager to serve. "What you say here is confidential. You're only judge is the Lord, and He already knows. Please go on, my child."

The secrets of what happened in Texas crawl beneath her chest, a jail of ribs and flesh that wane with each passing day as their prisoner strains to escape.

"I've got to go, I'm sorry Father." She presses on the door latch but finds it secure. Amara pushes against the door, but it doesn't budge. "Father, my door is stuck. It's not opening—Father?"

Smashing, pressing, prying, the door fails to give way. The confessional feels smaller than when she first arrived. Amara pivots on her butt to kick the door open, smash the confessional wall through to get to the priest, but the booth might as well be concrete.

"Are you sure you don't want to confess?" The priest's voice now has a sharper tone, a hiss. The booth begins shrinking. Amara tucks her legs up underneath as she tries to press through the ceiling. The wood paneling flexes, bends, and ultimately snaps.

A wave of feculent earth pours into the confessional booth, filling her mouth, blouse, and ears, forcing her eyes shut. The weight of the soil pushes in on her chest, on her back, working its way into open wounds that tear and bleed and—

Amara wakes in a startle, jumping from her chair to her feet and spitting what's left of the nightmare soil from her lips onto her living room floor. She feels the air with out-stretched arms to verify that this is reality. The blinds on the apartment window are open, and she looks down on a sliver of Arlington, lights twinkling, sirens faintly making their distance known. Finally oriented, she puts her clammy palms against the cool glass and breathes a patch of life into the window. She draws a frowny face. It quickly vanishes, leaving a reflection of her own face in its place.

The nightmares came daily for a long time, but Dr. Hariri assured her they would fade—and they did, until to-night. Perhaps the incident hadn't fallen behind her just yet, or the therapy insufficient, or perhaps a medication side effect extracted it. Amara's hopes for a quick recovery are clearly short-sighted. Hariri would say *the mind is complicated. Nightmares have many triggers.* He would attribute it to stress, to shock. But he can't attribute it to the shootings, to the killings. For, him, as for many surrounding Amara, these are secrets never to be unearthed, never to be resurrected.

"Otto, what time is it?"

"It's just after 3am, Amara. Are you alright?" the virtual assistant responds in its consistently polite British voice.

"Yes, Otto. I'm having trouble sleeping is all."

"Would you like some bedtime music, Amara? I believe you fell asleep to *Clair de Lune* rather quickly."

Amara scoffs. "Otto, I'll be fine."

She shakes a pill loose from the prescription bottle and swallows it down with the remains of a flat soda. A search for dog videos in shelters yields a calming distraction. Dogs riding horses. Dogs caught destroying sofas with guilty expressions. Dogs equipped with synthetic voice boxes saying everything wrong. Dogs telling their owners they want a cookie fifty times in a row. A video of Keith and Bella snuggling with his old dog. She places a smiley face next to it and shuts her screen down.

Seven months have passed since Texas and the only thing keeping her sane are her sister and dog videos and the distractions at work. A handshake and sixty second conversation with the President followed by a three week debriefing with State, FBI, and DHD. *No, I didn't see who killed them. No, there was no indication who set the bomb.* Another promotion to sergeant signals to everyone she's on the fast track, but nobody knows why. Nobody will ever know about the bomb with the big red switch and the yellow key. It's a demon in a box summoned to our world by Hank or Lucas or the Chinese or the Cartel... And now she gets to play pretend it never existed.

"Otto, voice code recognition: Michael, Gabriel, Rafael."

"Encrypted journal is ready for your input, Amara."

"Begin recording." The recording is kept locally on a drive hidden in the apartment. While it's possible somebody could find it and decrypt it, the chances are far higher she will drive herself insane by holding onto every secret she has learned. The pressure on her soul releases with each word as she confesses her sins to the one person who cannot judge her. Not yet, anyway. Amara knows eventually he will see this though, he will read her facial cues and see the poorly hidden anguish. But if she fails, he will never see any of her messages anyway.

"Hi, Daddy. It's really late, or early, or whatever, but I can't sleep. I figured we could talk—well, I could talk, and you can listen to this whenever you're better. But this has been a really frustrating week..."

Chapter 34

I was a cat studying a bird from the window, planning, preparing, ready to pounce, but conclusively divided from my prey. I watched the drone monitor, both directional mic and camera aimed squarely at my target. I shifted in my seat to avoid a spring poking through the cushion into my thigh, the small discomfort threatening my focus on Kacela Fantine.

She leaned against the cargo container, hands in her pockets, breath steaming from her lips, her smooth voice like a serpent even while chatting it up with her cohorts. Kacela's nose chain dangled just above her upper lip, and every minute or so she flicked the tips of her forked tongue against the snakehead bobble on the end.

Port Newark-Elizabeth Marine Terminal felt eerily quiet through the hypersensitive mic—even considering the already diminished activities due to the most recent trade war. The November sky had grown black in a way that somehow surprises everyone, even though it happens every year, and seemed to bring with it heightened doldrums of silence.

My team and I sat parked in an old warehouse about a quarter mile outside the marine terminal, geared up for anything, expecting nothing. Along with Department of Justice and State elements down the road, we formed a surrounding net. Boats stationed in the water buttoned down any unforeseen escape routes, but wide enough to allow the bait to arrive.

That night was the result of months of joint operations and vectored with our Counter-Terrorism task force investigation to unearth Bukum Yilani: the Twisting Snake. Rooted in Istanbul, the organization slithered across the globe, abducted children of state officials in every country and inserted them into the human trafficking networks. They extorted money, consolidated power, and affected government policy that favored BY's maritime trade endeavors and cargo inspections. Those who didn't comply had their children returned with explosive vests strapped to their chests, manipulated into the very government buildings where their parents worked.

Those who even hesitated in complying had their kids returned worse for the wear, and not just from repeated sexual abuse. The evidence we discovered in Philadelphia revealed that Bukum Yilani used a black market nanotech treatment called *Sublime* to render its victims compliant to a shocking level. Hondor Labs originally designed the dust-sized robotic particles as a drugless anesthesia, but dark-world elements found a method to jailbreak the source code, bypass the manufacturing restrictions, and redirect their functions to target the basal ganglia and temporal lobe. The end result essentially allowed for the zombification of the victim, and we suspected Stephanie Bartles was their first known American *Sublime* suicide bomber.

The drone's directional mic picked up the sound of movement on the dock. Kacela's group fell silent, and our target slipped a sawed-off shotgun from her boot holster and moved forward. I could see her tattooed hand gripping the pump, finger already on the trigger, eyes wide as she hissed for the men to spread out.

I ordered Everett, 'E'. "Get eyes on whatever made that noi..."

"On it. Drone Five moving east to grid 415 –no- 416, elevation 50."

"Ascend to seventy-five," I said.

"It's dark, and they're not going to see anything in this fog."

"Hope not."

Everett kept Drone One on Kacela as I adjusted the gain on the mic. Corporal Agent Pamela Hamilton—"P"—our newest member, issued warnings in low tones on the comm to DOJ and State Department crews.

Kacela Fantine was nowhere near the top of the BY organization, but after her arrest she became well connected to those who were. An uncommon female in the sex trafficking trade, she seemed to move from one section of the serpent to the other, making a name for herself by combining ruthlessness and guile in even measure.

Two years had passed since the last time I saw her in Philadelphia. She had been arrested shortly after our encounter at the pizzeria and was offered a plea bargain to give up information on her higher-ups. She could walk away, expunged record and witness protection program: the red-carpet treatment for her testimony. Instead, she served eight weeks of an eight-year sentence and was released due to a shit job by the agent who swept her up. Fantine never spoke a word, never made a phone call, never made a jail house confession, never penned a single sentence, never typed a single email. Kacela wore the same stoic expression for fifty-seven days while eating and shitting and burning holes into the skulls of the correctional officers with her dead gaze. She walked out of county jail squeaky clean.

But that night we had her. *I* finally had her. We watched Drone Five follow her to the edge of the pier where a silhouette coalesced from the mist and limped into existence. Plastic bags filled with decayed unknowns dragged behind like prey from a hunt, layers of failing clothing to block out autumn, uneven beard, unstable posture.

"Hey!" one of Kacela's men shouted, "Who the fuck are you?"

The unkempt figure hobbled his way obliquely past them, glancing their way but never staring, never answering.

"DOJ is asking if we have any undercover assets out there," P relayed.

"Where did this guy come from?" Everett mumbled. "We cleared the area with thermal imaging..."

Pamela shrugged. "Containers might have masked him. Looks like an indigent..."

"*Puñeta!*" I turned to P, "Let DOJ and State know we are monitoring. Hopefully this douche clears out."

Kacela's henchman continued to engage, admonitions for a crossing an unseeable boundary. Aggressive movements meant to intimidate only agitated and confused the wanderer as he dodged erratically. Long steps, shuffling, rapid zig zags as he failed to discern the best way out of their hunting grounds.

I was desperate to clear him out, and if I could have reached through the screen and plucked the man out of reality, I would have done it. Kacela Fantine seemed to share my sentiments as I watched her point her shotgun at the homeless man. We couldn't quite make out what she yelled, but their unwanted visitor meandered away.

Her henchman followed, assault rifle unslung, and fired it multiple times at the ground. "Dance, puta! Dance!"

"Stand by, do not engage!" Pam repeated, "Shots fired are at the ground, do not move in. Maintain positions."

I stole a glance at her and she covered her mic: *the DOJ agents are idiots*, she mouthed, and then went back to her communication duties.

One of the other BY thugs scouted ahead, pointing and laughing as the terrified man skittered away, and then looked around for any other intruders, troublemakers, or witnesses.

Kacela approached swiftly and grabbed the man around the throat. Once again, her soft voice made it impossible to determine what she said, but the expression on her henchman made it clear he crossed a line.

We watched and waited; Drone One's AI kicked in and auto-followed Fantine's confident strides away while I adjusted the camera pan and mic. Hopefully we would capture something that linked to another crime we could dig into. Our last op had pulled audio-video of Kacela bragging about kidnapping thirteen-year-old twin daughters and convincing them to take *Sublime* without a fight. She told the technician that she didn't want her "double trouble paycheck" having unnecessary bruising. DOJ never ran with it. No evidence of twin girls being abducted in the U.S., just criminals bragging to criminals, hearsay which—if pressed through the court—would amount to harassment against Kacela Fantine after the previous botched arrest. So much for our military authority violating civil rights.

"CIC coming through," Pamela announced.

I clicked my headset and identified myself.

"It's me, A," Captain Darren Franciscus said, "Stand down."

My stomach tightened, "What's going on?"

"DOJ identified a boat approaching two miles out. It turned around right after the rifle was fired."

"Two miles? How do they hear it two fucking miles—"

"A, A, A. The terminal is quiet. It's cold. Sound is gonna travel."

"*Puñeta...*"

"I know. Feel free to leave a skeleton crew, but we aren't catching a fish tonight."

"Leave a skeleton crew? We *are* a skeleton crew!"

"Put Orev on. He loves overtime." The last comment highlighted that—sometimes—the best person for the job isn't always likeable. While O showed deference to me, he seemed to take delight in contradicting anything our now-captain suggested or ordered. Darren and Orev locked horns on more than one occasion, so when shit rolled downhill, it landed on O's boots.

"I still don't understand why we don't just go get her. She's right-fucking-there. We don't need probable cause anymore."

"But we kinda do, and State says we do this old school or we don't do it at all." Darren added, "We all want her, and we all know what a solid arrest leads to, but we can't screw up again."

"*We* didn't. *Wadsworth* screwed the arrest."

"We're not rehashing this. It's done. We move forward as one department."

I hung up in disgust and asked Pamela to communicate with DOJ and State. As I tossed my headset onto the console, I could see she was unsure why the night ended so abruptly. Everett stayed on drone controls, but the rest of us started packing up. We worked in disappointed silence, removing our bullet proof vests and securing weapons in our tactical van parked inside the warehouse.

I distanced myself from everyone, stretched, then practiced an Aikido move I'd been struggling with, a variation on the *aiki-otoshi*. Eyes closed, envisioning an opponent, I did everything I could to mirror what my soke taught me. Stepping inside, maneuvering their hands away, driving the knees together, torquing your opponent's legs up and close to your body. It made perfect sense in my perfect imagination and—in class—it looked masterful.

Orev walked past me toward the door on a mission to pollute his lungs. He barely looked at me, his stride never broke as he commented on my form. "That move is shit," he said, then disappeared outside. Only O could get away with that talk. Prior to Homeland Defense, he was with the Israeli Defense Force and had killed with his bare hands. How many? Darren saw his file but never confirmed a number. He only said it was a lot.

"Amara, hey!" Iván popped out from the surveillance control room and waved. *Shit!* He must have been waiting for Orev to step out for his smoke, for a modicum of privacy that came in short supply these days. Only some of that was accidental.

I turned toward the door and tried to make my escape, but he was already jogging over with a hopeful smile. I'd be lying if I said I didn't find him attractive, and I couldn't think of anyone who treated me better. The man saved my life twice in as many years.

"How's it going? I was just headed outside..."

"Yeah, I was checking on you. You sounded pretty pissed talking to the boss..." He saddled up to me, hands in his pockets.

"Yeah. Well, Darren just sent me a message that DOJ will be monitoring, which means we all go home. It also means it will get screwed up somehow."

"That sucks."

"*Qué gacho*," I suggested to him. We repeated it back and forth until I was sure he got it. One thing about Iván few people knew was he was nowhere close to fluent in Spanish. It wasn't essential for our job, but he admitted to me one night he lied on his application, and nobody bothered to question him because his parents were Puerto Rican. Still, if anyone found out he falsified his application, it would be the end of any government job. Ever since, Iván and I spent every private moment working Spanish into everything we could. There were differences between Mexican Spanish and Puerto Rican Spanish, but I'd been around enough boricuas (including Darren) to pass for an islander.

"*Bien hecho, Pocho.*" It was a mean little nickname, but an accurate one.

"*Gracias.*" He smiled at me as he inched a little closer. "I'm still a pocho though?"

I stepped back a bit, "Yup. But keep working."

He must have sensed my attempt to escape, leaning in. "Hey, A, you think I can take you out for dinner again? You know, to work on my Spanish and all."

I squeezed my shoulders together, gritted my teeth. "Iván, I don't know if that's such a good idea. You know, we work together..."

He put his hands up, "No, not like that! I meant, you know, just as friends. Like last time."

"Last time you made me a mix tape..." My cheeks didn't know whether to make a frown or a smile and they ended up making both. Or neither. I probably looked gassy.

"Oh, you got the wrong idea! No, that was just some music I was sharing with you, that's all." He backed off a bit, the gentle giant retreating in the face of a rebuke.

This time I stepped forward, arms squeezed across my chest. "Okay, let's just take your collection of ballads and put a pin in it for a moment. I need you to understand that my life has zero room for romance. I work, I go to the gym, I go to the dojo, I go back to work, I go home, I sleep three hours, and I go back to work. There is no room for a man in all that."

"Are you- I mean- you're not interested in...?"

"Woah, not that you need to know, but I'm not gay either. I'm just saying there is no free time for you or anyone else. I'm busy *all the time*, okay?"

"You can't be busy *all the time*."

"Well, I am. You've seen me. When's the last time you saw me go out the crew?"

"You take some long trips," he said, looking away from me. The comment came from a place of hurt, and I should have let it be.

"What's that supposed to mean?" I asked.

"Nothing."

"No, not nothing. What do you mean by that? Am I supposed to check in with you, Iván?"

"No, of course not—"

"Are you sure? You know my sister lives in Pennsylvania, and I spend time with her. Is that okay with you?"

"I didn't—"

"No no no, if you want to be my boyfriend and all, maybe I should check in with you to make sure that my road trips meet your standards for appropriate amount of time away from you."

"Amara, I'm sorry—"

"Well, *Corporal* Fagundes," I snapped, "As much as I'd love to advance our friendship into a closely monitored relationship, let me remind you I'm your *sergeant* and in charge of our little team of killers, and department policy prevents me from crossing that line. Is that good enough for you?"

"Amara, I don't know why I said that. I'm sorry." He stepped back, hands up in surrender. "I'm going to go help Everett bring the drones in, *bien*?" Iván turned around and slinked away, wounded by the one person who he protected at every turn.

It became harder to apologize for chewing his head off with each footfall, for not leveling with him that my trips also involved my father and his top-secret condition. What did I expect? Of course it looked weird to an outsider, and anyone on my team had to know my time away had nothing to do with vacations. By the time I tried to take it back, Iván had disappeared behind our parked van.

"Fuckity fuck fuck," I whispered.

I stepped outside to find Pamela—who told us she wanted to quit smoking—taking a drag off Orev's cigarette.

"Smash any cigarettes in my possession to pulp!" had been her exact words. When she and I made eye contact, she flicked it back at Orev who shriveled from the unexpected projectile, the surprise wearing off when he saw me walk up.

No exchange of words took place, only my reproaching gaze meeting her head hung in shame. When I gave Orev the same look, he rolled his eyes and derided me. "She's a grown woman."

"She's a teammate who asked for our help quitting those cancer sticks. Something you should be doing, O."

"When you can beat my fucking PT scores, I'll quit. Until then..." He picked up the cigarette from the ground, closed his eyes and took a long drag, then let it out in a slow, rhapsodic release.

"I do have higher scores," I said, sitting down next to them and kicking my feet up on an old tire, a hobo's otto-man.

"You have higher *female* scores." He offered the cigarette to Pamela who refused it. He finished it off, burning it down to the filter and flicking it away. "Pamela, in the IDF, women are judged the same as men. This bullshit American idea that women must be treated different isn't equality. It will get us all killed."

"I almost beat your three mile," I said.

Orev laughed, "Almost. Amara, I kick your ass in everything, including in the most important metric: kicking your ass."

"That's not fair," Pamela said.

"Why?" Orev lit another cigarette and puffed it to life.

"Because she's..." she started to defend me but stopped.

"Because she's a woman? Because she's smaller?" Orev made childish faces at our newest teammate, "Oh no! I'm a woman! I need things to be fair! You think that the degenerate abortions we arrest keep things fair? You need to train to compete with the strongest, and the strongest are men."

Pamela screwed her face up. "How are men like you still alive, let alone employed?"

I started to interject but Orev waved at me. "Pamela, this is not me hating women. I love women! I love them too much. Ask my ex-wife! This is me telling you the truth. Women, on average, are weaker. Smaller. You have no testosterone. You don't have muscle mass. You must be able fight a man *despite* these things."

"Are you saying a woman can't beat a man?"

"No. I'm saying average man will beat average woman every single time."

"You are unbelievable, Orev." Pamela shook her head, turned to me and gestured as if she wanted me to weigh in.

"Don't look for sympathy from A. She knows. I teach her right. I teach her the Israeli way. Fight dirty, fight brutally, make every encounter catastrophic for your opponent. I make Amara a machine. Give me three years and I'll make you a killer too." He gives her an up-and-down. "Maybe four years."

"Oh, screw you. And we aren't supposed to be killers. We're supposed to be defenders."

Orev climbed into Pamela's personal space. "Think you can be one without being the other?" He scoffed and turned away.

"Pamela," I broke in, "I have been doing Aikido since middle school. I can—and have—thrown men around who were twice my size..."

"See?" Pamela pointed at me.

"...But he's right," I finished.

She looked at me like I ran over a sack of kittens.

Even though I trained twenty hours a week in firearms, martial arts, and physical fitness, Orev truly came with a reputation of do-not-screw-with-me. I almost felt sorry for whoever crossed paths with him. Under his tutelage, I'd managed to take my studies to a new level. He taught me to fight with a knife, baton, brass knuckles, han-bo, baseball bat, anything we could get our hands on. He broke two of my ribs in training once and insisted I fight on. And I did.

Pamela took to her feet, snatched the new cigarette from Orev's lips, and puffed away, hellbent to burn it away to nothing. "You people are a disappointment." Her finger wagged at us both, but she aimed the comment directly at me.

I looked back at her.

"It isn't just about *this*, Amara," she raised her voice and gesturing fitfully to Orev. "We identified a boat, probably with trafficked kids onboard. But because they aren't going to Bukum Yilani, we let it go? How is that okay?"

"It isn't okay, but there's a bigger picture. Bukum Yilani is the target. If we don't catch them in the act, we can't get them to roll on Millennial, and that's the fish we all came out to catch."

"So Millennial is more important than a boatload of kids being sold?" Pamela exhaled some smoke. "I've got friends at the Bureau, and they would be *losing their minds* over how you people operate."

Pamela stomped over to Orev and grabbed the pack from his pocket. He instinctively tried to stop her, but she smacked his hand like a mother swatting a child reaching for a cookie. "I'm taking these. Unless you want to go back to work and have to explain how a helpless woman beat your ass for a pack of Marlboros."

Orev and I sat together in silence. The real disappointment for the night was not Orev, not Iván, not Pamela, not even missing the arrest of Kacela Fantine. The real disappointment was that a boat filled with trafficked boys and girls had floated away and, until Pamela said something, I never gave it a second thought.

Orev sighed. "Do you have any gum?"

Chapter 35

Sergeant Agent Amara James awakens after a typical sleep deficient night, finds the strength to prepare for work in the bottom of a dark stained mug, and pilots herself to work in a haze. She and her team spend two unproductive days sorting through hours of video taken from the drone flights, listening to recordings of conversations and eaves-dropped phone calls. Their attempts to squeeze circum-stantial evidence for an arrest fails to impress the feckless State Department and their endless placations of the Türk-ish government, and the Secretary of State invokes presi-dential influence to safeguard their interests.

Everett steals Amara away for lunch in the cafeteria on a day of wildly unpopular dish of SalmonEc: grown salmon protein that is supposed to taste like the real thing, but in-stead tastes more like a bear claw snatching it out of a river. The empty tables give him a chance to size up into why their historic chumminess has dwindled to shortchanged conversation. He brings up Wadsworth, he brings up Fantine, he asks if Pamela's typically communicative nature has returned. She responds that Pamela's entire list of interactions have been 'good morning', 'have a good day', 'you got it', and 'I'm fine.'

"You know if she says she's fine that I'm fucked." Amara takes another mouthful of the SalmonEc and washes it back with a gulp of bravery.

"P shouldn't be blaming you. It wasn't your call." Everett moves the grown meat from the left side of the plate to the right as if its position will improve its palatability.

"Well, she's not blaming me. She's not saying a damn thing to me."

"Listen, I get it. It sucks when somebody you love and trust doesn't just tell you what's wrong."

Amara glances up. Everett stares down at his plate.

His delicate and sideways broach has announced his intentions to listen, to be confided in, and her silence is a trembling hand closing the door and latching the lock. "So, what happened with Iván?" Everett asks.

"Iván is seeing me in a way that is unprofessional and really fucking uncomfortable," she answers immediately.

"Yeah, that's tough."

"I mean, do you think made up the whole 'can't speak Spanish' thing to just get me to go out with him?"

"The man told me he was pregnant."

"Okay, fine. But then he starts approaching me about my personal life and actually tried to touch my hand..."

"Was that the first time?"

"Yup. Well, I held his hand in Orev's class, but that was before I flipped him on his back."

"Maybe he's into that kind of thing?"

"Well, that's about all the hand holding I can manage."

"I know," Everett says, reaching out to touch her hand, exaggerated puppy dog eyes aimed at her. "And I want you to know I am here for you."

She pulls her hand back, "You're such a dick."

"I know."

Their phones vibrate simultaneously, then again. Both phones fall into syncopation until they're both forced to review the notifications hammering them. Ringtones echo from every angle. Heads twist and murmurs grow from the few stalwart goers of the cafeteria as Amara and Everett share a moment that they both know they'll remember forever.

The specter of distraction spreads across the office, as phone, tablet, and monitor buzz to life. Media outlet reports on the divisive maneuvers by Governors Hollister and Khatri to embolden their state legislatures toward an attempted secession of Texas and Oklahoma. Various news agencies refer to it as a political stunt, a desperate attempt by Hollister to swing for the White House in the next election, a passing mood that will burn out like so many other movements. Department issued memoranda forbidding direct communication to resources in those two states tells a different story.

On more than one occasion, Captain Darren Franciscus shuts down an argument between personnel before it escalates, but most agents ridicule the idea of the Union fracturing. Amara's experiences in Fort Worth, however, tell her that Austin and Washington are filled with sincere individuals holding substantive goals, and at least one group is willing to commit mass murder as a means to an end. Even if what happened in Texas remains top secret, the resulting policies are apparent to all.

Everett can see her face drained of color, sees her demeanor shift, but she literally turns her shoulder toward him, avoids eye contact with everyone as she fixates on the news feeding in from every direction. An hour passes and she's accomplished nothing but parse the bits of regurgitated news that every hombre with a phone can produce. The bomb is occupying the right side of her brain while the ghosts of Lucas Machado and Hank Taylor wrestle on the left. Then the biggest block of news strikes, and she can no longer sit in her chair: Dyess Air Force Base wing commanders declare their loyalty to Governor Hollister. Some declare it throwing off the shackles of an oppressive government, others call it the first high ranking act of treason since the Civil War.

Amara steps into Darren's office unannounced the minute the news breaks. Her mouth is agape. Darren reads her distress and knows what plagues her mind. "Is...?"

A single word is all she utters as Darren shakes his head slowly to ward off the interrogative portion of the sentence. He rises, gently places a hand on her shoulder, opens the door, and gestures for her to leave. She turns around, desperate to know her place in the world, to know if her saving Dallas has played a part in any of it. She sees Lucas Machado's dead eyes staring at her from across the room. She turns and sidesteps the spirit of Hank Taylor's occupying the center of the hallway. *Stop! Please!* She runs to the lavatory, dashes her face in cold water, her head cleared of nightmares, but her makeup smeared like a mishandled oil painting. She returns to her cubicle, reapplies, and attempts to bury herself back into the investigation.

Orev pops by, drops a file on her desk, announces his retreat for another cigarette. "Shit just got real," he points at the nearest screen. "How long before we start arresting our own people you think? I give it until the weekend."

Another comment from Mitch stirs the pot, and another, and the direction of the country isn't the only point of contention in the office. Pamela's criticism of the BY surveillance snowballed from a passionate disruption to a full-blown argument with Darren during their After-Action-Review. Human Resource alerts ping her inbox with AAR Grievance dispositions. Each chime coincides with a micro-step through the process. Initiated, filed, completed. Supervisory acknowledgment. Supervisory review. Supervisory response. Amara puts her headset on in an attempt to parse the audio files taken from the surveillance, but the occasional recorded comment from Pamela is enough to fracture her concentration. With the headsets off, she is subjected to the news cycle feeding from every desk and coworker, each with competing messages of liberty and unity, each with their unparagoned reputation for journalistic integrity. *I shot them both.*

She turns off her laptop, snatches up her purse and coat, and walks out of the building.

Washington D.C. still pulses with cars and buses, but November rain has tapered foot traffic to only stalwart Washingtonians carrying black umbrellas above their black raincoats. A text message from Pamela is followed by another, then another, but Amara can't bring herself to open them. Instead, she sets her phone on mute and dumps it in her purse. She feels it shuffle and slide to the bottom, doesn't care that it might be easier to dredge the Potomac than dig it out later.

Her escape takes her to Washington Circle where she is able to enjoy the bronze statue without tourists huddled around it in a photographic scrum. It's one of the first statues in DC to have its patina removed permanently, allowing the bronze to shimmer as if it were newly sculpted. A glance at the date amazes her that its endured for almost two hundred years. She thinks of her father sitting near motionless in his chair, wonders if he'll still endure if she fails to find the antidote. The thought ejects her from the circle and further westward.

Amara passes the Embassy to the Mongolian Republic, skirts the edge of Georgetown, passes a group of students engaging in a lively conversation about Texas rednecks and nukes and how they better get out of the city because they love their guns so much. *I almost died in a fiery blast that would have incinerated a hundred thousand of those rednecks. Would any of this be happening if I hadn't found the bomb? Why didn't you listen to me, Hank?*

Restaurants and embassies and apartments and everyone is inside chattering away, their conversation spilling outside only long enough to find shelter from the moistened gloom. She sees Orev's favorite bodega, glances in, unimpressed. An antique camera store has a sale on VHS machines, a technology she has never even heard of. Her curiosity isn't enough to fight the desire to keep moving, and so Amara's pace quickens and she turns south to take the Anita Sabado-Domingo Bridge. The renaming of the bridge from Francis Scott Key sparked what they thought would be changeless division in the city... Little did they know!

Amara knew nothing about this woman, but hated the bridge renaming for far less important reasons... *Who allows their family name to become an entire weekend?*

The cars inching by cast a regular spray into the air that mists her and the other fools that dare go out today, but she's beyond caring. You can only be so wet before you can't be wetter. The view of the Potomac is stunning, even in the rain, even with most of the color fading from the riverfront trees.

How does Pamela not see the larger picture? How can she not understand that BY was their only gateway to Millennial? Would she feel the same had her children been killed by one of Millennial's attacks? Or her husband injected and her life turned upside down? The imaginary confrontation rages in Amara's head. *Sometimes you have to make terrible choices, Pamela. Sometimes there's no right way to handle things.*

Amara's tears flow and she's thankful that they're hidden by the rain, that the average onlooker is gazing down looking for puddles than straight ahead. And now she's walked into Virginia and is on Wilson Boulevard and her pants are soaked and she doesn't care.

Gazing down at her is the crucifix that hangs above the entrance to Saint Charles Borromeo Catholic Church. She feels compelled to enter, despite having to cross the street in the rain, despite the time away. With the exception of her nightmare confession, Amara has not been to church since her sister came to visit, and only then because of Bella's insistence at attending mass in the city.

Amara fidgets with her new spring bladed brass knuckles in her pocket, feels the holster of her Casull pistol against her hip, and worries about sullying the holy house with her weapons. It feels like she is already adding to a long list of sins by merely walking through the door but enters regardless. She shakes her umbrella off and crosses the threshold, double-checking that her holster isn't visible. God may see everything, but there's no reason to share her secrets with mankind. Within the narthex are two older gentlemen donning raincoats, sharing pitiable smiles. They depart with consolatory embraces, leaving her alone to drip on the tile.

"Hello there." The voice comes from behind, and Amara turns to see an unfamiliar priest approaching. His skin is black as coffee, his smile as white as sugar.

"Oh, hi, Father."

"Are you here for confession?" he gestures to the confessional booth.

She glances over her shoulder, sees the wooden door slightly ajar. "I'm going to decline. Can we talk though? Just talk?"

Amara learns Father Akunyili has taken over for Father Gravemore in what sounds like a typical rotation of assignments. His English is pristine and rich with Nigerian accent, and Amara is happy to swim in the tamber of his syllables. He tells her of how he came to the United States for cancer treatment and, after a miracle response, dedicated his life to the church. Amara shares nothing of her background or her profession, only that her dad is ill and she is worried. Father Akunyili prays over her and with her. In the silent moments that follow, she reveals the nightmare of the confession to him, and he offers to meet informally until her comfort level returns to normal. Their conversation lasts less than a half hour, but it is enough to clear the stressors inhabiting her headspace.

The weather lifts for her return from Saint Charles: umbrellas have transformed into walking canes. She hails a cab anyway, finally aware that she's wandered away for over two hours without notifying a soul. When she returns, the lobby squeaks with soggy block heels, the elevator is empty. She returns to her floor and all is quiet: the department is nose-to-the-grindstone, the news is turned off.

Amara plops down into her chair, she looks at the crucifix Bella bought her as a gift and smiles with a moment of joy that has been missing in her life for months, maybe years. A prayer of thanks silently leaves her heart and lifts to the heavens.

Darren walks up behind her and gently places his hand on her chair. "How was church?"

She looks up at him. "Did you track me?"

"You left without checking out. Department policy."

"Oh."

"Feel better?"

"Much."

"That's good. Because Pamela is filing for a transfer."

Chapter 36

Arm wrapped in a sling, face dark with fading bruises, Amara removes the black overcoat that she draped over her shoulders and flings it half-assed onto the coat hook. It barely catches, slips infinitesimally over the plastic ball end, then delivers itself to the floor in a heap. She picks it up, retrieves the funeral service sheet from the pocket and drops it on the table.

Eight days since the news of Texas seceding and Pamela submitting for transfer. Four days since the devil tried to steal her soul. Two days since she was suspended indefinitely. One hour since the funeral, the burial, the scrutinizing glares through tear glazed eyes.

"Otto," Amara clears the rasp from her throat and says, "Michael, Gabriel, Raphael."

*　　*

Our team of four organically developed from the department. Me, Everett, Iván, Orev. A, E, I, O... The running joke was that we were looking for 'U,' but we desperately needed a support agent with any first name. Pamela seemed to fit: old school FBI, levelheaded, married ten years, mother of two, and an honesty that came from experience rather than ignorance. Balancing her family with work threw some small wrenches into the gears, but she showed up and got the job done. She started in the Bureau's Anti-Trafficking Task Force, but confessed she couldn't look at her kids and 'those kids' in the same day. Nobody blamed her. The turnover there was three times the other departments, and seasoned agents would rather transfer to Demolitions than deal with those horrors.

What began with her pervicacious resignation slipped into a tempered-yet-still-unyielding conversation over lunch. She agreed to finish up the month with us at least. I pressed her to reconsider, conceded sadly when she declined. But knowing what happened that night, knowing what I know now, I wish we fired her on the spot.

The five of us engaged in a final spot check of our surveillance gear prior to hitting the road when the van's comm system buzzed.

"A," Pamela called out, "Red line call coming in."

I shook my head and turned my eyes back to our drone rack. "Pipe it over the speaker."

"Team one-niner, 13-71 in progress at SAYACH Corp. Immediate reallocation and response required." The dispatcher's voice sounded human, and although it could have been a synthetic operator, I doubted it. Not on a 13 Code.

I snatched the radio up. "Dispatch, Team one-niner is prepping for assignment. Request reassessment of dispatch."

"A! Get your team, get your gear, load the Demolisher, and move!" Darren boomed through the radio.

I jumped to my feet. Bukum Yilani surveillance was canceled, something none of us expected.

"Okay everyone," I slapped my hands together. "You heard the Cap! The Demolisher takes up a shit ton of space. P, O, E, you'll take the van. We'll go ahead and find out what's going on. Get moving people!"

"Want me to drive?" Iván asked.

"Sure, let's see the new car."

He waved me over to his waiting black Trans Am Retro, pressed his watch, and the doors opened to reveal a shotgun already locked in front console.

Iván spoke to his auto-navigation system, "Kitt, map us to Chapel Avenue, Jersey City, Avoid the Turnpike."

The map appeared on the screen with alternate route available. "Okay, Michael, course is mapped out. Make sure you strap in. Would you like me to drive?"

"Nah, I've got it."

I dropped myself into the passenger seat—comfy, leathery and with that new car smell. The acceleration and handling impressed me, a sports car down to its frame. Once we were moving, the dashboard display faded and a projection of pale guidelines appeared on the windshield. "Michael, I have plotted the optimum route for you to arrive at the SAYACH Corporation in 18 minutes."

"You still haven't renamed your car?"

Iván shrugged, his deep New York voice cut with boyish humility, "I like the show."

"Mis abuelos watched it when they were young. It wasn't good then. It's regurgitated trash."

"You haven't seen the new show. It's clever."

"So, you're keeping its name Kitt."

He shrugged.

"At least change it so it calls you Iván."

"Maybe just let me enjoy my new car?"

"Fine..." I said. In retrospect, my treatment of Iván had been pretty awful ever since the pseudo-date we enjoyed. Maybe because I could still sense his interest in me, maybe because I felt I needed to remind him with every interaction that we couldn't be together the way he wanted. Maybe something else. "So can I call you Michael then?"

"Can you just drop it?"

"Fine..."

I took my phone out and called Darren. He answered, told me to standby, and placed me on hold. I bit my nails, picked my cuticles, watched the traffic build to uncomfortable levels. He had to know we would be missing an opportunity to arrest elements of BY and find out how they funneled explosives to Millennial. The more minutes that ticked by, the fiercer my blood pumped.

Iván's car screamed across three lanes of Interstate 78. We swerved briefly into traffic before jumping into the fire lane. A driver ahead of us—probably a civilian tired of people cutting him off five miles before the exit—swerved over the solid line to run blocker. I hit the lights and wailed the siren for a solid ten seconds—well after the driver pulled back into his own lane and was staring at our taillights.

"I'm sure the Cap knows what he's doing," Iván said, eyes focused on the road.

"Well then, where the hell is he? He ...better not be ordering fucking takeout while I'm-"

"I'm right here, Sergeant. And I'm on speaker." My stomach tightened— 'speaker' meant somebody else was in the office with him.

"Yes, Captain. Sorry, Captain."

"Sergeant James, I am uploading TAC SIT to you now. Active shooter in the SAYACH facility. SWAT en route to the location but is not authorized entry."

SAYACH was a defense contractor that took over the old Department of Army building, and a 13 Code dealt with top secret facilities where, to put it bluntly, loss of life took a backseat to national security concerns. No local police, no Staties, no SWAT—only special operation teams with top secret clearance. Police would secure the perimeter and provide support, but the insertion team had to be a DHD task force, regardless of equipment or experience. Governmental madness.

Darren continued. "9-1-1 call came from Dick Gastrono, a vendor who was filling the soda machine in the lobby about thirty minutes ago. Security doors locked him in and snoop killers kept any cellphone calls from getting out."

"How did he make the call then?"

"He says he punched a hole in the drywall and pulled the vending machine back in place. Said he heard somebody come into the lobby from the interior door but couldn't see anything. When the suspect left, he busted through the drywall on the other side and into an unsecured area."

Clever. Most people panicked in an active shooter situation. Maybe this Dick Gastrono character had a bigger part? Captain Franciscus went on with the anemic details of our mission.

Number of shooters: unknown.

Number of personnel: unknown.

Number of victims: unknown.

Types of weapons used: unknown.

Status of the assailant or assailants: unknown.

Even more concerning, however, was that we had no information from SAYACH on what the facility was used for. Genetic alterations? Advanced weaponry? Robotic Warfare? When I asked, he told me they were looking into it.

"Is this some bullshit clearance issue again? What's the point of having a special response team if you can't trust us?"

"Sergeant James," a softer, calmer voice cut in, "This is Rena Edison of the SAYACH Corporation. You are not being stonewalled, I can assure you. We are doing everything we can to get you the answers you need, but our network has been hacked and all access to our files are down. We're trying to reach anyone who wasn't at the facility when the shooting started."

Rena Edison identified herself as defense attaché and described SAYACH's contributions to the military as running the gamut from anti-jackal software to intelligent body armor.

"Is the hack related to the shooting? Is it Millennial?"

"Possible," Darren replied. "SWAT is deploying sniffers that will feed to your TAC SIT. If there is any indication of explosives, you get your team out *inmediatamente*."

Iván swerved in and out of the dense traffic, racing across the Newark Bay Bridge. I fixed my grip on the oh-shit handle and tried to stay focused on my call while fighting the urge to wrest the steering wheel out of Iván's hands.

Chapter 37

Emergency lights cut the darkness, spinning reds and strobing white-blue agitation behind us cast our shadows in 3-D patterns on the ground. SWAT teams stood by in mild agitation, guarding the outside of SAYACH and flanking our procession to the front doors. Dozens glaring at us, every single one of these professionals thinking exactly what we already knew: we were the least qualified people here to perform this job. Only our clearance placed us higher on the pecking order, and all for reasons we still did not understand.

Pamela remained behind at the command center to orchestrate information funneling out from us to the safe zone and from SAYACH to our team. Our remaining four bookended the Demolisher G44 robot, a central monstrous figure of vaguely human design, and approached the double doors in a V shape. I ripped six hand-length pieces of duct tape off a roll, slapped each onto my right thigh, then tossed the roll to Iván. He did the same thing. Then

Orev, then Everett. Our guns at the ready, we waited for the robotic siege weapon to position itself.

I pointed at the door and said, "Breach."

Orev activated his haptic rings and the robot moved to action. Its machine eyes had already scanned for structural weaknesses using algorithms running a thousand times faster than a human could think to determine the optimum strike point. Two thousand pounds of brutalizing demolition tech swung into action. A battering ram jutted from the robot's lower abdomen, hydraulics jack-hammering the steel phallus a dozen times into the outer door in a perverse assault of the building. Were it not so terrifyingly destructive, it would have been grotesquely comical.

The Demolisher advanced into the main lobby, straining servos screaming to move the mechanical giant. Orev's hands reached out and, in kind, the robot lurched forward, felling the inner doors in a like manner. Responding to human control, it extended its hydraulic arms past us, ten feet, fifteen feet, and tossed the doors into a pile of rent twisted debris.

The hallway open for all to see, I eyeballed the vending machines: each was slightly off kilter—aligning with the vendor witness's escape narrative. In front of me, Iván kept his assault shotgun at a low ready position. Orev kept his X-38 Taser slung as he used the haptic rings to pilot the Demolisher as forward as he dared maneuver. I couldn't see Everett behind me but knew he and his carbine stood ready.

I held my .454 Casull pointed straight up near my temple; the faint unctuous mineral smell still clung to it from this morning's cleaning. My left hand remained free, but my fingers tickled the baton I kept strapped to my thigh.

Millennial. I drew the conclusion from pattern—not obsession. I knew how they thought, how they chose their victims, what they wanted to destroy, eradicate, cremate. Others may have been guessing, performing their due diligence, collecting their data, collating, comparing. I was using my intuition, leaping to where I knew a step would be to capture my conclusion. Their targets held meaning. Cloning facilities that experimented in contagious plagues, data centers used to spy on people, genetics labs that resulted in painful terminal outcomes if Millennial had set their mind to destroy the workings of this facility, it meant that whatever lay beyond these doors held potential to be worse than their destroyers.

I unslung my pack from my shoulder and rolled the softball-sized sphere down the hall. Internal gyros pushed it forward as it bounced gently off the walls, feeding vapor analysis back to the incident command post outside. We waited sixty agonizing seconds for the readouts.

SWAT had deployed sniffers along the outside earlier, and the likelihood of a shooter at this facility having explosives was low, but I couldn't get over the feeling of Millennial's involvement. Pamela radioed us back that the analysis came back negative.

"Vamos," I queued over the open comm, and the four of us stepped from the relative safety of cover behind the Demolisher. A section of the hallway narrowed, jutting from the wall and looking like a Metro attendant station booth. The guard shack must have been made with security glass, as someone or something had smashed the clear surface into opacity, yet nothing managed to break through. And yet the door sat ajar and the security officer lay in a gooey puddle of blood, his holster sat empty.

The hallway dimmed to emergency lighting twenty yards up, and we came upon the body of a woman in a smart business suit beaten so badly that her bloodied skull concaved. Her right knee angled unnaturally. Details that would take up residence in my brain before the day's end.

Double doors stood in front of us. Two short hallways left and right ended in single doors. All three openings appeared security locked with biometric readers, but Iván pointed to the right side of the double door with his shotgun barrel—it appeared just the slightest bit ajar. I stepped around Iván and grabbed the handle gingerly. With the minutest of pressure, I tightened my grip and pulled. The door had not latched. I nodded my head and performed a finger countdown: three, two, one...

I swung the door wide open and stood for a terrifying two seconds as Iván, Everett, and Orev filed past me. No shots, no sounds of struggle, only an 'all clear' from Iván as I pulled one of the strips of duct tape from my pant leg and covered the locking mechanism of the door before letting it slide closed behind me. But it didn't.

Looking down, I saw the crumpled body of another fallen SAYACH employee, positioned just enough to trigger the latch verification light but not actually engage the mechanism. Whoever felled this victim must have assumed the door secure merely by peering up at the light—a level of familiarity with the facility that pointed to the attacker coming from the inside... Exactly how Millennial leveled Innovo Pharmaceuticals.

It had to be Millennial. Professionals, scientists, military personnel, janitors, dock workers. Their numbers were unknown. Their participants diverse. Attacks frequently came from within. Millennial rewarded their ranks with a type of artificial immortality bestowed upon themselves or their loved ones or both. The only quality these terrorists had in common was their goal of stopping specific technological advancement, and by what means they prioritized their targets remained a mystery.

I made a mental note that this third victim had gunshot wounds. The first had been shot, the second beaten, and active threats rarely switched weapon types. From shotgun to semi-auto, sure, but from blunt weapon to gun?

"I'm thinking we have at least two attackers," I spoke low over the comm.

"Was thinking same," Orev said.

We came to the first door, found it open, taped it, and quickly cleared it front to back. Two computers, both smashed open, were missing hard drives. There was a waste can filled with paper and water and stinking of bleach. Everett armed a two-inch motion sensor and flung it against the ceiling. The device strobed a bright green light three times then went dark. If anyone double-backed on us to hide in this room, our little snoop would ping us.

Second, third, fourth room: all came back empty. Fifth and six rooms each held a body, each one bludgeoned to a horrific death. I radioed Pamela and the incident commander outside to keep them abreast of our progress. They had nothing new to report from the perimeter.

"Commander, we still need eyes on the second floor," I reminded him.

"No drones for twenty minutes."

"What's the holdup?"

"Sorry, Sergeant. The equipment van got stuck in the Lincoln Tunnel traffic."

"Pamela?"

"Yes. We've got one launching... Now. We'll have heat and motion in sixty seconds."

We moved on. We had been in here less than three minutes, but each passing second without a confrontation only made me feel that what would come later would be far, far worse.

The hallway elbowed left, then right, then right again. Destroyed documentation was everywhere, and every other room held bodies of SAYACH employees. Some stabbed, some beaten to death. Nine casualties so far and no indication as to how many employees were on shift when the killing spree started. Two more victims in front of a secured elevator brought the tally to eleven, only these were U.S. Army. The military frequently loaned personnel to defense contractors, so how the attackers got the drop on these men we could only guess.

I spoke to the open air over the comm, "Commander, first floor is cleared and tagged. P, anything from the drones?"

"Nothing, Sergeant. Second and third floors are empty. Only four signatures, all matching your transmitters. Floor plans are still unavailable, but we have a lieutenant here who worked here when it was DoA. Says there is an extensive basement level. Drone scans won't penetrate."

Orev and Everett exchanged heavy looks while Iván searched the fallen soldiers. He stood up with two access cards and fanned them out in his hand like playing cards. Orev grabbed one. Iván "They're waiting for us down there," Iván said.

I nodded. "We're splitting up."

"You sure?"

"Yes."

Chapter 38

A pulsing organ of red light staccatoed with lightning flashes of white through the emergency stairwell as soon as I opened the door. The audio aspect of the alarm repeated in alternating Spanish and English to ascend to the next level. I could hear the partnered voice from thirty feet above advising just the opposite, directing any foot traffic to the ground floor.

Iván and I rapidly descended. I took the lead, pulled a flashbang grenade from my belt, armed it, then popped the door slightly ajar. A quick toss and I yanked the door shut. Even when protected and prepared, the concussive wave shook us through the door, and I couldn't help but recall the explosion in the stairwell back in DC.

Iván counted down with three fingers then pointed at the door. I kicked it open wide, expecting—almost hoping—that our targets would be waiting for us.

"*Aquí*," I almost yelled over the comm line while scanning the halls. One extended thirty feet to our left and then bent out of sight. The second ran straight ahead then bent to the left, presumably to loop around. Through the smoke I could see the blackened pattern of the flashbang's detonation on the floor and walls, but no people, no bodies. I reached into my bag and grabbed another sniffer, set it, and rolled—

Two shots rang out, scattering cement fragments right above my head. I looked to my left and saw a man in slacks and a tie spattered in blood not thirty feet away, both arms straight aiming a pistol at my face. Iván body-checked me, aimed his shotgun, and fired. His aim went high and murdered three rows of LED lights.

Three more shots cut the air as we jumped out of the field of fire and into the hallway straight ahead. The elevator doors in front of us opened and I called out, "E! O! Step out now—change of plans!"

Everett poked his head out, saw us pinned to the wall near the corner, his carbine at the ready. Orev followed, close to the wall. I held a fist up, one finger, brought an okay symbol to my wrist, held up my thumb and index finger. *Stop. One target. Armed with a pistol.*

Everett looked down the hallway that bent to the left and signaled he would loop around and flank the gunman. I gave the go ahead and Everett vanished. Iván took the opportunity to launch another flashbang toward the man with the pistol.

We held our ears and opened our mouths, waited for the compressed wave of filtered air to pass us, then followed the explosion with barrels out. No man. No fallen figures. My ears rang and my head ached from back-to-back concussive shocks, and my chest felt tender from the blast force.

"E! Report position!" I called out.

"He went into a secured door between us. Clear the hall."

We turned the corner where the shooter disappeared and saw Everett and Orev standing by a heavy-duty wooden door, card reader to the side and a window opaque from rusted wire mesh. I took a chance and pushed my eye against the glass for just a moment. A tall figure and a shorter figure. I pulled my head away just as the pistol fire spidered the glass.

"I think he's got a kid in there."

"Are you sure?" Everett said.

"No, but we can't get this wrong."

"No flashbangs," Iván warned. "O, you think the taser will make him flinch or bring him down?"

Orev frowned and teetered his hand.

I radioed an update to the incident commander then pointed to the door. "Open it."

Iván reluctantly nodded and tried the prox card we had taken from the dead soldier three times. The light never turned green. I pointed at the doorknob.

Iván flipped the switch on his shotgun from semi-auto to burst, then pulled the trigger. A triple blast from the barrel sent splinters flying and the handle a kilter. Iván drove his massive frame against the door and dropped to a kneeling position as the three of us drew a bead on the bloodied shooter.

White male, maybe late forties, sandy blond hair, face sprayed with dried blood, crouched behind a small boy. The kid had to be nine years old, ten at most, towheaded, eyes wide as saucers. The pistol was pointed at the base of the kid's skull.

"Drop the weapon! Drop it now!"

I could barely make out his words as he shouted against our cacophony of commands, "Get the fuck back! I'll kill him! Back off! Now!"

"E, do you have a shot?"

"Pistol," he mumbled.

The hammer on the pistol was cocked, the man's finger on the trigger. We could have pushed for Orev to take a crack with the taser rifle, shocking the kid and the assailant simultaneously, or for Everett, the best sharpshooter eye on the Eastern Seaboard, to take a shot. But people who are tased or shot sometimes flex their muscles: an unintended trigger pull was likely with either choice.

Departmental doctrine specified that we don't recognize the hostage; you took the kill if available, but we all knew that was bullshit. I knew what it was like to be on the hero side of that coin, but the zero side meant a civilian death hung around your neck forever.

"Back off or I will shoot in three! Two! One..." The man's face twisted in rage and I couldn't be sure if he was calling our bluff: or not. My father would have known. He could have told whether the stranger was blowing smoke up our asses or would be blowing this little boy's brain out.

I was a neophyte with a hunch, a coiled up emotional wreck trying to analyze an unknown person under questionable conditions in a mysterious setting. I looked straight into the shooter's one exposed eye and tried to focus on what I knew. He had killed before, his face exhibited fear mixed with rage. But his grip on the child seemed familiar, as if holding his own son or a money bag or a prized heirloom. The whole picture unsettled me enough to sign his death warrant.

"*Cógelo*," I instructed Everett.

The vulgarity translated into Everett squeezing the trigger with immediate and deadly precision, his carbine battered our eardrums in the tight quarters. My eyelids flinched, and I watched the man slump behind the boy, the red dot on his forehead joining the crater in the back of his skull in the spilling of blood.

"Shooter one is down! Repeat, shooter one is down!" I ran for the gun, disarming the corpse before it struck the ground. I could hear Orev behind me consoling the child, guiding him to the corner and away from the body. Blood pooled unevenly on the linoleum. I kicked him in the groin to make sure he was dead.

"So, who are you?" I whispered to the corpse.

We left Orev with the child while the three of us cleared the rest of the basement. No second shooter ever manifested, most likely escaping before the lockdown. Nearest the main doors and the tightest collection of carnage, one left while one remained behind, but why?

The last basement room stood guarded by a wide steel door with a heavy-duty frame and a security lock that would not budge for any of the recovered ID cards. Even Iván's initial shotgun blasts failed to allow us entry. No window allowed us a peek this time, but the blood splatter and body fallen at the base of the door indicated something of interest within.

Iván loaded a mini drum of his prized magnetic frangible rounds. Everett and I backed up to a safe distance to watch twenty-four slugs vanish in less than five seconds, leaving behind a sunburst opening of smoking shrapnel.

Iván waited for us to join him, then brought his bulk against the portal, breaking through into a room unlike any other in the facility. A stench poisoned the air so thickly that we considered donning breathers before we cleared the room. Sterile lights illuminated an array of Qputiv mainframes tethered like mountain climbers along a steep pass. Each could have provided smart controls for a city, yet a dozen of these often prohibitively expensive computers were dead.

Data drives bobbed in a large, stinking janitorial waste bucket nearby—murdered information. Each one still hissed from their sulfuric bath. The housing units themselves hissed from within, their doors unscrewed and the surfaces doused with sulfuric acid. Hell, someone even severed the thick channels connecting the mainframe units. The sheer cost of destruction had to be enormous.

Across the room lay a hospital bed, complete with IV, ECG readout, and a rigid plastic harness that appeared as if it would wrap around the skull, neck, and back. We encountered similar harnesses in illegal biotech chambers, but this one held all the hallmarks of state-of-the-art tech, hundreds of colored wires, beautiful craftsmanship, meticulous design.

"What is this place?" Everett whispered.

I shook my head. We would need a forensic team in here to even venture a guess to that question.

Chapter 39

We spent the next hour securing technological aspects. Placed lockouts on a dozen pieces of equipment, bag-and-tag on fifteen intact computers, scoured drawers in desks for unknown proprietary items, searched corpses for data straws in pockets or microcards tucked into folded over socks. By the time DHD's forensic team arrived, we completed a third of their prep work. The destruction throughout the facility conducted thoroughly. SAYACH suffered incredible, possibly permanent, loss of research.

Pamela waited for us outside after wrapping up with the DOJ. She sat in the back of an ambulance with the rescued boy, holding his hand, tucking the emergency blanket around him.

"How's he doing, P?"

"He's going to be fine," she said, more for the child than to be truthful. "He's a tough young man. You can see it in his eyes."

Pamela had two boys at home, four and seven, and she brought all her maternal nurturing to the table for this kid.

What was he doing in a classified defense contractor building? Was it Bring-your-kid-to-super-secret-work Day? I grabbed the closest paramedic. "Any ID on him yet?"

"Nothing," he shrugged. "He's not talking and doesn't have a Know-Me chip. You guys will have to run DNA, retinals, or prints."

"You can't?"

"The network is hairy. Another cyberattack has everything running spotty."

A lot of kids came chipped these days, a not-so-simple solution to the burgeoning abductions nationwide. RFID readers at gas stations, supermarkets, and toll booths rolled out patchwork across the country as government incentives made costly equipment almost desirable, but less than five percent of targeted locations had jumped on board so far.

The Know-Me program was a banshee in the Texan Separatist manifesto, used by Governor Hollister to highlight the overreach of government. Initially mandated for newborns—the government now merely recommended its usage for children over twelve months old. This kid looked nine-ish. He likely hadn't been implanted, and Texans weren't the only ones opposed to such measures. Had he grown up in New Hampshire's libertarian alcoves or Carolina's blue dog backwaters, he might not even be in any database.

I called for an ID tech from DHD to help us out. Twenty-four years old, four foot eleven, and all too enthusiastic for a mass murder scene, Hailey Commich had sprung out of the academy plastered with permasmile, ready to make the world a better place. We called her Hailey Comet. She blew over to us like a bubble with her backpack, pulled out the palm reader, and knelt at the boy.

"Hi there, kiddo," she beamed, pulling the slick plastic device from her bag and dangling it playfully from its lanyard. "You want to play a cool game? This is a palm scanner. Just put your hand right here and it plays music!"

Hailey made a gentle play for the kid's hand, but he wouldn't have any of it.

"Oh, don't worry, buddy," she sang, "It won't hurt you. Look." Hailey pressed the button on the side and the ivory surface lit up, casting an almost magical light on her smiling cheeks. She then placed her own palm over the reader, waited for it to glow sky blue, and then showed the boy the bottom readout. There in perfect color showed Hailey Commich's DHD image next to her credentials.

The demonstration seemed friendly enough, but the boy shrank to the back of the ambulance and curled up on the gurney. Pamela crawled in after the child to console him. I guided Hailey away, disappointment a rare state for her.

"Well, shucks!" she said.

I wanted to ask her who in her life was cruel enough to teach her the word 'shucks.' "We'll just put a pin in that one," I told her. "Any word on our shooter?"

Hailey paged through her slate before stopping on an image of the man who held the child hostage. "Jackson P. Serfass, fifty-five, lives in Hoboken, married, holds two addresses so my guess he's got a vacation home..."

"Or he's separated or divorced or cheats on his wife."

She grinned, "...Working for SAYACH Corporation for just shy of twenty years, holds a T.S. clearance with the DoD, PhD in Neuroengineering... I don't even know what that is... Uhh, had an assault charge four years ago that was dropped, an aggravated assault charge that was also dropped three years ago, five moving violations in the last seven years, and two outstanding parking tickets."

The shooter finally had a name. I watched them load Serfass' body into an ambulance and bit at a hangnail. "Any indication what the assaults were? Domestics?"

Hailey strummed her slate for a few seconds, "Simple assault was his wife, who dropped the charges three days later. The aggravated assault was against a Jonathan Vantucci, looks like he might have been a neighbor. Vantucci accused Serfass of beating him with a baseball bat, put him in the hospital for three weeks. They arrested Serfass, who posted bail: four weeks later the charges were dropped."

"Get me a last-known for Vantucci."

She scrolled, paused, then read on, "Vantucci... died yesterday. Jersey City PD posted it as a robbery gone wrong this morning. Cause of death..." She looked up at me and raised her eyebrows. "Most likely beaten to death with a baseball bat or pipe."

"Get digging."

Franciscus called in and told Everett to report to the field office in New York City—standard practice after a kill. I waved over the team for a huddle. "Pam's in the ambulance with the kid. He's taken to her, so I want her to ride with him. Maybe he'll open up. Everett, you're heading to Midtown..."

Iván had turned away, his attention on the media drones that descended upon the parking lot in a veritable swarm. Police deployed buoys to delineate where they could and could not cross, net-gunning any that violated the boundaries.

"Hey! Hey, Iván!" I snapped, spinning him around. "Thanks for paying attention."

"I'm listening," he sneered. "I can do two things at once, you know."

"All right, Knight Rider, show off your multi-tasking on the way to New York. You're interviewing the witness Dick Gastrono and you're Everett's ride before you both go for debriefing. Orev and I will follow the ambulance to the hospital in the van and we'll catch up with you after we I.D. the boy."

Chapter 40

New Jersey traffic qualifies as the sixth fundamental force of the universe and the least understood. I sat in the passenger seat of the van, Orev drumming his fingers on the steering wheel as the waves of cars oscillated along the state route, haptic rings still worn, occasionally adding a distinctive rhythm to the song. I imagined what the roadway looked like from above, a giant inch worm rippling along, with various portions moving and gripping the pocked asphalt.

Two trikes next to us sat side by side, not quite fitting into the narrow lane as the drivers jockeyed for who would get six inches closer to the flatbed in front of them. Orev and I watched in mild amusement as the two screamed at each other for roadway dominance. The guy on the left screamed out a long string of Spanish profanities which summoned the bird from the guy on the right.

Orev and I exchanged disgusted looks before he put the window down and blipped the siren. They both looked over and Orev held up his badge. "Hey, shut the fuck up or I'll dump your shit trikes off the fucking bridge! You hear me?" Orev's thick Israeli accent must have thrown Left Guy for a spin because he fell into silence with a confused stare. Right Guy couldn't get it through his skull though and jumped out of his trike.

"Hey, officer, what did I do? Hey, what did I do? Hey, officer! Hey! I'm asking what did I do? Hey...!" Right Guy stood there, hands up in a giant Y with his fingers wide open, gums flapping in obnoxious repetition.

Orev shook his head and rolled up the window, but we could still hear Right Guy shouting "*What did I do?*"

"E won't be the only one who shoots somebody today," Orev growled.

"Please don't. I can't do anymore write-ups." I laughed and turned away, staring at the side mirror and the line of headlights behind us, hoping Pamela had made some headway with the boy. I fought the temptation of calling her, not wanting to interrupt any momentum she built in her work with the child.

A set of headlights broke from the queue behind us and charged up the fire lane. The driver had to know the lane would disappear in a hundred feet and they would be forced to merge into a line of disgruntled commuters, but the car pushed onward anyway. It didn't surprise me—this was Jersey after all.

But it did not slow. This guy had to know every car behind us and in front of us had no room to maneuver. Hell, the ambulance with lights on moved ten yards in ten minutes. A motorcycle could barely maneuver between the bumpers and nobody could accommodate him cutting the rest of the drivers off even if they wanted to. But this driver sped up, filling up the emergency lane with brights now piercing the dark.

The car flew forward past murderous looks, blaring horns, and wagging middle fingers. Our van's active safety system sensed an imminent collision and jerked forward as far as the program could take it, but it couldn't reconcile striking the ambulance in front of us and avoiding the crushing blow from behind.

An explosion of dusty white slapped me across the face. My ribs compressed in a painful blow. The world vanished from sight as the airbag stretched out in every direction. When the pressure loosened, Orev's curses replaced the sickening shock wave of plastic and metal crumpling. In my disoriented state, I somehow realized my seat now inclined unnaturally forward, even if only a few degrees.

I heard Orev struggling and a sound like a sweaty body sliding onto a leather sofa. I grabbed my brass knuckle rings, locked the three-inch blade in place, and cut at the curtain airbag along the door. Beneath the sound of honking horns, I heard footfalls—two or three sets—that stopped at the passenger van door. My door. Someone yanked on the handle and access to my stunned body swung open. I heard two rounds go off, one of which certainly connected and struck me in the back. I ducked as low as I could only to find someone prying the door open to drag me out.

I've never seen red when angered—what I do see is a tunnel, closing in on all sides, and my target stands in my way, foiling my attempt to leave, to escape, to survive, to gasp for breath. Their purpose mattered little to me: their intention to stop me is all the information I needed to react. This would not be the end, some shitty stretch of Jersey highway is where my sister would lay a wreath, only to have it covered in litter and dust and mud. With only an inkling of awareness, I saw a pistol within arm's reach. My vision still blurred from concussion, I managed to grab hold of a wrist. I unsheathed my baton with my left hand and swung upward in a wild arc. A bone-cracking connection was followed by unintelligible curses.

Dizziness pulled me downward, but instead of allowing it to conquer me, I dropped to the ground, planted my elbows, spun, swept my leg out, and connected with a set of ankles before a desperate kick from the second man knocked me onto my back. I heard the gunman hit the ground, semiautomatic pistol still in his hands. I spun on my ass, wedged his arm in between my thighs in an *omoplata* submission hold and bent his forearm obliquely. The pistol fell, but I continued to apply pressure until I felt his bone snap.

Three pops of gunfire went off followed by a gasp-stealing triple punch to my solar plexus. I doubled over, gripping my chest reflexively, releasing the man's broken arm. He wailed even louder now, detangling from our scrapping. I traced the edges of my liquid armor vest in a panicked check. They came away slippery... Dead center over my heart. I dug desperately to figure out if I was hit, then realized that the second shooter managed to nail his friend through the arm, adding his inept insult to my purposeful injury. The entirety of my upper torso ached, but my vest (and the assailant's forearm) absorbed all three shots.

I reached for my holster and my fingers found the snap undone and my pistol missing. Lost in the collision? On the ground? As I glanced around, the (mis)shooter grabbed his buddy by the collar, speaking apologetically in a language I didn't understand. The man whose wrist I'd broken with the baton refocused on me and grabbed for his fallen pistol with his uninjured hand. I swept my dropped baton up and brought it across his gun before he could manage a solid grip, loosing the weapon from him for the second time. The whir of my weapon cutting the air ended with twig-smashing his already busted knuckles in the process.

My gun was gone. His gun was mine. I snatched it up, fired three shots at point blank range, ended one variable, then turned to see the remaining two men who ambushed us scurrying away. I aimed the pistol—a Glock was my first guess—and fired, kept firing, the rounds either striking ineffectually or missing. The register on the gun froze open as I watched the injured man collapse two dozen yards from me in dead weight and his would-be rescuer disappear behind an SUV.

Another handful of shots came from Orev's side of the van. A battery of shots fired in return. Yelling. Screams from nearby cars. More snaps from around the ambulance. Somebody called out "Where is he?" and I flattened myself to the ground.

My comm chirped and Pamela's excited voice transmitted, "242, Dispatch! Officers down! Officers down! I-78 northbound, north of Jersey City! Agents in contact, multiple assailants!" So loud, giving my position away...

The dispatcher gave a calm response that backup was on the way. Crouching at our crumpled van, I winced in pain as my shoulder connected with the undercarriage. I flattened out and shuffled along on my stomach. A set of running shoes came into view, shuffled, dug in, bent, then sprang—the choreography of exchanged gunfire. His shoes vanished from sight for a moment, then reappeared with his bleeding body. Glazed eyes staring right at me, he held his throat, a futile attempt to hold back the pulsing river that poured between his fingers. As his breathing shallowed, I slid out from underneath, sheathed my baton, and opened the driver door.

Orev sat surrounded by airbags, pistol in his grip, register wide open. "Fucking Russians caught my leg!"

I looked at his thigh. "Yup, right past the armor. Shit."

I grabbed the med kit from between the seats and tourniquet his leg as best I could before gunfire struck the driver's door, inches from my body.

"You're good. Stay here and call in for support. You have extra ammo?"

He felt his empty holster, looked around, and shook his head. "It's all in the back."

One glance at the van told me I wasn't getting back there without a crowbar. "You see somebody, comm me." I ducked away in search of the fifth shooter, not knowing if a sixth or seventh lingered behind, or if the third returned. I radioed Pamela as I ducked and moved to the trike beside us, "P, status?"

"Pinned inside the ambulance! Gunfire from outside. Driver is critical, paramedic unconscious, low on ammo."

The ambulance perched on the edge of the overpass. The passenger door opened to a twenty-foot drop, and the twisted back doors—even if they could open—were blocked by the front of our van. One tiny window in the back looked broken, the doors pocked with bullet holes. I could see movement inside, no idea if it was the boy or P or neither.

I followed the sound of a man's unintelligible voice. Peeking through the broken window of the trike, I could see he was maybe ten feet away with what was maybe an Agram 3000 in his grip.

"P, fire a shot," I whispered.

"I've got two rounds, A. Here's one of them."

I took two deep breaths and scurried around the tapered back of the trike. Seconds stretched until Pamela's first shot rang out. The shooter ducked, fired a burst toward the wrecked ambulance, then dropped down once more after P's second shot. I sprinted around the back, and he turned toward me a moment too late.

I grabbed his weapon in my left hand and slashed the brass knuckle blade on my right across his thigh. He pulled back and yanked the submachine gun from my blood-slicked grip—I had no idea where I'd injured my hand, but the blood was definitely mine. I shoved hard against the weapon, driving the butt into his chest, then swept his feet from the right. I drove my body forward again as he fell, pushing my fist upward as we fell together.

I hugged the weapon with my whole body, pointing the muzzle perpendicular as I elbowed him repeatedly in the ribs. His grip refused to yield, even after we both hit the ground. His knee smashed me in the neck, then bent me off of him with ease. One punch, two punches to the face—he only hit me in the forehead, but it still managed to rock my consciousness like nobody had ever done before.

Dazed, dizzied, I loosened my hold on the weapon, but somehow maintained a single lucid thought, knowing he would try to jerk it free. When he did, I craned my neck forward and bit down hard on his forearm. He screamed and thrashed. Even when he let go of the weapon, I continued to clamp down until his flesh separated from his body into my mouth and both his arms windmilled free.

He bludgeoned my skull with rapid blows before pulling back on my hair. I obliged, brought both arms in tightly, spitting the chunk of meat out of my mouth into his face before driving my blade sharply up his abdomen. He thrashed and spattered and flailed but strength poured from him and onto the oily asphalt. Heavy, so heavy his body became, thrashing living hatred becoming dead weight collapsing at my feet.

Footfalls came from the ambulance and I saw Pamela running away from the fight and carrying the boy in her arms. How she pried the door open was unknown, but she was now out of the ambulance and running forward, away from the fight. The boy wriggled like a fish desperate to return to water.

"Move! Move!" I heard Orev's voice on the comm.

Bullets ricocheted as the third shooter returned. I dropped and rolled until I was able to jump over one of the trikes towards the edge of the overpass, smashing into the cement and steel guard rail on the opposite side of the highway. I grabbed the rail as best I could and swung my whole body over to dangle 25 feet in the air.

The fall would certainly break my legs—and that was the best-case scenario. My left grip was failing, my own life force betraying me with a slippery end, and my right grip was weakened from both injury and carrying the brass knuckle blade. The shooter approached, weapon swinging. The laser sight zigzagged along the asphalt before catching me in my left eye.

Then rending metal cut the air.

Our van was split asunder as the Demolisher spread its arms and lengthened its legs, hatching from the van in a violent mechanical birth. Once dislodged, it grabbed the closest trike, lifted it high in the air, and launched it towards the gunman. He fired a dozen ineffective plinks at the Demolisher but remained in place. Perhaps out of fear, perhaps not understanding the gravity of his decision.

The trike arced with deadly precision, crushing the shooter, then bounced—dear God, it actually bounced—and continued toward me. I swung my legs up, hooked the guard rail with my ankle, and fell back onto the overpass as the mangled trike struck where I dangled a second ago, then plummeted off the overpass.

I scanned the area, hoping nobody was dumb enough to remain in their car during the attack with the hopes of streaming the latest act of police brutality on social media. I glimpsed O's hands waving in the crumpled cab of the van, then another gunman appeared, moving toward the boy and Pamela. I would never catch him.

Orev, however, maneuvered the siege robot, then extended its right arm on hydraulic pistons, one, two, three meters, and snatched the armed attacker from the road. The arm retracted with gasping howls bellowing from the captive stranger. Drawn to the mechanical torso, I watched the robot's left arm grab the man's lower half and then both claws pulled in opposite directions. Legs and hips separated midair from his torso as each half slapped against wrecked cars in slickly wet thuds.

I ran to the upper remains, pried the submachine gun from his death grip and popped the clip. At least two rounds, probably more. I popped it back and ran toward the car that rammed us. The laser sight dot bounced across the empty seats and closed doors. Up the fire lane I could see a second car zipping backwards, too far away to target and too fast to chase. They'd abandoned the hit, leaving us all worse for the wear.

Once backup arrived and emergency matters were tended to, I returned to the van. The entire attack lasted maybe four minutes. It felt like thirty seconds. Or an hour. I searched for my Casull and found it underneath one of the dead assailants, new scuff marks to add to its battle scars. I checked the safety and slipped it into my holster and secured my weapon.

I climbed out of the cab and, surveying the carnage, tried mentally sorting the order of events for a debriefing with Darren—and ways to spin how I let everything fly sideways so quickly. I wiped tears on my newly bandaged hand, giggled and wept simultaneously, and braced for the shit storm I knew headed our way.

Chapter 41

Surrounded by the muffled, sterile, brightly lit environment, I bounced on my toes and paced a path into the linoleum. The physician assistant admonished me several times to breathe, relax, and sit still while he took my blood pressure.

"Did you get punched in the mouth?" he asked, pointing to my face.

I looked in the mirror, dried blood on my cheeks and chin. "Yeah, but the blood is somebody else's."

"Did you bite somebody?"

I nodded vigorously. "It's been a crazy night, bro."

"You're in shock, Agent," he said. "I recommend relaxing, maybe lying down."

"I feel fine!"

"That's euphoria. Don't confuse this with being well. You're pretty chewed up. I'm going to order a scan and a triple H panel since you've been exposed to a lot of someone else's blood."

The PA told me to lay down on the bed, but my legs shook and fingers twitched. I bounced off the bed and flipped the curtain away. The people behind the counter barely acknowledged me leaving my room, and I texted the team to find out where they were.

Iván responded first. Dick Gastrono, Mr. Vending Machine hero, checked out. His story matched with everything we knew and nothing we didn't. They released him with the caveat to not go too far in any direction. Iván asked how we were doing.

"We're alive, standby."

Orev lay in the hospital bed, healthy leg hanging over the edge while elevating his bandaged thigh. I caught Darren in the midst of a tirade. "... And now a Mister Devick Franklin said you threatened to throw his trike off the bridge, then shot at him, and then you actually hurled his trike by throwing it off the overpass with your DHD assigned robot. How are you going to defend that?"

"You weren't there! You didn't get shot in the leg by some piss-faced Russian mafia abortion! You were riding in a fucking limo with that SAYACH whore while I was bleeding in that shitty van you got for us, you cheap fucking bastard!"

"You ripped the van in half! You ripped a *man* in half! Do you know what Transworld News will do with our balls once they've put them on display?"

I mockingly wagged my finger at Orev, "This is why we don't have nice things..."

"*Yo brego contigo horita*, Amara." Darren shot me a look to get out, then turned back to Orev. His voice turned from anger to frustration. "You can't keep on wrecking our stuff. This might fly in the IDF, but this isn't Israel. We don't have the budget to deal with your recklessness..."

I spun around, snapped my fingers with a little wink, and sashayed out of the room, bumping a cart with my hips like it was my dance partner. That silly little maneuver did wake me up to how much everything hurt. My left hip felt bruised as well as the small of my back. The red patches on my forearms would undoubtedly purple in the next couple hours. With the heavy liquid armor vest off, I poked myself to see how badly the bullet strikes got me—pretty much everywhere felt tender.

My phone battery signaled it was low, so I dumped it in a charging basket at the nurse's desk before heading to the private room from where Pamela messaged me. A State Trooper guarded the door: I flashed my badge and went in to find Pamela consoling the child. He cowered away from a rather distraught looking nurse gripping her wrist.

"Everything okay?" I asked her.

"Your mystery boy here bit me while I took his DNA swab."

"I bite people all the time. Don't take it personally." Despite my mouth covered in blood, my joke fell flat. I looked over at the boy, now snuggled into Pamela's bosom, eyes fiery as he glared at the nurse. I turned to her. "Anything on the palm scanner?"

She shook her head, "This boy is not in the database, I can tell you that. Not even a partial match. No prints, no bioheat sigs. My guess is he's international."

"How long for the DNA swab?"

"An hour at the most."

"We need any results as they come in, please. Relatives, last knowns, anything. Don't wait to button up the report."

"I'll deliver it stat by drone right now. It will leave within the minute. In-flight time to the lab is... I'd say seven minutes tops. Fast enough for you?"

I signed the nurse's slate and fingered in my authorization code for the tests, then—as a precaution—I put Hailey as a secondary contact. Hopefully she'd be able to cross reference with her own searches to point us in the right direction.

With the nurse departed, I crouched next to Pamela and reached out for the boy. He cowered, so I left some distance. I looked to Pamela whose wide eyes focused on me. "You're in a freakishly good mood. Did you get hit in the head?"

"Multiple times. Doctor said something about euphoria. I don't know."

"Well, aren't you the life of the party."

"I'm just glad we're all alive."

"Orev okay?"

"Well enough to be arguing with the captain."

She shook her head, "Glad you two are doing so well."

Her despondence echoed in her voice, and for the first time walking in, I saw Pamela was legitimately shook. I sat beside her, took a deep breath, and tried to mellow. "How are you holding up?"

"That was really scary, Amara. I'm not going to lie."

"I was scared too. Honest. I know I don't look scared, but this is me coping. Are you hurt at all? You? The boy?"

"Fine," she frowned, "Mac is fine too."

"Mac? He told you his name?"

"No, but I couldn't keep calling him 'boy', and he seems to respond to Mac. Don't you, Mac?"

The boy glanced from her to me then retreated further into Pamela's bosom. I noticed a bandage on her neck. "What's this from?" I asked.

"Cut myself on the ambulance door. Stupid. I'll probably be in pain tomorrow, but nothing a box of wine can't fix. Any ideas about who or why?"

I shook my head.

"How's the ambulance driver?"

The bullet meant for Pamela cut through his shoulder. Should have been an easy patch-up job in the ER, but bullets are finicky—hell, they're goddamned magical at times. They turn, they fragment, they tumble. Once they hit a target, it's a coin toss to see if they actually do what you want them to do. In the case of our ambulance driver... "Bullet struck his shoulder blade, bounced southward and cut an artery."

Pamela frowned again and shook her head. "I'm sorry about the transfer request. It's just... This job isn't what I expected."

"I know. And I'm sorry. If it will change your mind, after tonight, I don't think we'll be in the field for a while." We stood there for a pregnant moment as she stroked the boy's hair gently. I tried to talk lower to keep from upsetting our new guest, "Orev thinks they were Russian mafia. I couldn't tell if they were targeting...."

"Why...?" Pamela let her gaze linger on Mac for a long second.

I shrugged.

If I had to lay odds, I'd put Russians finishing up the hit job started at SAYACH. But the total tech destruction ran contrary to a mob job—it screamed Millennial. Too damned little intel on a case that for all accounts should have a lot more answers.

The hospital shook with a violence known only to earthquakes. And explosives. Lights flickered before returning to a fraction of their previous luminosity. Worse, the floor tilted—barely perceptible, but it still meant a massive force shifted the footing of an entire hospital. The boy looked to me and then Pamela and then jumped to his feet in a bolt. We scrambled to nab him before he made it to the doorway. Fire alarms blazed across the hospital floor and the building lurched again.

"A, we have a detonation in the lower level," Darren's voice thundered in my ear. "I've got O and we are heading for the stairwell."

"I've got P and the victim," I responded. "Right behind you."

Pamela grabbed the boy by the scruff and guided him down the hallway, "Come on, come on, nothing to worry about... Just a small change of scenery. We're going to have some fun and take the staircase, okay? You want to race Amara down the staircase?"

Mac stared at P like she had gone insane. I snagged my phone on the way out, stuffed it in my pocket, and then put my elbow out in front of me to form the tip of a wedge to escape.

The hallway quickly filled with nurses and doctors moving patients to lower, presumably safer, ground. We literally ran into Captain Franciscus assisting Orev into the stairwell, knocked shoulders with a dozen blurring figures, and practically rappelled to the ground floor. The sprint down three flights of steps made my ribs ache—the left side acutely bad. Sirens filled the air, mixing with multilingual automated messages.

I glanced back to see smoke curling up from the ambulance bay and a donut of cement dust billowing outward.

Metal groaned in answer to concrete's bellowing protests, the hospital's death rattle. Fissures ran up the hospital's main structure, starting at the epicenter and extending out like lightning.

Personnel heroically filed patients and employees into groups according to emergency designations a safe distance from the building. As we reached the parking lot, I found the nurse who took Mac's swab and hook-armed her as she headed back into the building. "Tell me you sent the DNA swab!"

"Are you kidding me right now?"

"Did you send it?" I yelled.

She shook me off and backed away, "Yes, I sent your damned test! Now help us!"

We fled with all the others.

"Somebody wants this kid dead," I managed to puff out to the captain as we continued to run.

"I'm starting to get that impression," he pointed toward the east parking lot. "I'm in the valet section. I'll get Orev clear of here then come back to assist. You head to the communals, get the kid to the safehouse in Edison."

"Can't we take him to the office?"

"Do you see what they did to the hospital?"

"How about an Army post?"

Darren shook his head, then reached into his wallet and pulled out a business card for a urology office. "This is the address."

"I've never been there."

"It's okay," he assured. "The door is a heavy bastard, but it will take a rocket launcher to get through it. Get there. Stay there. Radio silence on the road."

I nodded, guided Pamela and Mac to the communals: two-seater automated self-driving cars with trunks barely big enough for grocery bags, used and abused by anyone with a credit account. We scanned the green lights on the dashboards to indicate availability. The ocean of green lights slowly winked to red as staff and visitors sought ways home.

I waved my creds in front of two available communals: the lights turned from green to red to blue. Blue always meant government usage and the auto companies billed the feds later at a premium. Pamela opened the door and ushered the kid in.

"Where are we going?"

I grabbed a pen and wrote the address on her palm. "Dogleg to at least two destinations in the auto's mapping before you hit the safehouse, okay?"

"Got it," she nodded with a nervousness I had never heard from her before. "No problem. No gun either, but whatever."

"Wait. What?"

"I checked it in the holding locker. The clerk said—"

"*Puñeta*, no... Never listen to those people. You can't... Fuck."

We looked back at the smoke and dust from the hospital, watched the numbers in the parking lot grow. Panic festered in every direction, but then there were others who walked casually, who stood having conversations in the shadows where their faces and intentions couldn't be read.

I drew my Casull from under my arm and handed it to her with two clips from my cargo pocket. "I know it's not department kosher, but there isn't a lot of time to screw around, so take it."

She nodded.

"P, you've got this. Okay?"

"I know."

"I'll be right behind you. Hell, I'll probably be there before you."

"Okay." Pamela looked at her phone, a screenshot of her kids.

"Don't make any calls home right now. Radio silence 'til you get there. Then use cells only to stay in touch with the comm center and me and the Cap. You good?" I gripped her by the shoulders—I couldn't manage the hug, even to assuage her fears, even here in this moment.

Pamela gave me a shallow nod. Just as her eyes became glassy, she switched to beaming mom filled with adventure: "Hey Mac, you ready for a fun trip? We're going to be spies..."

Her voice trailed off as she climbed into the communal and rode away. I followed seconds after, joining a caterpillar of communals making a peristaltic crawl to the main road before our automated rides diverged under separate navigational instructions.

Chapter 42

I spent more time staring in the rearview than the windshield, focusing on headlights through misted glass and failing to discern which—if any—followed me to my first stop. I parked at a defunct strip mall in Hillside, spying through cycling blasts from the rear wiper jets clearing the rain away. A car behind me slowed, then continued along US-22 at a snail's pace.

Maybe they were lost? Maybe they were gang members looking for a score? Maybe I was followed? I applied a new navigation point, closer to Edison but still far enough from the safehouse. My communal's electric motor pitched high as it sped up and turned me onto the Garden State Parkway, eventually kicking me out near the golf course. Local PD called it Yellow Acres after squatters took up residence on the green and turned it into a shantytown. We had to interview a homeless woman there once who swore she found a Millennial crypt, but her lead turned out to be a dead end.

As I pulled into Yellow Acres, the familiarity was eclipsed by fatigue, injury, solitude, and me armed with a blade instead of a pistol. Only shadows and flapping aluminum panels resided here now. The bulk of the structures lay flattened by bulldozers, a pathetic end to a final refuge for social outcasts and self-inflicted homeless. I half-wished to be surrounded by gutter punks off their meds, stumbling out of their rickety huts and twitching for a fix—at least there would be witnesses. The wish turned to trepidation as headlights followed me into Yellow Acres.

"667, Dispatch, 10-24 agent in distress," I blurted into my radio. "Morris Ave, abandoned golf course! Request backup!"

"Dispatch, 667 say position again."

The vehicle's lights filled up the night, and I jumped out of my tiny death trap before I could respond. It was the same car I spied at the strip mall. I made a quick turn behind a tree. Their doors opened and I ran. I managed to fit my brass knuckles on my hand—blade closed this time—and sprinted into the ruined shantytown.

Footfalls, two sets, maybe three, followed. I cast myself away from their headlights, hoping I could catch a visual. No gunfire, no sound of weapons actuating. I figured somebody should have shot at me, unless they wanted a clean kill with no stray bullets.

A furtive glance revealed there were two of them. I allowed the footfalls to catch up. Then, reaching out my bandaged hand, I grasped a young tree, swung around its narrow trunk, and landed behind one of my pursuers with fist raised. He never had time to turn as my knuckledusters connected with the back of his head. His arms went limp on the way down, but I swept my foot along his path to assist his connection with the ground.

When the second figure was close enough, I flicked the blade open, grabbed his wrist with my free hand, and drove the tip into the center of the palm. Muscles twisted in resistance, pressing back against my blow, his body torquing. But momentum was on my side. The steel spread flesh and curved bone apart, parting the center of his hand until the razor-sharp edge met resistance. Metal reached sapwood of a large tree, crucifying the hand that reached for me.

He screamed and his free hand grabbed my hair. Yanked me askew, landed his knee solidly into my spine. I heard—felt—a sharp snap as my body fell, my weight pulling the blade from his impaled palm, dragging a trench of blood along his forearm. The two of us landed in a heap of plywood, my ribs and breasts making contact with a rusty sharpness that I hoped to God didn't puncture too deeply.

"Amara!" I ignored him and spun to get on my feet. A nail penetrated my boot and, while I never felt it, it stuck me to a piece of plywood long enough for him to land a brutal kick to my abdomen and collapsed me.

He approached, one hand bloody and open in a sign of peace, the other hand concealing something in the darkness.

"Just wait," he said, familiarity of his voice growing.

"Studious Stanley?" I pointed the blade with a shaking, feebled arm. "Why didn't you just say it was you?"

He looked different enough from the last time I saw him that I might not have recognized him on the street. Cheeks were fatter, eyebrows bushier, but the voice was the same. Shaggy hair, suit twenty years out of style with narrow lapels and thin tie, handlebar mustache sculpted with too-modern accuracy, the man I called Stanley squeezed his hand into his armpit as his face wrinkled in pain. "I couldn't let my colleague know we knew each other."

"Why aren't you worried now, then?"

Stanley gestured and I saw his colleague's body twitch slightly, face buried in the leaves, hands palm up.

"So, no gun today?"

"Don't need it. I'm lined head to toe," he answered, holding up a hand trigger. "If I set it off, they'll be swabbing what's left of us out of the tree bark."

"Then why haven't you? Do it. You, me, and your bitch boy can die together, if he's still alive that is." I'm fairly convinced I said 'ditch doy' in my fatigue but couldn't bring myself to correct the retort.

He spoke slowly, "I need the boy. We lost him but found you. Quite by accident, actually."

"Why do you need the boy?"

"We're going to kill him."

"And if I don't tell you where he is?"

"I don't want to kill you."

"You seemed pretty determined tonight at the hospital."

"Unfortunate, but necessary."

"And on the highway."

He laughed. "That was the Russians. They were trying to save the boy. Trust me, when you find out what he is, you'll want him dead too."

"Doubt it. I'm not in the habit of blowing up hospitals or murdering children." A long pause grew. "He's just a kid. He had nothing to do with whatever SAYACH was working on."

"Exactly how do you know that? Have you identified the child yet? Figured out who his parents are? Determined why he was there? What do you really know, Sergeant Agent Amara James?"

"I know I radioed for backup right before I got out of the car. Tell me what's going on now or you're going to be in a world of hurt when my friends realize you're with Millennial."

"We'll both be dead long before that happens." Studious Stanley looked around. "That boy represents the first Whole Brain Emulation. Cloned by SAYACH, raised in a lab, mind wiped and replaced by a copy of the consciousness of his creator. Too bad SAYACH didn't realize their lead scientist is a pathological murderer who sold his secret of immortality to the Russians."

Doctor Jackson Serfass. The man who killed every single one of his researchers and destroyed every hard drive in a top-secret facility, invented a new technology that allowed a mind to be uploaded to a different body? Ten years ago, I would have shrugged it off as preposterous. But...

"That 'child' represents the first step towards the end of humanity as we know it, Amara. The rich and powerful who control this technology will retain immortal lives, create dynasties without end, and the world will bend to their rule."

I reached for my mic and felt the pieces of my radio held loosely together by the wiring within. The blow to my back destroyed it, and I was left once again with the cell. I fished my phone out of my pocket, battery at three percent, and called Comet.

"Commich here, go ahead Sergeant."

My ribs ached, but I mustered, "Comet, you get a response on our SAYACH boy?"

"Yeah. Not what I expected. The DNA returns back to Doctor Serfass."

"He's his son?" I asked.

"No. I mean the DNA is identical. The boy is a genetic match for Serfass. I thought cloning was illegal..."

My eyes drew to Stanley's. The DNA match didn't confirm everything he said, but it confirmed enough. "Comet, listen carefully. My radio is busted and I am almost out of juice on the cell. I need you to get a hold of the captain and get somebody over to the safe house in Edison. Pamela's in danger. Got it?"

I waited for her response then saw the blank screen of my phone. "Oh, you've got to be kidding me! Fuck!" I screamed, lifting myself to my feet and stumbling into a bush before regaining my balance. I held out my hand to Stanley, "Give me your phone."

"You're kidding, right?"

I reached for him, but he held up a trigger in his palm. My whole body froze. "If you're telling me the truth, my teammate is in danger."

"Then you better tell me where she is."

I had to get to her but couldn't risk taking Studious Stanley to the safehouse. I couldn't outrun him, couldn't lose him, couldn't arrest him, had no idea if my dispatch call went through, no communication, and no energy to fight.

I ran to the fallen terrorist and shook him to semi-consciousness. A groan, a flickering eyelid. Flipping him on his back, I yelled to Stanley, "Go get your car! I'll help you load him in."

"You'll help me?"

"So long as you give me the cure for my father."

"I can't guarantee anything."

"But you'll try?"

"Yes."

"Fine. Do your best and I'll bring you to the safehouse. My backup will be here any second. Now go!"

When Studious Stanley ran toward his headlights, I only had a few moments. Once he was out of earshot, I sprinted deep into the shantytown and hid close to where my communal waited. I watched until he drove to where I left his comrade then rocketed to my communal, slowing only to scoop up two handfuls of mud.

I caked it onto all three taillights, peeked up to see Stanley's sedan still navigating delicately into the shantytown, then covered the headlights and dash light with what remained on my palms. I heard Stanley open his door, his calls for me growing louder.

With a swipe and a command, the communal exited Yellow Acres. My head pivoted, looking for signs of Studious Stanley's pursuit or the arrival of the police. I saw neither. I hoped that Stanley had lied or at least been misinformed. If not, Pamela sat in the safehouse with a nine-year-old copy of Jackson Serfass.

Chapter 43

I had my auto drop me off a block from the safehouse. With fingers slipped securely through the grip-holes of my brass knuckles, I walked past the parking lot of the Cedar Heights apartment complex: the communal Pamela used was nowhere in sight. No cars anywhere. Of course, she could have (should have) sent it on its way to the nearest carpool. I held out hope that she had taken a circuitous route which allowed me to beat her here, despite my run in with Millennial.

A gaggle of laughter coming from three blocks up appeared beneath one of the few functioning street lamps, a throng of youths moving out of sight. I made as sure as I could that no other eyes were on me then entered the safehouse's building. I fished through my pockets for my keys, found the tiny LED light I hung on the ring and illuminated the hallway before me. My right hand's fingers felt bruised and barely fit through my weapon. My ring finger struggled to bend at the tip, but I forced the shape of a fist through the pain and continued to the basement, as per the business card address.

I found my way to the safehouse entrance and ran my badge over the reader. I inhaled painfully and pulled the door with a thrust. It barely cracked. The door couldn't be opened with any subtlety, so I heaved against it. Grinding, squealing, it opened only enough to get my hand through. I struck my eye against the opening, glanced around to see a dimly lit area obscured by an office divider.

"P?" I whispered.

Nothing.

I shoved my fingers into the opening and leveraged my body, pushing my legs against the wall. The door finally gave way, allowing the stale air inside to push away the fetid stench of the hallway.

I called out again, "P, it's A."

Still no answer. I stepped boldly into the room and closed the door before anyone could follow behind. The light switch on the wall was inoperable, but the lamp from the back room illuminated the space sufficiently.

Two mismatched couches with a coffee table between them marked the living area. A stack of folded military wool blankets sat undisturbed on the edge of the faux leather arm, with one wrinkled blanket and sheet laid out like a makeshift bed. A small container of cookies had been emptied and discarded on the table next to a glass whitened with milk.

I called louder, "Pam?"

Boxes stacked against the wall held old military supplies. Uniforms from the Army dating back to before they suspended Posse Comitatus, metal canteens going back thirty years, canvas belts, defective boots, sheets, yellowed pillows flattened by their own weight.

Catty-corner to the boxes, the bathroom door sat ajar, a sliver of light escaping from inside. The kitchen lights were off, but the microwave clock read past midnight. I stopped but heard nothing.

"Mac? Hey, Mac, are you in here? It's okay. It's Amara. Remember me? I'm Pamela's friend." No answer. *I'm the one that saved your scrawny ass from SAYACH, you little shit.*

If 'Mac' was indeed Jackson Serfass, why was the big version of Serfass threatening to kill him? Holding him hostage? Was that part of the ruse? Or did something happen to Serfass after his consciousness transferred? Maybe the boy was some aspect of Serfass, but not a criminal one. Maybe he was truly a boy.

"Mac, are you in here?"

I stepped carefully to the kitchen where I found Pamela's phone sitting on a charging pad. I touched the screen and found the security lock engaged with the warning '9 failed attempts' displayed across the top. I took my own phone out, placed it next to hers on the charger, and then moved toward the bedroom.

As I stepped closer, I recognized the sideways light of a tipped lamp. I tried flicking the blade open my knuckle-dusters, but my thumb was swollen and fatigued: my left hand had to assist. With a small shove, I pushed the door open and saw Pamela lying face down on the comforter, a black and red wound splitting her face open.

My tears began to build, but I shooed them away, pushed it all down, focused on finding the boy. This room had no closet. Hell, it wasn't even a bedroom. Just a shitty square fastened together with haphazardly hung drywall. There were few spots to play hide-n-seek. I got down on my knees, whipped the dangling blanket back and found that the boxspring rested on cinder blocks with nothing beneath it but dust and an old book.

My search became more harried as I pushed the bathroom door open and found nothing but two new toothbrushes and a travel-sized gumball flavored toothpaste tube. I whipped the shower curtain back, found nothing, and then ran back into the bedroom to search Pamela, the heat from her body still lingering, the last of her motherly warmth dissipating into the cold basement room. No radio, no weapon. My tears started again.

I spun out of the bedroom and ran for my phone. The green power bar barely reached above the bottom line, but I booted it anyway. Two long seconds later the screen lit up and I heard the chime in my earpiece tell me I was connected. I pulled off the brass knuckles and swiped through my contacts, looking for the Dispatch number. I was about to connect when I heard it. Not from behind or to the sides.

A horror movie creaking door emanated from beneath the counter. I looked down and saw the cabinet at my knees open a wee bit. A tiny eye peeped up at me from the smallest of hiding places. The pupil contracted in the kitchen's dim light as it hovered over a glint of subdued gunmetal.

"Peekaboo..." the boy whispered, and then the safehouse rang with gunfire. The first shot went high, struck the drop ceiling, and showered the kitchen in white foam dust. I dropped back automatically. The second shot splintered the pressboard cabinet door and flung it open. A woody shard cut across my neck, and I ducked behind one of the couches. The third and fourth shots cut across the safehouse to parts unknown, but I knew exactly where the fifth shot landed.

The radial bone in my left ulna shattered and I felt my blood sting my eyes and sprinkle my mouth. I landed on the ground, pulling my wounded limb close to my chest.

From beneath the kitchen counter, the boy emerged like a moth from a cocoon, unfolding from a seemingly impossible cubby to stand erect and purposeful, my own pistol— the one I gave Pamela to protect him with—in his trembling grip. He walked with an unsure stride, using his free hand to pull wads of toilet paper from his ears and discard them on the ground.

"Holy shit! That's loud!" he beamed. "Man, this is a great gun but *not* built for kids. You must have man-hands, bitch!"

I shuffled back as best I could with one arm bleeding, my right hand wrapped in carbon steel and extended blade. The boy followed, Cheshire smile overtaking his small, pale face. My head bounced against the wall, and I turned and side-crawled till my back struck the piled up Army boxes.

"Where are you going... Emily? Amelia? Whatever the hell your name is?" The boy's voice cracked a little, but the timbre of his words came off as mature. "You really screwed things up for me, you know that?"

"I know you're Jackson Serfass. I know all about your experiments."

He stopped, the boy's eyes darted back and forth.

I continued, laying it on thicker. "DHD knows too. It's over."

Worry clouded his face, but his hands still held the gun straight out. A second later his smile returns with a chuckle. "You know what? Whoopty-fucking-doo! I don't care who knows. Because I'm the only one that can do it. That makes me the most valuable person in the world. Once I'm out of here, that is."

His resumed his approach and I collapsed backward, head rapping against the concrete floor, my legs curling up until I formed a ball surrounding my bleeding arm. The boy came closer, "How does it feel to be bested by a nine-year-old, you stupid b—"

With all my remaining strength, I kicked out as hard as I could, smashing my left heel into his jaw. The blow drove his little skull upward with a force that lifted his body off the ground, casting him elliptically backward till his tiny head smashed against the floor. I watched as his pre-teen grip on my pistol relaxed and his feet fell to either side.

Blood dripping, nerves screaming, I leaned against the boxes and righted myself. I left a speckled crimson trail on the way. When I reached his unconscious body, I kicked my pistol clear and snap-kicked his ribs. He grunted but did not move.

"To answer your question, it feels pretty shitty."

Chapter 44

Streetlamps blurred by as the communal carried us northward on the Garden State Parkway. I brushed my left hand's fingertips against the door controls, felt nothing, and blamed the tourniquet I fashioned from old military canvas belts. Lack of circulation, maybe nerve damage—I couldn't be sure.

Fat lip, swollen jaw, Jackson Serfass's mini-me came to and grabbed for the door handle. Even with wire wrapped snuggly around his wrists and waist, he managed several solid tugs before he realized the lock would not disengage.

"Good morning, sleepy head," I taunted.

He looked down at the smeared blood covering his trousers and puppy dog shirt, his hands spattered with reddish-brown. "What did you do to me?"

"Don't worry, it's my blood," I raised the soaked make-shift bandage that wrapped my purpling arm.

"Let me out of the car."

"*Out?* Do you have any idea how hard it was to get you

into this matchbox? Why do you think you're covered in my blood, dumb ass?"

"Let me out of this fucking car!"

My chest ached with an exhausted laugh as I watched his temper tantrum thrashing through my faded vision. Even as the auto slowed for the exit ramp, the boy turned and landed tiny fists against any part of me he could reach with his bound wrists. Every pattering blow seemed comical save for them aggravating some already tender part. When he connected with my shattered left arm, however, I leaped upon him and pinned him with the bulk of my body, driving my good elbow down into his thigh.

"Are you going to behave, little Mister Jackson Serfass?"

"Get off me, you greasy whore!"

I leaned back into my seat as more blood dripped down my elbow. My eyes dipped again. Through foggy vision, I could see the boy's sinister smile form as he sat sideways to face me.

"You think turning me in is going to do anything?" He put on an exaggerated pouty face to go with a whiny voice. "I'm just a little kid who's been traumatized by SAYACH employees for years, then abused by DHD agents in a gross overstep of power. They beat me, your honor! They kept telling me to be quiet because I saw them steal some computer thingy at SAYACH, and if I didn't, they would take away my teddy bear!"

I rolled my eyes at him.

"You don't think I'll get away with this? I fooled that soulful mama you had protecting me. I even felt up her big brown titties while she hugged me, and all she did was shrug it off. Oh, and how did she die? Oh yeah, with your gun!"

I shook my head, my anger the only thing keeping me awake. "They'll figure out what you are, then stick a big needle in that tiny little arm of yours, and it will be lights..." I faded momentarily. "Lights out."

"And how will anyone know? I'm still not sure how you know, but I'm beginning to think you got your 'information' from an inscrutable source. I think they'll bury you long before they bury me."

Doubt crept into my fading consciousness. Could I ever prove that this freckle faced nine-year-old boy killed twelve people? Thirteen now that Pamela was gone. And Jackson Serfass could continue to feign innocence, play the victim, and convince enough people that he would never pay for his crimes. If I revealed my source, it would be the second time a Millennial terrorist sought me out, gave me information, and asked me to defy my oath to free my father. How many times could that happen before I was relegated to a desk job, or removed from DHD, or—worse—brought up on charges?

"You are an evil fucking human being, Jackson. But there's... There's justice waiting for you. Don't you worry..."

I pressed the navigator menu, rerouted the auto, and watched little Jackson Serfass screw up his young face. Through the auto's windows I watched the skyline disappear, replaced with double-stacked cargo containers that played out like a maze in every direction. The fog had somewhat cleared by the time the communal slowed to a stop.

"Where are we? What is this place?"

My hand fell on the controls and the door locks disengaged. I could barely keep my eyes open as I watched the boy assessing me, weighing his chances of beating the system or fleeing. My vision blurred again, and when it returned, I saw him jumping out of the car, his tiny form trussed up, waddling toward three figures approaching slowly from behind the cargo containers. I could hear Jackson's young pleading with the two men and the woman.

They were armed, and with my last remaining strength, I pressed the emergency services option on the navigational controls to bring me to the nearest hospital. The auto flipped around and rolled out of the Port Newark-Elizabeth Marine Terminal before the men could reach me, question who I was, beat out whatever meager life remained in my shell. In the rear view mirror, I watched the boy become smaller and smaller, guided away by the helpful hands of Kacela Fantine.

Chapter 45

Lieutenant Fitzsimmons of the Criminal Investigative Division tapped his stylus on the desk as he reread his own notes.

"Explain again why you gave your service pistol to Agent Hamilton. You said she lost hers?"

"No, I didn't say that. I said she secured hers in a locker at the hospital." I pictured my voice like a placid lake, nary a breeze to disturb the waters.

"And she did so, why?"

"Because she was holding the boy."

"The clone, you mean."

"Yes, the clone."

"And you felt it necessary to violate department policy to loan her your pistol?"

"Yes, to protect her and the clone."

The other lieutenant chimed in, "The same gun that killed Agent Hamilton."

"And the same gun that shot me, right here." I adjusted the cast in the sling.

"A shot from close range, the doctors reported."

"What are you implying, Lieutenant?"

"We're not implying anything," Fitzsimmons said. "We're simply trying to get to the bottom of matters. We have two injured agents, one dead, and one clone child that belongs to a defense contractor who has gone missing. We have a top-secret facility destroyed, a dozen casualties, a related murder, a major hospital closed, five dead from the hospital parking lot, dozens injured from the explosion, hundreds of thousands in damages to civilian and governmental vehicles, a man crushed beyond recognition by a flying trike, and a dismembered body belonging to a known Russian hitman."

"It wasn't the best day I've had."

The other CID officer scooted closer to the desk, "Can you describe the attacker who shot you at Safehouse 141?"

"I didn't get a good look at him."

"Not one descriptive aspect of an intruder who shot and killed your teammate and friend, who..." He referred to his notes, "Who—and I quote—'kneed me in my back repeatedly, then threw me into a crate which splintered and cut me in several locations, then shot me with what I later determined to be my .454 Casull service pistol.'"

"That's correct."

"You're saying that a decorated agent and combat expert with the DHD could ascertain nothing of her attacker? Tattoos? Scars? Facial hair? Latino? Caucasian? Black? Asian? Young? Old? Anything about the attacker would be helpful, Sergeant."

"He was short."

W. Lawrence

Chapter 46

Amara stops her recording, turns off the stove, and pours the hot water over the teabag to allow it to steep. She checks her inbox, sees four unopened messages, each with the word 'Suspended' in the subject line, leaves them unread.

"Otto, resume encrypted recording."

Sitting in her chair, she ruminates over her actions, her confession to the only person she can share it with as she wipes the tears from her bruised cheeks. "I hope you can forgive me, Daddy. Maybe I was wrong leaving Serfass with them. I know you would say two wrongs don't make a right. But I think of Pamela's boys and her husband at the funeral and.... And then I think of Serfass with those monsters, using *Sublime* on him, selling him to the highest bidding degenerate, and it makes me feel... I know I shouldn't want him to suffer, but I do. It's justice, right? It has to be. It has to be...

"He deserves it. Killing him would have been too easy. And I knew, *I just knew* he would get a pass if I turned him in. Nobody in the legal system understands this tech. I don't understand it. The only ones who understand are..."

She wipes her nose on her sleeve. "Daddy, I'm worried. I'm scared of everything. Of failing. Of succeeding. I can't take back what I've done, but I hope you can forgive me, understand why I did it. If I can't at least tell you here, then I don't think I can ever come back from this."

The sonorous rumbling of an overhead jet pervades the apartment, and she pauses the recording she has logged for the last hour. She runs her hands through her curly hair and pulls at giant handfuls, her jaw clenching, grips tightening, left forearm aching in its lattice cast.

"Otto...Delete journal entry."

W. Lawrence

Act 2 Preview

Amara tears headlong into the dust cloud as she covers her face, dodging survivors from the front while two more police cars speed past her from behind.

"Iván!"

Her feet crunch over shattered glass and broken plastic, kick through discarded bags of food and even a bag of weed. A police officer is waving people out of the building across the street, an apartment bellowing smoke from the third and fifth floor.

A woman wraps a man's arm around her shoulder and bolsters his steps, limping past her carefully.

Two competing calls from two worried strangers in two different languages fight to fill the sky against the approaching emergency vehicles. Amara adds to the cacophony in increasing shouts. "Iván!"

Drawing closer to the roundabout, her feet splash and then squish and then slosh the closer she gets to the epicenter. Dust gives way to steam, a vaporous reminder of a fountain that no longer exists. Millennial scooped a section of the roundabout and replaced it with a crater twenty feet across. Earlier, the concrete was hot from the summer sun—now it's steaming from the thermobaric explosion. A stream spills from the broken fountain and sizzles its way down into the crater to create a hellish sauna.

The statue hasn't just fallen but bounced at least twenty feet from the toppled column that held it aloft for a hundred and fifty years, the stone smashed and scattered across the roundabout. The flagpoles bend at odd angles, flaccid beams of steel stripped of their garments. The trees are cracked and blackened and stripped of their leaves, their remnants thrown so far that a ten-foot branch juts from a store window across the street.

"Iván!" Amara cries.

A fire engine has just blocked off North 3rd Street and a volunteer in an emergency vehicle has blocked off Northampton Street to the west. The young man couldn't be more than 20 years old, but he's amongst the first to arrive and he approaches Amara with purpose.

"I'm sorry but I need you to leave the roundabout," he points to the north. "We're setting up an emergency station on 3rd Street by the bookstore. Miss? Miss! Are you able to—"

"Iván!" she lets out in a long shriek, spinning around in search of any sign of him.

And then she finds one.

What's next?

The question was posed long before Syncing Back published: is this a sequel or a prequel to Syncing Forward? The answer is "yes." The fancy-schmancy word to describe their relationship is a *diptych*. Whichever story you read first is going to give you some spoilers for the other, but also provide revelations. They stand alone well, but the two stories together are more than the sum of their parts. Diptych.

Syncing Forward came out ten years ago. Somewhere along the way, really bad things happened in my life. Dramatic, bad things that shouldn't happen to anyone. So bad that I'll write about it someday. Not today though. Today I need to write about something cheerier: like Amara James going off the deep end and killing people. Ironically, ten years is the same the length of time between when Martin James was attacked and Amara began her career working for the government. Coincidence?! Well, yeah, it really is. But ten years is too long to make me (or any publisher) happy.

Stay shiny! Not to fret! Act 2 is already written and Act 3 is mapped out. Even if I die, I have somebody who can finish the story for you. Feel the love! More importantly, purchase the love and give it a good review.

Comments? Questions? I would love to hear from you how you heard about Syncing Back and what you thought. Feel free to e-mail me at syncingforward@gmail.com. I'm especially curious to hear from readers who have not read Syncing Forward yet.

A review is the lifeblood of a book's success, so please consider leaving one where you purchased it. Unless the review is terrible, of course, in which case be kind and leave a fake good one. You can call it your good deed for the day. Also, there is no greater compliment a writer can receive than when a reader tells his or her friends about our books.

You can find more information and free stories on my site bywlawrence.com. See you in Act 2!

The world is what we make of it.
W. Lawrence

Acknowledgments

There are only so many hours in the day, and even as part of a married couple collaborating to make a household run, the day is a zero-sum game. For me to take time to write means my wife needs to give up time someplace else. It lacks glamor, it is frustrating for her, but the work is no less important. For this, she has my deep gratitude. And the gift of coffee. I buy her really good coffee. And I'll probably have to pick up a pie while I'm out, now that I think about it—

John Crye has been a marvel of a professional as well as a good friend. He is truly the only person deep enough in my head to understand my world, and for that act of bravery alone, he deserves my praises. And if you need help building a story, reach out to him. Seriously. His professional services are well worth the money. He will dedicate serious hours to you. He's also a really good author, so check out his Elect Stories.

Blake Edwards is a decades-long friend and a fantastic editor who straightened me out like a piece of wire. He also is one of the wittiest men alive and a brilliant levelheaded mind. I'm a better person for knowing him.

Thanks to Tom Edwards for the stunning cover work on Syncing Back, and being freakishly fast in his ability to distill my 'want list' into a working piece of art.

Finally, thanks to Victoria Gerken at Podium Publishing for giving me the motivation I needed to get back in the saddle.